Serpentine

**A novel by
Catherine Edmunds**

Art is the proper task of life
(Friedrich Nietzsche)

Circaidy Gregory Press

Copyright information

Cover Art
'Serpentine' by Catherine Edmunds

ebook ISBN 978-1-906451-62-2
paperback ISBN 978-1-906451-63-9

Printed in the UK by
Berforts Ltd

Published by Circaidy Gregory Press
Creative Media Centre,
45 Robertson St, Hastings,
Sussex TN34 1HL

www.circaidygregory.co.uk

To Antoine Watteau (1685-1721)

Chapter One

Victoria fixed a fresh canvas to the easel. It was time to commit the unsettling memories of José to paint: to tie them down for good so she could file them away in the ex-boyfriend compartment along with last year's historian and at least three members of the university rambling club. She picked out a fat tube of cadmium yellow – perfect to show her Spanish lover's warmth and take away the dull pain of his absence.

Foolish girl. This portrait that you will paint – why you choose yellow? Am I a lemon? A banana?

Shut up, José.

You are wrong and stupid. Put down that paintbrush and come to bed.

Bugger off.

The weight of the tube nestling in her palm was familiar and encouraging. Victoria squeezed and darkness slid out, lubricated by a hint of amber oil. Brush or fingers? Fingers, definitely. She smeared the paint with her hands until the canvas glistened and her lover's body began to appear. Where thigh met hip there were valleys and curves to be recreated in paint as her fingers caressed his landscape, blending and sweeping over his reclining form.

An hour later she stood back and contemplated the image. José might want to leap from the canvas and into her bed, but he couldn't now that she'd bound him there for good.

Oh no you haven't, he whispered. She felt his breath around her in the sweet fumes of linseed and toxic turpentine.

Shut up, she said. Shut up, shut up, shut up, shut up.

Her phone buzzed and she jumped. It was a text from José. Was the man psychic? She flushed and read the message.

Today the cathedral is dressed in white rags. You will find this pleasant I think. For me it is foolish. The men work, that is all. Do you smell the sea? Talk to me sometimes. J.

The cathedral "dressed in white rags"? What was that supposed to mean? And how could she smell the sea in the middle of London? The man was an idiot. Now she'd be unsettled until she replied, and then she'd be unsettled until he returned the message, so it would go on and on. She texted, *Go boil your head* back at him and switched off the phone.

The rest of the morning was taken up with making potato prints, the logic being that she could eat the potatoes once she'd cut off the inked bits. Artwork with an edible end product. Great use of resources. Perfect.

Food and José had always been a problem area. *You must wipe your fingers, so*, he would say, demonstrating with a napkin. *Do not eat with your hands. You have a knife and fork. Use them. Your fingers, your clothes – they are not for food. Your mouth is for food. Your cutlery is for transport the mouth to the food. Yes? I show you.* He would demonstrate, as if she were a little child needing to be shown how to eat properly. She would tell him that next he'd be instructing her to cut everything up and then swap the fork over to the other hand, and what was wrong with eating naturally anyway? He would sigh and drop his head into his hands, running his fingers through his hair, and she'd wriggle on her chair, knowing she'd forgive him anything. Then they'd go back to the hotel and make love and everything would be all right.

Except that it had never happened like that. She'd always been annoyed by his desire to mould her to fit his formula for perfect womanhood. Their lovemaking had been perfunctory and uncomfortable, despite her best efforts – possibly *because* of her best efforts. She kept expecting to be told that her technique was crude, that she should do this with her fingers or that, and not to wipe them on the bedclothes but use the tissue at the side of the bed.

Oh, bugger off José. Now then. Potatoes. The method was straightforward enough: slice a large potato in half, pat dry with kitchen paper, paint with acrylics, print, wash, whittle away, paint in contrast colour, print, repeat, rinse well, bake in a moderate oven until done (or microwave if in a hurry), serve with butter and grated cheese. She covered two large sheets of cartridge paper with the repeating potato pattern, allowed them to dry while she microwaved and ate the potato, and then returned with a black fine-liner to work over them. This part was laborious and would keep her going for days. After an hour of going cross-eyed, it was time for a break. She stood up, stretched, grabbed her handbag and let herself out of the flat and into the dust and humidity of mid-July in London.

Victoria had intended to visit Doris Salcerdo's *Shibboleth* – the "crack" in the Tate Modern floor that everyone was talking about – for ages. A short tube ride and stroll across the bridge from St Paul's later, she was staring at Louise Bourgeois' *Maman*, a thirty foot sculpture of a spider, which was still on display in front of the old Bankside power station. Victoria walked around it, wondering if she would ever have the confidence to put that much honesty into her own artwork.

Feeling suitably humbled, she entered the gallery. *Shibboleth* started as a hairline crack at the end of the turbine hall. She knelt down to touch it, not sure whether it was painted on the concrete or real at this point. Definitely real. Tourists parted at random to reveal the ever-widening crack. Victoria followed its course with care, looking up now and again to see how it fitted into the vast space of the hall.

Most visitors were taking photographs or laughing and jumping over the crack, fooling about. Victoria wished they'd stop, but one man stood still and looked with the sort of concentration this artwork demanded. She thanked him silently before changing her mind when he turned and she saw who it was. John. John Wotsisname. What the hell was the guy's surname? She should be able to remember. He'd married her best friend Emma a couple of years ago and Victoria had gone to the wedding. She remembered her shock at seeing bubbly Emma drooling over this cold stick.

Dammit. He'd noticed her. He nodded an acknowledgment and turned away stiffly. Good. At least the dislike was mutual.

Victoria hadn't emailed Emma for ages. They'd shared a flat in Durham as students, but after graduation Victoria had moved back to London to try to be a "real" artist while Emma had stayed on in the north. They'd missed each other and had written reams at first, so Victoria had learnt how Toby, an Adonis-like youth, had nearly broken Emma's heart before she'd fallen on the rebound for a sophisticated older man – antiques dealer John. Emma's emails had been full of walks on the moors, wind in her hair, and the sensuous curves of Serpentine furniture. And then there was the kitten. Victoria knew how much Emma must have been touched by such a gift and was pleased to discover John had a cuddly side. She'd looked forward to meeting him. The wedding invitation duly arrived and Victoria had headed up north, expecting to find a rugged fell-walking type with a sideline in antiques, probably bearded, wild-eyed and passionate, who climbed mountains searching for priceless old furniture and came back with kittens for his lover. John was a disappointment, however – unexceptional, and with a manner that could best be described as repulsive, in the old-fashioned sense. He rarely smiled, except in an unsettlingly knowing way, and had no pretensions to being a fell-walker.

Victoria walked to the centre of the hall, ignored the milling crowds and sat on the ground to examine the portion of crack in front of her. It was several inches wide at this point, but not the bottomless fissure that it appeared to be when standing, unlike the cracks in the rocks on that Spanish beach. Oh God – why did she have to think of José now? Go away, go away! She clenched her fists and shut her eyes tightly, willing the tears to withdraw.

'Are you all right?'

The voice sounded more annoyed than concerned. Victoria looked up. It was John. Typical.

She sniffed noisily, found a piece of kitchen paper covered in splotches of paint lurking in her pocket, and wiped her nose.

'Yes thanks. Fine.'

She stared mesmerised at his shoes – black patent leather, old-fashioned and so shiny she could see her reflection in them. No, this was not a man who climbed mountains, sought serpents and won fair maidens.

Was he ever going away?

'It's like an open wound.' He spoke quietly, staring at the crack. Victoria wasn't sure if the remark was intended for her or not, but the man was uncanny. Was he reading her thoughts? She got to her feet.

'Yes, I, err –'

'Have to go?'

'Yes. Meeting someone.'

He raised his eyebrows, clearly not taken in for one moment, before turning and walking away.

'Don't say goodbye then, you supercilious git,' said Victoria, as soon as he was out of earshot.

Back home, Victoria decided to email Emma. If John was in town, then maybe Emma was too. It could be awkward, given the lack of correspondence since the wedding, but they'd been best mates once, so it should be easy enough to get chatting again. She booted up the pc and wrote before she could change her mind.

Hi Emma
Just bumped into John in Tate Modern. Forgot to ask if you were up in town too. Let me know, and we'll have a coffee or something.
Cheers,
Vic xxx

That would have to do. She wasn't about to write what was really on her mind: *Hi Emma – just bumped into that priggish husband of yours in Tate Modern. What the hell were you thinking of, marrying him? I hoped he'd twist his ankle in the crack, but he didn't. Never mind. Better luck next time. Love and hugs, V.*

Victoria shivered at the memory of John's composure. She glowered at the computer for a few minutes. José might have vacated her head for the time being, but John was inhabiting the part of her consciousness that became overactive when she was stressed. His morose face stared back at her from the screen. She stuck out her tongue, panicking for a moment as she realised the webcam was pointed at her.

Come on, Emma, reply.

But Emma didn't reply, not that day, nor the next. It wasn't until a week later that Victoria received a response.

Hi there – no, I'm not in London, but I'd love to see you. Any chance you could come up some time? I'm at the cottage. Let me know.
Emma xxx

Why no mention of John? Maybe the bastard was having an affair with someone in London and Emma had kicked him out. Victoria considered the possibility for a few minutes and then replied.

Hi Emma – I'd love to visit. Haven't visited the cottage in ages. Been catching up with a load of arty stuff here. I got behind cuz of a trip to Spain where I met this total stud, José – you'd have swooned – snake hips, dark chocolate eyes, the lot. Thought he was my type at first, but OMG! You can guess the rest. Nothing much changes where me

5

and men are concerned.
Saw John looking at "Shibboleth". Cheery stuff. What've you done
to the poor man? I almost felt sorry for him (but not really). What's
the craic? Maybe he just had indigestion.
Vic xxx

Emma's reply came within minutes.

Christalmighty, how dare you! How DARE you write to me about
John like that! You have no idea! NO IDEA!!! DON'T YOU EVER
WRITE TO ME LIKE THAT AGAIN!!! I mean it. Get out of my life.
You don't know anything about it. Get out get out get out

Victoria read it twice. What the fuck? Emma had never written like
that before, even when they'd been having rows and silly jealousies
about boyfriends back in their student days. Victoria felt a lump in
her throat – she who never cried at sad stories or films or anything.
She would have to apologise, but not right away, or she'd write
gibberish.

She leaned out of the studio window and tried to sift clean air
from the confusion of petrol fumes. This flat was too small, but the
rent was just affordable, thanks to the remains of the legacy from her
parents. Oh, how she missed them; their advice, their good sense –
their love. Eyes smarting, she turned back into the room and looked
at the painting of José. She'd left it upright to dry when she should
have laid it flat on the floor, with the result that the colours were
sliding down the canvas in great fat oil slicks. Bloody typical. Even
the painting was crying. She took a paintbrush and tried to stop the
descent into ruin. It didn't work. Christ, what a mess. Plan B? Yes.
She took a rag, soaked it in white spirit, and rubbed at the painting,
removing virtually everything, until just the cadmium yellow
undercoat glared at her with the faint ghost of José's body. She
stroked it with her fingertips, but there was nothing there – no
reaction.

What was it John had said? "It's like an open wound." Precisely.
Hurt a friend and the wound stays open, festering until you deal with
it. Right, strictly no more paintings, not even a thumbnail sketch,
until the job was done. She returned to the computer.

Hi Emma, Sorry, sorry, sorry! Not sure how, but I've put my foot in it well and proper, haven't I. Won't happen again, promise. I'm free next Saturday and could come up to Durham for the day – maybe you could travel down, and we could meet and eat cake and drink coffee and eat more cake. 11:30 at ArtBooks sound ok? Let me know. Kicking myself here
Vic xxx

She sat at the computer for the next hour playing endless games of tetris, anxious not to miss Emma's reply.

Good idea. See you Saturday. Love, Emma xxx
PS sorry about my last. Feeling crap and lost it for a moment. Better now. Honest.

Yes! Victoria leapt up from the computer, spun round, whacked her hand on the mantelpiece and swore loudly.

Chapter Two

A postcard arrived two days later. Victoria noted the Spanish stamp and steeled herself to read the neat handwriting.

I wonder – should I boil my head as my beautiful lady desires? Then I think, no – she is fractious because the promise of a postcard is broken. So here is the card. All happy now. I visit soon. You not worry any more. I remember waves on the beach and the wet feet and the running. Do you? Do you still want to catch me? I think so. José

Great. A Spanish lover running across London with wet feet was all she needed. Christ! Could the man not understand he wasn't wanted any more; that she had no desire for him to walk his fingers down her spine, to warm the skin just below her ear with his hot breath, to whisper obscenities in a language she didn't understand? She shivered, then put the postcard on the mantelpiece and considered it. The picture was attractive, but the words were meaningless. He'd never visit. Of course not. Would he? She took it off the mantelpiece and turned it over, running her fingers over his writing.

Your words are charming and your picture well-chosen, but you are a nothing, a piece of paper, ephemera.

She was ready to paint. A new canvas; a new thought. What though. She needed a contrast. John wotsisname? Yes, why not. Cold and clever, icy blue, hard and harsh as the South Atlantic. Not jagged though – nothing sharp edged. Curved in subtle and deceptive ways. Unexpected and secretive. Serpentine.

The painting was difficult and she struggled to depict her vision. She didn't know this man, not really – so how could she paint him? With a shrug of her shoulders, she added a penguin, and then another, and another. They looked absurd, but she couldn't stop – she added more and more of the slippery beasts until instead of being quaint and amusing they became horrific; crowds of them falling off the ice and drowning, crushed beneath icebergs, blood spilling out over their white feathers, turning the sea a deep crimson that appalled her.

Another postcard arrived the following day. Victoria looked at the photograph of a tree stump in a field, a few cows, and nothing much else. On the back, José had written,

I am cut down. I am a log. The cows are beautiful, but they are not you. Text me. Besitos
José

Beautiful cows, eh? Victoria wondered whether the English tourists who José no doubt herded around every day – and night – with a crack of his whip would be flattered at the description. Who or what was "besitos"? She couldn't be bothered to look it up. Yes, she could. Oh, dammit, he was getting to her again. She turned on her computer and entered the word into a translator. Little kisses, apparently. How sweet. He'd never signed like that before. Maybe he was bored. Maybe the English tourists really were bovine. Victoria put the postcard with the other one in her handbag.

She rose early on Saturday, packed a small sketchbook in her bag, and hurried down to Kings Cross. She found an empty seat on the train next to a businessman who spent the entire journey making frantic calls to sort out a crisis at work that had erupted late on Friday night. Victoria listened, fascinated, to the minutiae of the situation, and was privy to much gossip about his colleagues as they sped north through Peterborough and Grantham. By Doncaster the crisis was coming to a head. The man left the train at York, to Victoria's intense annoyance.

Not far to Durham now. Victoria chewed a rough bit of nail and longed for the man with the crisis to divert her, but the southern accents at the start of the journey had given way to Geordie, and there was no escaping the fate of having to share cream cakes and coffee with her best friend in one of her favourite bookshops.

She strolled down from Durham Station and up into the ancient peninsula that was the City, with its winding streets and quirky shops selling a mix of academic necessities and New Age tat. The shops eventually ran out and she turned the corner past the Victorian pillar box and onto Palace Green. One of the towers of the cathedral was swathed in white cloth and scaffolding. Ah yes, of course. That was what José had meant when he'd texted her. What was it he'd said?

Today the cathedral is dressed in white rags.

She glanced at her watch. Nearly half past – time to go. She walked back down the bank to ArtBooks, pushed open the door, listened to the well-remembered chimes and ran up the stairs.

'Hey, you beat me,' she said, slipping into a chair beside Emma.

'Hi. Long time.'

'Oh cripes. What happened?'

Emma's face showed the mottled remains of bruises, sending Victoria's imagination into overdrive. Had the bastard been beating her up?

'What?' Emma put her hand to her cheek. 'Oh, that. It's nothing. Why don't you get some coffee? And cake. I haven't eaten yet today and have an overwhelming desire for over-indulgence.'

She grinned and Victoria remembered her friend's addiction to vast dollops of cream and sticky cakes. She tried to hear a note of hysteria in Emma's voice to justify her supposition about John, but there was none. She looked happy, bright and cheerful. Blooming, in fact. Pregnant? Could be. Hard to tell. She'd always been a bit curvaceous.

'Okay, what would you like?' said Victoria, trying not to stare at Emma's bruised face.

'Black forest gateau. Gotta be. What about you? Banoffee?'

'Of course.'

Two absurdly large cappuccinos completed their treat. The sugar rush gave Victoria the confidence to say what was on her mind.

'So – you pregnant then? You look like you might be.'

'No, thank God. Just fat.' Emma giggled. 'Enjoying my food. Trying out a new experiment.'

'Experiment?'

'You know, like those women in the Arabian Nights, fed on Turkish Delight to plump them up and make them gorgeous.'

'You're gorgeous anyway.'

'Yeah, whatever.'

'You know you are. Look at the way all the boys at uni fell over themselves to be noticed by you. Older blokes too. Your tutor. Then there was that shrink – what was his name?'

'Evan.'

'Yes, him. He had an almighty crush on you for a while.'

'Evan was sweet. Far too old for me though. He ended up

marrying Toby's mother. Did you know?'

'Weren't he and John much the same age?'

'Mmm.'

Emma's non-committal answer could be explained by the mouthful of gateau. Victoria tried again.

'So what was John doing in London? Antiques fair?'

'Something like that, I should think. Right time of year. P'raps. I dunno.'

'Emma! How can you not know?'

'That's his side of things. I sit on chairs. I don't ogle them.'

'You're jealous of a chair. That's a new one.'

'Gosh, yes, just imagine. John goes down on one knee to the chair. Swears undying love. Talks of re-upholstery, French polish and God knows what else. The chair goes all serpentiney and squiggly, and begs to be sat upon, crushed beneath the sacred weight.' She frowned and stared at the remains of gateau on her plate.

'And then what?' said Victoria.

'And then John gets bored with the chair for its lack of conversation, its wooden construction, its low intellect and its inability to swing from chandeliers.'

'So what does he do?'

'Throws it across the room. Smashes it to bits. Goes out to look for a table instead. Fails to find a table. Comes back. Glues the chair back together, but it's never the same again. I need more cake. You want another one?'

'No thanks. More coffee, perhaps.'

'Good idea. Best not have any more gateau. Might be sick. No point in that, is there?'

'None at all. Emma –'

'Yes?'

'Oh, nothing. I'll get the coffees.'

'Cheers.'

Victoria stood in the queue at the counter and tried to get her thoughts in order. Emma had told the entire story of her marriage in a nutshell, and Victoria had no idea what to do about it. She couldn't pat her on the head and say: "There, there – okay, so you weren't clever enough, or sexually adventurous enough for your husband, so he slapped you about a bit – not to worry, dear."

She went back with the drinks.

'Those bruises on your face? They're not really "nothing", are they?'

'They don't hurt.'

'Oh, bloody hell, Emma! That's hardly the point, is it?'

'No, it is the point. I used to fall off horses all the time. Remember? Black and blue. It didn't matter. I still loved going riding. Never put me off.'

'Hardly the same. The horses didn't throw you deliberately.'

'Zack did. Nasty brute, that one. Handsome as hell, and didn't he know it. Wonder what happened to him. Dog food by now, most likely.'

'Yeuch.'

'Well, that's what happens, isn't it?'

'Emma, you've grown hard.'

'Maybe.'

'Why? What went wrong? I thought you were so happy.'

Emma shrugged, and Victoria tried again: 'John gave you that kitten. Your emails were full of it. You sent me photos.'

'It got run over.'

'Shit.'

'He offered to buy me another, but he doesn't really like cats. It was a gift to win me back from Toby, that's all. It worked. No point buying another. He's clever, is John.'

'Too bloody clever.'

'Tell me about it.'

'I still don't get it though. I thought you'd found the love of your life, and that it was mutual – that he was absolutely besotted with you.'

'He was. Then.'

'And now?'

'His little miss perfect was too stoopid. That's all.'

'Emma, you're not stupid. You got a first.'

'Not the point. Okay, so I could research stuff and write good essays; I could sit in an exam room without panicking; I now know more about art history than I did before entering university; I can even draw a bit. So what. So bloody what. Despite all that, if I go to an art gallery and see a picture that really speaks to me, I say something daft like: "Ooh, that's lovely," or "Isn't that pretty," and

12

John goes ballistic. He doesn't do "pretty" or "lovely". Or rather, he did once briefly, and ended up married to me. Learnt his lesson. Won't make that mistake again. I'm divorcing him. Must be insane.'

'Ah.'

'Irretrievable breakdown, that's what we're using, or some such. Forget how they word it. I've moved out. That's why I'm at the cottage. I'm not going back to him. It'll take a while to sort out, but ...' Emma blew her nose on the paper napkin. 'But it's okay. Really. I'm fine. Devastated and hopes dashed and all that sort of pathetic stuff, but I'm fine. The bruises don't hurt, not really. I'm okay.'

'For God's sake, Emma! You're not even remotely okay. Come on. Let's go and look at some books. Drink up and we'll find some ghastly Fra Angelico reproductions and point out what's wrong with the text or something.'

'Yeah, good idea. I need to distract myself. Been having bad dreams.'

'Nightmares?'

'Sort of. I have this recurring one where I'm walking along the wooded bit round the back of the cathedral and John takes a swing at me and I fall down the bank and it's bloody freezing and I die of internal haemorrhaging and exposure and all that malarkey.'

'Blimey. That's a cheery one.'

'Yes, isn't it. Right. I've finished.'

They made their way downstairs into the main bookshop. Van Gogh and Monet prints glowered down at them in the unforgiving fluorescent lighting. The stairwell contained a display of books showing local views.

Emma picked one up and turned it over. She pointed to the illustration on the back. 'There. That's where he pushes me down the bank.' She ran her fingers over the scene. 'It's a beautiful place to die.'

'Don't be daft. It's just a dream. A nightmare.'

'Not sure if it is a nightmare really.'

'How do you mean?'

'Maybe it's wishful thinking.'

'What? You *want* him to push you down the bank?'

'P'raps.'

'Oh for God's sake, Emma.'

'Haven't you ever loved anybody like that?'

'No! No, I haven't.'

Victoria thought about José's postcards in her bag. Would she want her handsome Spaniard to knock her about a bit and then murder her? Yeah, right. What the hell was the matter with Emma? The odd thing was, apart from a few weepy moments, she didn't seem particularly depressed. She was eating well. That was a good sign, wasn't it? She was happy to talk about things, and was getting a divorce, prising herself out of an unhappy relationship.

'Emma, I don't understand.'

Emma opened the book and folded a photograph of a wedding sharply along a diagonal, and then tore along the crease. 'It's simple. I love him. He doesn't love me. Did once, maybe, but not any more. Nothing anybody can do about it.'

'Yes, but you can't want him to push you down a bank – that's absurd.'

'Is it? To push me, he'd have to touch me. These bruises – they're signs of him touching me. I goad him and goad him until he touches me. It's all I've got.'

'Christalmighty.'

'It's not good, is it.'

'No, it isn't.'

'I took advice. Women's refuge. They explained how I could get out of the situation. It made sense.'

'Of course it did.'

'But they had it all wrong. John doesn't want to hurt me. He hates it. I make him do it. It's not his fault.'

'Emma, of course it's his fault! You can't *make* someone hit you. That's bollocks. It's like you said. He fell for you because you're young and lovely and sweet and all the rest of it, and you were flattered – all that attention from an older and distinguished man – and so you fell in love back, but then ...'

'Yes. But then. What then?' She bent the book back until the spine cracked.

'I don't know. I wasn't there.'

'Exactly. But don't worry. I'm okay. I'll bounce back. Look at me. Plump and jolly. I've applied for a job in Newcastle. The Laing Gallery. You never know – might even get it. That'll take my mind off things, as my mother used to say whenever I split up with a boyfriend and she persuaded me to go shopping with her at the Metro

14

Centre.'

'Oh lord yes. With mine, it was a massive breakfast at a Little Chef. Bloody mad. Didn't help anything.'

Emma grinned. 'Filling though. Tell you what, let's see who can find the worst edition of Vasari. Makes as much sense as anything. Double points if it's the one with that awful engraving in the front.'

She slipped off between the bookshelves and Victoria trotted after her, with fleeting images of racing after José in her mind.

Always running but never catching. You must go faster, I think, he whispered in her ear, so she deliberately slowed. People were starting to stare.

She caught up with Emma round the next bookshelf.

'Have you ever painted that view?' asked Emma, pointing at a picture of the cathedral in the now mangled book.

'No,' said Victoria. 'It's too corny. I've been tempted, because I know it would sell, but I dunno – just can't bring myself to do potboilers like that.'

She studied the crumpled picture, working out how she would tackle the tree branches in her own way to show their grace as they leaned over the river, balancing this natural movement against the square certainty of the towers. There were possibilities in the scene, but it was also the classic picture postcard view, which reminded her – she still had those cards in her bag. She was tempted to tear them up and throw them in a bin. Should she or shouldn't she?

Emma turned to her. 'So, what sort of things *are* you painting nowadays?'

'Oh, a mixture. Abstracts mostly. Potato prints.'

'Potato prints? You're joking.'

'No, not at all. Think about it. Has a potato print ever won the Turner Prize?'

'We could find out. There's bound to be a book here. But no, of course it hasn't.'

'Well, there you go. The next Big Thing.'

'Isn't that a bit, you know – primary school?'

'Wait until you see them. You'd be surprised. I'm going to try them out on one of those art-selling sites. See if I can get picked up by a top dealer or something. Discovered.'

'Yeah, but potatoes? Sounds unlikely to me. Mind, you're looking very smug. Must know something I don't.'

'Not really – I just like them. They work.'

'If you say so. Good luck, I suppose. Tell you what, when I'm a gallery owner, I'll offer you a potato opening if you haven't managed one already.'

Victoria snorted with laughter. 'The mind boggles. Maybe I could get sponsorship from the British Potato Council. Is there such a thing?'

'Wouldn't be surprised.'

Victoria picked up a book. 'C'mon. Thought we were looking for Vasari.'

'What? Oh yeah.' Emma dropped the illustrated book, now very much the worse for wear, into a bin of remainders and gazed around at nothing in particular.

'It's not easy, this painting business,' said Victoria, wrinkling her nose at a coffee table book of Jack Vettriano reproductions. 'Making money, that is. Producing the artwork isn't the problem. Selling though. God ... if I were prepared to make dozens of identical postcard-sized paintings of Durham Cathedral, I could sell them by the cartload and have a useful small income, but I can't bring myself to do it. Soul-destroying. I don't know. Do you think I'm being a bit precious about it all? That's what worries me.'

'No, I don't think you're being precious at all. You're a proper artist, whatever that is. John always used to say ...' Emma stopped mid-sentence.

The silence was awkward. Victoria was about to change the subject when Emma continued: 'I do need to learn to say his name in ordinary conversation, don't I.'

'Yes. Definitely.'

'Can't though. As soon as I say it, I get this icky feeling of desire and revulsion churned up together in my guts. Makes me feel like I'm about to throw up.'

'That'll be the gateau as much as anything, but I still think you should try and use his name once in a while as otherwise it'll become The Thing That May Not Be Uttered and will start festering.'

'You're right. I'll try again.' She took a deep breath. 'John ... used to say that only an original one-off painting could contain the soul of the artist, and that those painters who made several versions of the same work – and he even included Rembrandt and Monet, for goodness sake – were prostituting their art for filthy lucre, and were

16

artisans, not worthy to be spoken of in the same breath as true artists.'

'Oh.'

'Oh indeed. John's not one to mince words.'

'A man of strong opinions?'

'Very. And unforgiving of those who dare to hold different views, especially if they refuse to be taught the error of their ways.'

'Taught? As in beaten into submission?'

'God, no. John may be many things, but he's not a violent man.'

'Oh really? That's not how it looks from here, Emma.'

Emma glared at Victoria. 'He hit me, okay? But I've explained that – I goaded him. Now *leave it*.' She turned away. 'Please let's not talk about that again. I can't bear it.'

'Sorry. Hey, really sorry. Don't cry. He's not worth it.'

'Not worth it? Isn't he? How the hell would you know? You've barely met him – you can't possibly know. Oh God, why am I doing telling you all this stuff? This was supposed to help me: meet a pal, talk it through. It's crap, though, isn't it. What sort of a pal are you anyway, with all your snide comments? What were you doing in the Tate with John, that's what I want to know. Did you arrange to meet him there? Why? What did he say? What did he *really* say?'

'Shh … Nothing much – just a few words. Emma, we –'

'Oh, "we" now is it? "We" as in Vic and John having secret meetings at art galleries, then shedding crocodile tears to put poor little wifey off the scent?'

'Christ no, nothing like that. It was pure chance, us meeting. We barely spoke. Emma, for goodness sake, calm down. People are looking.'

'Let them bloody look. Bastards!' She spat the word at a passing mother with a baby in a buggy. 'I shouldn't be here at all. I should be at home, telling him I'm sorry, begging him to take me back. He would, too, I'm sure. He's an honourable man. He's – Oh God – what am I going to do?'

She struck the nearest bookshelf with her fist and then drew back in obvious pain.

Victoria winced at Emma's words as much as her action. So John was an "honourable man"? Funny sort of honour, she thought, looking again at the fading bruises, knowing that there would be an extra one on Emma's hand now – though this would be self-inflicted.

For one horrible moment, she wanted to give her friend a hard slap herself, but resisted the temptation, and put an arm round her instead.

'Hey. Emma. It's okay. You're doing the right thing. Really. Maybe he'd take you back, but what then? Doesn't sound like either of you can make the other happy. You're hurting, he's hurting –'

'He's hurting? What do you know about that? What do you mean?' Emma shook herself free of Victoria's arm.

'Just something he said about it being "like an open wound". I thought he was talking about the infamous "crack" in the Tate, but it looks like he probably meant your marriage as much as anything.'

'So you think I've wounded him? It's all my fault? Is that what you're saying? Suddenly you're the expert on my marriage? You, who's never managed to keep a boyfriend for more than a few weeks. Know all the details do you?'

'I never said that. There's no blame on either side, I'm sure.'

'Oh, but there is. It *is* my fault. Must be. He gave me everything, but I let him down. I didn't understand how much I was irritating him, with my stupid opinions and my inability to learn anything. He wanted to teach me so much, show me so much, open my eyes to possibilities; but I wouldn't listen, wouldn't be taught, just wanted to keep to my own silly theories about everything.'

'Emma, there's nothing silly about your theories. They're just – I don't know – different from his. Look, you're not in some bloody novel by Charlotte Brontë – this is real life. That whole teacher-pupil romance thing is sordid at best. It never works. Not in real life. You know that. Now come on. Let's have another look at the local books. See what the amateur artists have been churning out.'

'Yeah, right, let's laugh at the poor stupid amateur painters and their hopeless efforts and tell ourselves how superior you are, even though they're making money and you're broke; you with all your wonderful talent, too full of yourself to paint pictures anyone might actually want to buy.'

'Emma, that's not fair!'

'Bloody is, but okay, I'm in a bit of a funny mood, as you may have noticed. After all, it's not every day I bare my soul to a "best" friend who hasn't even bothered to write to me in two years.'

'I –'

Someone in the shop cleared their throat noisily.

Emma stuck her tongue out at them and then dropped her eyes,

18

unable to meet Victoria's. 'Sorry, sorry, sorry. Didn't mean it. Not really.'

'Didn't you? Emma, if you had problems you could've written to me any time. You chose not to. How was I supposed to know there was anything wrong?'

There was no reply other than an unforgiving glare from Emma's bloodshot eyes.

'Do you want me to go?' said Victoria.

'Yes. No. I don't know. Yes. Just bugger off.'

There was a loud "ahem" from somewhere near the till.

Victoria made one last attempt. 'I'm sorry I didn't write. Really. Time just slipped away. You know?'

Emma didn't reply. Victoria willed her to speak, to say it was all right, they were still friends, even though a small voice inside her kept saying that if Emma hadn't been so whiney then maybe John wouldn't have grown tired of her. She remembered her own impulse to slap her friend, and wondered about John's side of the story. She wished she hadn't been so rude to him at the Tate.

Emma spoke at last: 'When's your train due?'

'Not for a couple of hours.'

'Well you'll have to amuse yourself until then. I gotta go. I'm sure you'll find plenty of amateur artists to laugh at down by the river. Bye.'

'Emma – wait!'

It was no good. Emma strode back towards the shop entrance, knocking books off shelves and breaking into a run after a few yards. She didn't look back.

Victoria bit her lip and swallowed. She felt the same as she had when Emma's furious email had arrived – helpless, frustrated, and wondering what she'd done wrong. Why couldn't Emma be fun, like she used to be? Victoria fumbled in her handbag and retrieved the two postcards. José's attempts to mould her to his way of thinking had caused a week old romance to falter, which had hurt in its way, but was nothing compared to what Emma had gone through. On the other hand, Emma had lived with John for months before they married, so she must have known what it would be like. Perhaps John had some sort of "honour" after all and had felt duty bound to marry Emma having effectively halted her career and turned her into a full time housewife. Was he really the sort of man who wanted one of those pathetic women who trail in their husband's wake, nodding and agreeing and smiling sweetly whilst dying inside? No, there must be more to him than that. Or was it simply that John, the dealer in beautiful things, had attempted to recondition an *objet d'art* which had refused the treatment and kept springing back to its original form?

If that were the case, whatever Emma might say, John wasn't an honourable man. Considering your wife only as an attractive object to be moulded to suit your desires wasn't honourable. Hitting her, for whatever reason, wasn't honourable. As for Emma herself – she was trying to extricate herself from the situation, true, but only half-heartedly. Perhaps they were each as bad as the other.

Victoria left the shop and wandered down to the market place where she retrieved the sketchbook and pencil from her bag. She drew the silhouette of a tree, leafless, stunted and broken. Behind it, she sketched a small country church where once there had been weddings, but no longer – the building was empty and the windows broken. She looked at the drawing for a few minutes, then tore it neatly in two, screwed up the pieces, and placed them in a nearby litter bin. And the postcards? They were nice pictures, she rationalised. Useful source material. You never knew when you might need such things.

No, that was a load of shite. She threw the postcards in the bin too, and used up the last half dozen pages of her sketchbook on studies of John's long legs with their shiny shoes bestriding a fissure like a colossus; then John's profile, John's eyes, such sad eyes, John's unsmiling mouth, and finally a peculiar piece of serpentine-style furniture that started as a chair, but morphed into a bed.

'Christalmighty,' she muttered, when she realised what she was doing, but she didn't destroy the pictures. Instead, she stuffed the sketchbook back into her bag, and walked, head bowed, up the road to the station.

Chapter Three

It was too quiet on the train. Victoria thought fondly of the business man from the morning's journey and wondered how his Very Important Meeting had gone. Maybe someone else would get on and sit next to her and be just as entertaining, but the train passed through Darlington and York without anyone interesting appearing.

Another couple of hours to London. Sleep? She could do. It was always risky on a train, but she couldn't spend the next two hours trying not to draw John. She arranged herself so that she was sitting on her handbag and facing into the window, leaning her head on the inner corner of the headrest. She'd probably pick up nits. Usually did on trains. Not to worry. There were worse things in life than nits. Divorce, for example. Shaky friendships. Disloyalty.

The train rocked her to sleep in no time. A herd of buffaloes roared past and a duck waddled up, sat on her lap, quacked a couple of times and peed.

'Oh my God, I'm so sorry!' said the duck in a posh accent.

Victoria awoke with a start, vaguely aware of wet thighs and someone patting her leg.

'Gerroff!'

She slapped at the hands, which were quickly withdrawn.

'I really am most terribly sorry,' said a man's voice, not remotely duck-like in intonation. 'You were asleep – the train jolted and I spilt my drink on you and was just trying – not doing anything untoward, please believe me. Gosh, I don't know what to say.'

Victoria looked down in her lap and then frowned at the man in the dark suit who sat red-faced in the seat next to her clutching a small carton of orange juice. She wriggled off her handbag, extricated a tissue, and started dabbing at herself.

'It's okay, don't worry about it. You made me jump, that's all, but you're forgiven. It'll wash out. Looks dreadful though. Hope to goodness it dries out before we get to London or I'll look like I've had a most unfortunate accident. Where are we anyway?'

'Just passing Ally Pally.'

'Oh shit! It'll never dry in time. What shall I do?'

'Have my newspaper. You can use it to cover yourself up, so to speak. If you place it strategically in front of you, nobody will notice.

And I really am most dreadfully sorry. Would you be frightfully offended if I gave you something towards a dry cleaning bill?'

'Yes, I would. That is to say, it's sweet of you, but these are jeans, for God's sake, and nobody bloody dry-cleans jeans.'

'They don't?'

'Of course not. But thanks anyway.'

'You look sad. Are they very special jeans?'

'What? No, nothing like that. It's been a long day.'

'Ah. I'm sorry.'

She was pleased he didn't ask any questions. The last thing she wanted to do was to dissect the day with a stranger.

He handed her his copy of the Financial Times. 'There you go.'

'Thanks.'

Another smile, a crinkling in the corner of his eyes, and Victoria suddenly laughed.

'What's funny?' asked the man, perplexed.

'Duck pee.'

'Pardon?'

'Just before I woke up I was having this dream where a duck was sitting on my lap and peeing.'

'How strange. No wonder you were disorientated.'

'Yeah. Don't suppose your name's Drake or Mallard, is it?'

'No such luck. It's Tovey. Simon Tovey. No feathers at all. And you are?'

'Victoria.' She thought about adding her surname, and it seemed rude not to, but strangers on trains were strangers, and whilst he'd probably just been trying to mop up the damage, how could she be sure?

'Delighted to meet you, Victoria.' He put down the carton of juice and a soggy monogrammed handkerchief, wiped his hands surreptitiously on the side of the seat, and shook hands with her.

Victoria was pleased to find his grip firm, if a tad damp.

'Hi there, Simon. Pleased to meet you too. So, what do you do when you're not pouring libations over innocent maidens? I don't suppose you're an art dealer by any chance?'

'Art dealer? No. Why? Are you?'

'No, I'm a struggling artist. The real thing. Got a garret an' all.'

'Really? I like art.'

'What sort?'

22

'Oh, you know, the usual thing – Bouchet, Chardin, a soft spot for Fragonard and his ilk.'

'That's not exactly the "usual thing".'

'Maybe not. I suppose I'm a bit of a dunce when it comes to anything more contemporary. I say, are you sure everything's all right? You're looking sad again.'

'I'm not sad really. Different taste in art, that's all. I suppose if you like Fragonard, you won't be particularly keen on potato prints?'

'Well, I like prints and I like potatoes, certainly – sauté, dauphinois, even the humble baked spud. Not sure about potato prints, though I suppose if you printed on rice paper, using food colouring they'd be at least be edible.'

'Nice idea. Hadn't thought of doing that. Wouldn't last long in a gallery though, unless kept in hermetically sealed containers, or frozen, or something. I dunno. Formaldehyde?'

'I have no idea. Not my area of expertise.'

'So what is your area of expertise?'

'Antiques. Mid-eighteenth century ceramics, to be specific.'

'Oh lordy!'

'Why, whatever's wrong with that? Don't you like ceramics? Or is it antiques generally?'

'Antiques are fine; it's just antique dealers that give me the shivers.'

'That's a pity, as I was going to offer you a glass of champagne when we arrived in town as recompense for the spillage, but if you really can't stand my profession, I don't suppose you'll want one.'

'Champagne? What, at St Pancras you mean?'

'Yes. I hope you're tempted? Just a little?'

Victoria looked at the quality of his perfectly fitted suit, caught a whiff of expensive cologne over the drying orange juice and wondered if perhaps she'd been a bit hasty in deciding all antiques dealers were the spawn of the devil.

'You wicked man, of course I'm tempted. Very. I've wanted to go there in preference to those over-priced coffee places downstairs for ages, but I've never quite had the nerve to go in by myself.'

'Well then – come as my guest. It'll be compensation for ruining your jeans, and if it helps, I can always pretend to be a bricklayer rather than an antiques dealer.'

'Really? What qualifications do you have?'

'I once built a small wall in my garden.'

'Okay, that'll do. I hereby declare you to be an honorary builder. We can discuss frogs and hods, or whatever it is you bricklayers talk about.'

'Lime mortar?'

'Yes please, that'll do nicely. Lime mortar and *Veuve Clicquot.*'

The train was slowing and swaying over points, passing under grimy bridges and through short tunnels. Victoria felt more cheerful. Antiques dealer or not, this Simon was a charmer, and he was going to buy her champagne. The day, unbelievably, was going to end well.

The train lurched to a halt, and they stood up to leave. Simon was taller than she'd expected – at least six foot two. Victoria carefully placed the Financial Times like a fig leaf in front of her crotch and left the train with a spring in her step, wondering why she had ever thought small hairy men like José were attractive when there were golden demi-Gods in the world.

Within a fortnight, they had settled into a comfortable routine. Simon spent the day at work, but came round to her flat nearly every evening, showing a commendable interest in her artwork before taking her out to dinner or the theatre. Sometimes he suggested they stay in and he'd cook something. He wasn't the world's greatest cook, but he had a knack of buying tasty items from the local delicatessen and combining them into something very acceptable.

He hadn't stayed overnight yet, but after her dysfunctional rapid-fire sex with José, it was a relief to be gently and quietly wooed – to be courted, in fact. Simon was old-fashioned in that way. He left her mind free to concentrate on her art during the day, without having to recover from the sexual hangovers of the previous night. She kept telling herself that this made perfect sense, but at the same time, she couldn't help wondering if a more vibrant sex life might improve her painting and inspire her to raise her game, instead of churning out tame and safe pictures. On the other hand, the scenic paintings and still lifes had started to sell. An anonymous buyer had even paid seven hundred pounds for the potato prints, to her astonishment. She knew they were good, but had never expected a casual visitor to the art site to agree with her, let alone enter into a bidding war with another visitor. The reserve had been only a hundred pounds for the pair. She was going to re-stock the "garret" with the profit, and looked forward to browsing through art supply catalogues.

Simon preferred representational art to abstract. He liked to be able to recognise the image at first glance and to read the picture without any difficulty. If he didn't understand one of her paintings, he would ask her for the "story". She knew he meant well, but she was reminded of what a schoolteacher friend had said to her once: that you should never ask a child what a picture is supposed to be because of the upset this would cause. The child would most likely be indignant, wondering why you were so thick that you couldn't see, but there would also be the danger of denting their confidence, making them think they were terrible at painting if you didn't understand their picture. Worst of all, you could be backing them into a corner where they would have to lie. Victoria hated being in that position. It had happened the other day with one of her abstracts, when Simon had asked: 'What's that supposed to be? That yellow bit?' and she'd had to say it was a piece of sandstone, inspired by Durham Cathedral. She couldn't very well say: 'It's an expression of my need to vomit when remembering sex with my ex-boyfriend'.

In the end, it was simpler to draw and paint "real" things: landscapes, bowls of fruit, cathedrals, doorways, and corpses. The corpses didn't go down too well. *Good grief, Victoria! That looks like a dead person. You'll need to give him a bit more colour if he's just asleep.* And she'd lie again by nodding sagely and agreeing.

Little white lies. That's all they were. They kept Simon happy, kept him coming round with bunches of roses and bottles of wine.

Then one day he turned up with the gift.

'You're looking very pleased with yourself today, Simon.'

'Am I? Always pleased to see you, sweetheart.'

He planted a kiss decorously on her cheek, and came inside.

'You're nice,' said Victoria, wrinkling her nose with pleasure.

'I know. Extra nice today as it happens, as I've bought you something special.'

'Oh, goody. Hope it's a cake.'

'No such luck, I'm afraid. Not edible. Talking of which, did you ever make those edible potato prints?'

'Heavens, you remember that? No, I didn't, but the non-edible version has just sold for a tasty sum.'

'How appropriate.'

'Indeed. Let's see my present then.'

He handed her a neatly wrapped box. 'Sit down, and handle with care. These are a bit special, and very fragile.'

'Ooh, goody.'

Victoria undid the ribbon, lifted off the lid, and carefully removed the tissue paper to reveal a gruesome pair of china figurines. She'd seen similar ones in the pound shop, though to be fair, these looked better made.

'They're beautiful darling,' she lied, lifting one out and turning it round in her hand.

'I should say. Beautiful, and very precious. Just like you.'

Oh, dammit, he was so sickly sweet. Banoffee pie with lashings of custard and sugar and more sugar and Cornish clotted cream on top.

'I've brought the valuation along, which sounds desperately crude and whatnot, but you'll need to insure them.'

Oh. Not pound shop then. Gawd. Prissy little pair of figures in various shades of shit – or more correctly, mostly likely nutmeg and umber – and she'd have to pay to keep them? She looked at the valuation. Bugger it. That was one hell of a gift. She swallowed. Having already accepted them, she was stuck. She took another look at the figurine in her hand.

'It's got a mark underneath – signature or something. Looks familiar. "L dot L".'

'That's the mark for early Sèvres.'

'Early?' Victoria remembered Emma talking about Sèvres porcelain when she did a module on the subject at university, but try as she might, no intelligent snippets of information came to mind.

'The Vincennes period of 1740,' said Simon.

'Yes, of course. Wow.'

'The costumes are the "Country French" style that nobles would wear when dressing down to ape the peasantry.'

'Gosh.' Gosh? She never said "gosh". Must've picked that up from Simon.

'They'd make an excellent subject for a still life.'

'Oh yes, wouldn't they!' Christalmighty, was she going to have to draw them, as well as pay the insurance?

'I'd love a picture of them.'

'Consider it done.' She placed the figure back in its box, went

26

over to Simon, sat on his lap and kissed him. 'Thank you for such a wonderful gift. You are the kindest,' *kiss* 'sweetest,' *kiss* 'boyfriend in the world and I don't begin to deserve you.'

'And you,' *kiss* 'know how to say,' *kiss* 'exactly what I want to hear.'

She considered the statement. Was he saying he knew that she knew she was talking a load of shit? Or was he being simple and sweet and loving? Or was he actually playing at saying exactly what she wanted to hear? And did she care? No. She stroked his hair, kissed him again, hopped off his knee and led him by the hand to the bedroom. He came without complaint.

There was a voice in her head. It had a strong Spanish accent.

I think you do not love this man, it said.

Maybe not, but I think you didn't love me. So, Señor, what do you have to say to that? Eh?

The voice didn't reply, didn't have a chance once she was lying on the bed and Simon was unbuttoning her top and dropping his head down to kiss her breasts. From then on, she really wasn't interested in anything else at all.

A few minutes later, he stopped. He stood up, straightened his shirt, and checked himself in the mirror, before turning back to Victoria.

'You are the most wonderful woman in the world, and I wish to take things slowly, one course at a time. You are a delight to be savoured.'

'A slow roast rather than fast food?'

'Yes. Yes, exactly. I knew you'd understand.'

He kissed his fingertips and then placed the kiss lightly on Victoria's forehead. She frowned.

'What's the matter, sweetheart?' he asked.

'I was hungry.'

'We can go out and eat if you like.'

Oh, good lord. Was he really that dense? Or maybe he was just shy. Inexperienced? Could be.

'Yeah, come on then. I fancy an Indian.' *Or a Spaniard,* she thought, naughtily. Sex with José might have been perfunctory, and designed purely for his own satisfaction, but at least they'd bloody *done* it.

She tried her hardest not to be grumpy through the meal, but couldn't help noticing how utterly gorgeous all the Indian waiters were and how handsome all the male diners were and in fact the females were pretty tasty too, and what was *wrong* with Simon? Maybe he was gay. Yeah. That must be it. No, he wasn't. Oh hell, she didn't know. Needed more to drink. This Cobra beer was decidedly yummy. She didn't usually drink lager, but it was just the thing with a curry and it did the trick. She relaxed and started to enjoy the meal. Simon's face by the light of the artificial candle on the table was more handsome than ever and *when the hell is going to sleep with me?* Shit, but she was drunk. Sober up, Victoria, sober up. She staggered to the ladies, splashed some water in her face, and looked in the mirror. Bloodshot eyes like an old lush. No wonder he wasn't interested. She was a sight. When had she last washed her hair? Always too busy during the day because of her art, and too busy in the evening because Simon was round. She was useless. Hopeless. In Spain, she'd been swimming every day, so at least she'd been clean. Right. That was the answer. Showers. She needed to smell fresh, not of turps and glue and sweat. No wonder he'd stopped so soon. Probably felt like throwing up at the stench of her. Talking of which – too much lager. Yeuch. Why had she ever thought she liked lager?

She ran into a cubicle and brought up the curry.

This was not good. She ran the cold tap, scooped some water up in her hands and sipped it, trying to clear her mouth. Someone else came into the ladies, and the smell of curry wafted in through the open door. She nearly threw up again, but just controlled herself.

Poor Simon. He'd given her the most genteel of gifts, and she'd acted like a tart in Bigg Market on a Saturday night.

For a moment, she wished she really were. Then she wouldn't have to be on her best behaviour; could throw up in the road and carry on partying with her mates, more curry, more lager, yay! Not with Simon, though. No – not with Mr Sensible Proper Simon, with his love of cold porcelain and his chilly perfection.

Victoria, pull yourself together. He's a sweetheart. A lovely bloke. Come on. Walk back out there and behave. Okay?

Okay.

She ran her fingers through her hair, and weaved her way back to their table.

'Sorry I was so long – not too well. Do you mind if we go?'

'Darling, of course not!'

He gestured for a waiter, asked for the bill, and they were out in minutes. He held her hand, and she wished he wouldn't, wished she could be alone, or with someone who understood who she really was.

Like me? asked a well known voice.

No. Nothing at all like you.

Chapter Four

Victoria was escorted home and chastely kissed on the cheek by an unusually silent Simon who left her on the door step and disappeared into the night with barely a word. She staggered up the stairs to her flat feeling queasy and dissatisfied. The box with the porcelain figurines lay open on the coffee table. She picked up the female figure, fumbled and dropped it. Bloody typical. At least it didn't break. Shit, but that would have been *so* embarrassing. 'Sorry, Simon, seem to have smashed your little china girlfriend. Don't mind, darling, do you? Oh, you do? Bye-bye then.'

She was still too drunk to do anything useful, so ran a bath, dropped her clothes on the floor and sank into the steaming water, sloshing it around the way she used to do as a child. Some of it went so high that it flopped over the rim of the bath onto the floor, leaving a puddle on the tiles. When she got out after ten minutes of blissful relaxation, she slipped on the wet patch and cracked her head on the wash basin. Rubbing the throbbing bruise, she decided it was not being a particularly clever day and the sooner she was in bed the better.

Once there, the dissatisfaction that had evaporated in the bath returned with a vengeance, along with the familiar, *What am I going to do with my life?* thoughts that she'd been having for as long as she could remember. Was it always going to be such a pain to sell a few pictures and hold onto a boyfriend? Not that Simon looked like straying. Not yet. Did she want him to? Perhaps. Anything to liven up the relationship. No, that was the stupidest thought yet. Simon was sweet and handsome and charming. Perhaps they just needed time. How long had it been – two weeks? Three? Something like that. Not very long, whatever. There was plenty of time for things to develop. With that consoling thought, she fell asleep despite the feeling of raw egg yolk sloshing around in her head.

She woke at three in the morning with a taste in her mouth like pickled garlic and cowpats. A drink of water in the bathroom didn't help. Shivering and nauseous, she crawled back into bed, sitting up to stop herself feeling sick. She pulled the duvet up under her chin and leaned back against the pine headboard, pressing the back of her skull against the edge so that the pain would take her mind off the nausea. It helped a little. She couldn't remember if she'd been dreaming or not, but Durham Cathedral was floating around the edges of her consciousness – this time tall and gaunt, rather than stocky and comfortable. She tried to imagine the organist filling the nave with glorious sounds, but instead of Bach or Buxtehude, all she could hear was the fairground music from *Carousel*. It went round and round and wouldn't stop. She resigned herself to its mesmerising flow and envisioned it curling like smoke round the pillars, forming long snakes and that tied themselves in knots around her neck and squeezed tight until her eyeballs popped out. No! This half-awake, half-asleep state was no good at all. She forced her thoughts outside the cathedral and down to the river, seeking consolation there, but inevitably she saw Emma and remembered her friend's desperation. What must it be like if love messes you up so badly that all you want is for your lover to push you off a cliff? What must that sort of distress feel like? Taste like? Not like last night's curry, that was certain. Victoria ran to the bathroom once again and retched. There was nothing left to bring up, but her stomach muscles complained and ached and she knew they'd hurt all tomorrow and maybe the next day too.

Back in bed, she gripped the duvet tight and sank into a troubled sleep. The cathedral enveloped her in darkness and she tripped, smashing her head on the edge of a huge crack that had appeared in its floor, stretching from one end of the nave to the other.

'Simon! Help me! Please!' she cried, scrabbling desperately for a handhold.

He came and stood at the side of the crack, squinting down at her. 'I don't understand this fissure, darling,' he said. 'What's it supposed to mean? What's its story? Tell me. Explain. I want to know.'

'No! Don't ask! You must never ask!'

'But you made it sweetheart. Why? Why did you dig this hole? What are you doing down there anyway?'

She burst into tears of rage and frustration at the impossibility of answering his questions, but in the end it didn't matter, because two hands came down and grasped her wrists and pulled her out. Only the hands weren't Simon's, and the arms that held her weren't his either, but the vertigo and pain slid away as she nestled into the duvet and slept.

She woke up at eight the next morning feeling surprisingly refreshed, if somewhat sore round the midriff. The sight that greeted her in the mirror was depressing. Bloodshot eyes, a greyish complexion and saggy skin. No matter. She felt better than she looked and was ready to paint. A commission for a book cover had come in by email a couple of days earlier. It was very specific – oil painting, impressionist style, Brittany coastal scene, two fishing boats, elderly fisherman in traditional garb with a boy assisting him, to be sent as a jpeg: 1913 by 2925 pixels, at 300 dpi. Sounded like the proportions had to be more or less two by three, so that would do for starters.

She took a large sheet of white card, measured it carefully, trimmed off the excess, and slapped a load of gesso over it as a primer. The whiteness hurt the back of her eyes, but it was work; real work with real money promised and a contract in the post.

Of course, there was that other commission to consider – the request to draw those blasted Sèvres figures. She could start on that while the gesso dried. It was unfortunate that she would sooner watch the paint dry than draw a delicate piece of porcelain, but that couldn't be helped. By studying the figures, she'd get to know them, maybe appreciate them better, which in turn could lead to further insight into Simon's character and taste. It was all to the good, as quite apart from anything else, she'd disgraced herself last night and owed him a sweetener.

No she didn't. She didn't owe him anything. The figures were a gift, not a bribe. She could draw them or not, as she pleased.

Having got that thought out in the open, she was happy enough to sit down and start sketching the silly things. Half an hour later, she was becoming familiar with their shapes, and the designs on their clothing; with their glossily perfect features and their nut brown and white colouration. They were still boring as art objects. Male and female by their dress, but ultimately sexless. Bit like Simon. The thought made her giggle. She put the delicate drawing to one side, took a new sheet of paper, and covered it all over with thick black oil pastel, until she had a slick, shiny surface, and her nostrils were filled with the spicy aroma of multiple colour; of black, darkness, the depths of a fire without light, just heat, waves of heat scorching her, igniting her hair and making it blaze, and – she tore up the drawing, scrumpled the pieces and threw them in the bin. The Sèvres figures watched and mocked her with their bone china perfection. Damn them. The desire to throw them on the floor and smash their smug faces was stronger than ever.

She picked up her pencil again. Draw, dammit! The pencil refused, and she threw it down in disgust, but then to her relief the phone rang, and okay, so it sounded like a thousand church bells pealing just two yards away from her head, but at least it was an excuse to stop. She answered, taking care not to hold the receiver too close to her ear.

'Hello?'

'Hi Vic, it's me.'

'Emma!'

'Yeah, look, sorry about what happened in Durham. I wasn't myself. Shouldn't have rushed off like that. It was very rude of me.'

Victoria forgot her hangover and frustrations and sat down on the carpet.

'Hey, you weren't rude. Well, not very.'

'Ha!'

'You were upset, which is perfectly reasonably under the circumstances, and I wasn't being too clever – should've been more sympathetic.'

'No, no, you were fine. It was me, but I'm better now.'

'Good. Getting stuff sorted out then?'

'Yeah. Just received some more bumph from the solicitor's. Another couple of months and it'll all be done and dusted, they reckon.'

'That'll be a relief.'

'That's putting it mildly. Look, can you come and visit? Properly this time? Stay with me in the cottage. Please? I know it's hard for you to take time off, but Bamburgh in early autumn's brilliant with all the tourists gone, and –'

'I know – been there often enough, after all, and you're absolutely right. I should come, and it just so happens that Simon – that's my boyfriend – he –'

'I didn't know you had a boyfriend? What's he like? Do tell.'

'Sweet as pie. A real poppet. Tall, fair and utterly gorgeous.'

'Yay! Excellent! Do you suppose he'd like to come too? He'd be more than welcome.'

'That's just what I was saying. He's got some sort of a "do" on next month at Alnwick Castle, and I was thinking, as that's not too far from you, maybe I can go to that with him and see you at the same time.'

There was silence.

'Emma? You still there?'

'Yeah, yeah, it's just that we used to go to an annual "do" at Alnwick.'

'Oh. Sorry. Didn't know.'

'It's okay, but I never want to see that blasted castle again.'

'You won't have to. Simon will expect me to go with him to the dinner thingy, but then I'll be free to see you. We can fix something up nearer the time, okay?'

'Yeah, that'll be fine. Vic?'

'Mmm?'

'Thanks.'

'For what?'

'Being a pal, putting up with me – you know.'

'Hey. Cheer up. Worse things …'

'Yeah, I know. Keep in touch, will ya?'

'Of course.'

'Good. And I promise to behave when you visit. Listen: "John". There. See? I can say it now.'

'Excellent. And handy – it's a very common name. Be awful if you had to avoid anyone called John for ever more.'

'True.'

'Right, I'll be in touch. Bye then.'

'Bye.'

Victoria put down the phone carefully. Simon's "do" at Alnwick was a gathering of antiques dealers. That meant it could quite easily be the same one Emma used to attend with John. Would he still go without his wife? Ex-wife? Whatever? Yes, of course he would; there was no reason why he shouldn't, but cripes – that could be awkward. No, why should it be? They would nod politely, Simon would say: 'Who's that?' and she'd reply: 'Oh, it's the ex-husband of an old university friend of mine. I don't like him much, so let's ignore him,' and Simon would say: 'Okay, no problem,' and that would be the end of the matter.

Back to the figurines. Victoria sat down at her art table, angled the two lamps so that there were no excessive shadows, moved a few pencils and brushes around, and considered the work she had done so far. It wasn't bad, but the angle of the female figure's mouth wasn't quite right. Not pouty enough. Insufficient smirkiness. Victoria took a pencil and lightly drew in a couple of fangs and a comedy scar. No! Naughty! She grabbed her putty rubber, moulded the corner to a point, and tried to remove the errant lines, but she could still just see them. Damn it! She'd have to rub the whole face out now with a heavy duty eraser and start again. There was a large eraser tied to the soft brush that she used for removing all the rubbery bits that were left behind, but the brush had disappeared. No – it had fallen into the bin. Bloody typical. Probably covered with glue and bits of paint and pencil shavings.

The drawing took the rest of the morning to complete to her satisfaction. She carried it to the coffee table for Simon to examine later. He'd like it, no question. The image was pretty and delicate. She'd shaded it with earth-coloured pencils, which gave a subtlety and richness to the nutmeg hues. She could almost persuade herself that she liked the figures, except for the way the female one's eyes followed her around the room. Couldn't be helped. It was done.

Chapter Five

Victoria stuck her tongue out at the figurines and went to make a cup of tea, turning the computer on as she went past. Might as well check emails, especially as there was no danger at the moment of a negative one from Emma. When she returned with the brew and logged into her account, she was disappointed to find her inbox contained just the usual rubbish: invitations to increase the proportions of an organ she didn't possess; a begging letter that required her to send a wood-burning stove to a family in Russia; and a huge win on a lottery she'd never entered, but which required her bank account details in order to pay in her prize money. There were no offers for a gallery opening in New York, or even a potato show in Bury St Edmunds. A few clicks and the annoying messages were consigned to spam and deleted forever. Google helpfully brought up a few Spam recipes, which she ignored, preferring to check the auction sites to see if she'd had any interest in her artwork. Nothing much was moving, except for a few sales on her postcard-size paintings on eBay.

Three games of tetris later, and without really thinking what she was doing, she typed 'Simon Tovey' into Google. There was a Detective Inspector, a Scout leader, and – yes. There he was. Dealer in Fine Ceramics. There were quite a few entries relating to his business, one way or another. And then – she couldn't resist – she typed in 'John Wotsisname'. She had to laugh. There were over 19,000 results, which proved she wasn't the only person who kept forgetting names. However, the very act of typing reminded her of his real name. John Stephenson. Of course. That was it. She typed it in. Crikey – he was important. Loads of entries. She looked through page after page of entries on antiques, Chippendale furniture, conferences, appearances as guest speaker all over the place – and even wedding photographs. She peered at them. Emma looked radiant. John looked possessive and not exactly smiley. She shivered. Enough. She turned off the computer and went to the kitchen for a slice of toast and marmite, which was all her delicate digestion could face at the moment.

After lunch, she packed her art bag and set off for her life drawing group. Some months ago, she'd joined with half a dozen like-minded artists to hire a studio and a life model for a few hours a week. The studio was a short walk and bus ride away, and provided a welcome opportunity to mix with other artists and talk "shop". It was also good to switch her brain into idling mode as far as her personal life was concerned, though that was becoming increasingly difficult to achieve.

Soon after arrival, she was deep in conversation with a couple of the other artists about the precise size of postcard paintings that was required for the American market, which was flourishing at the moment. They all agreed that it was foolish not to take advantage of the easy money that was available. Selling out? No. Artists have to live.

They arranged the lighting, set up screens to prevent drafts, and greeted Cynthia, the middle-aged woman laden with tins of dog food in a Tesco's bag who was today's model. She was one of their favourites – a part-time mature art student, who knew exactly what was expected. The session started with the model holding dynamic five minute poses. Victoria's pencil flew across the paper, capturing the sweep of an arm, the curve of a buttock, line, proportion, movement, swift cross-hatching to show form, *et voila!* The drawings lived, they danced across the page, and Victoria relaxed. This was what she should be doing; this was real.

The model then held a relaxed, longer pose of half an hour. Victoria drew quickly and finished ahead of time, so made lightning sketches of the other artists at work while she waited for them to finish. One of them, a young man known to them all simply as Mal – "My real name is unpronounceable just call me Mal," had been his way of introducing himself – had lustrous black hair which reflected the light. Victoria spent at least five minutes attempting to capture the effect. His hair could use a bit of re-styling, she reckoned, and then Mal would potentially be as attractive as José.

As attractive as me? I think not, said the familiar voice in her head, its lisping intonation making her lurch with desire unexpectedly.

Missing you, she whispered, silently.

Really?

Mmm.

I am not surprised. The boyfriend, this Simon, he is not a man of passion, I think.

37

Now hang on, José. Simon's all right. He's got plenty of passion. Just a slow worker.

You don't sound convinced, my sweet. I think you need someone quick and impulsive, not a snail who will slime around you for years before allowing you to crack open his shell.

Oh shut up. That's rubbish. We complement each other perfectly. A great match. You know, like Jack Spratt and his wife.

I don't think so, else why do you give your heart to this Mal, to this boy who reminds you of me?

Heart? Rubbish. I'm drawing. I love drawing. I don't love Mal, and I certainly don't love you. Now shut up and bugger off.

José laughed quietly, and put a vision into her mind of the two of them making love on a hotel bed. Victoria blushed but carried on drawing regardless, swearing out loud when the end of the pencil snapped off, as it was bound to do, she was pressing so hard.

And had it really been so great with José?

Of course, sweetness.

No, lover, it wasn't. You said all the right things, did all the right things, but your lovemaking was painting by numbers, not painting by passion.

I lack passion, you say? My kisses, were they the kisses of a porcelain person or a man of Galicia? I think you know the answer.

Yes, yes, I know all that, but where was the tenderness? The attention to my feelings? My needs?

I know your needs, my sweet. I see how you look at this boy with the black hair with such intensity, all the time dreaming of me. Why do you not simply empty your mind and concentrate on your art? Because you can't, my angel, can you.

Oh yes I can, but it's a good point, José. I shouldn't be dreaming of you at all. Bad, bad Victoria.

The enthusiasm had gone. Letting José into her head nowadays was a mistake, always depressing. She looked at the drawing. It was good, but overdone, as if she'd been trying to draw someone else entirely, and the imagined person and the real Mal hadn't gelled at all. She put her pencils away, closed the sketchbook, and sat for a while to see if she could empty her mind using will power alone. It didn't work. José lurked there in dark corners much of the time like a nasty piece of guilt. If she tried to think simple thoughts – a blue sky, a tree – then it worked for a while, but Simon's serious face would pop up and ask her what the tree meant, and she'd feel duty bound to give an explanation. And then something silly would happen, like an ostrich jumping out of the tree and telling her off.

This was a waste of time. She wasn't going to get any useful life drawing done this week.

'Sorry folks, gotta go,' she whispered, and picking up her bags, she sloped off quietly so as not to disturb the others.

Outside, the sun blazed down and the traffic had already slowed to virtual gridlock as workers tried to beat the rush hour by leaving offices at three o'clock. Victoria crossed the road and headed down to Trafalgar Square. She could usually find something to sketch there, even though the pigeons, which she'd love to have drawn, had been long banished. It was surprisingly quiet in the middle of the square, now that the traffic was restricted. She sat on a low wall and made a couple of rough sketches of Landseer's lions and a quick one of the springbok on the side of the South African Embassy, then decided she might as well pop into the National Gallery. She didn't often go inside, as she generally preferring more contemporary work, but the gallery housed some of her favourite paintings.

A few minutes later she was standing in front of Leonardo Da Vinci's *Virgin of the Rocks* reminding herself of the meaning of beauty, of real passion – not sexual thrills, but the real thing, the passion that defined who she was, what she was, and how her life had to be regardless of boyfriends and lovers and porcelain figurines and despite cracks through floors and cathedrals that could break your heart.

Neither José nor Simon spoke to her here, which was a profound relief. Although well aware that the voices were of her own making, she couldn't always shut them up. Here, in front of this masterpiece, she was free of them at last. Ten minutes was enough. She took some deep breaths, and made her way down to the café for black coffee – an unusual drink for the habitual tea drinker, but necessary this afternoon.

She caught a crawling bus back to the flat, working out a new canvas in her head as it trundled along. On arrival, with memories of beauty framed by rocks and her earlier life sketches still clear in her mind, she started painting movement and swirling shapes that morphed into life, then back into rock again, all within a cavernous womb-like shape. After two hours solid work, she knew she was succeeding in persuading the brush and the paints to follow her vision. She squeezed straight from the tube to the canvas, regularly standing back as far as she could – the easel was positioned so that she could retreat down the hallway for a full view. She left the painting for a while, had a cup of tea, watched a bit of TV, and then returned with fresh eyes. Another hour and a half she was exhausted, but relieved with the knowledge that the painting was definitely well on the way. She closed the door on the image, looking forward to seeing it again tomorrow and possibly finishing it. There was just time for a shower and change of clothes before Simon arrived. He'd like the sketch of the figurines – she was sure of that – and she'd balanced the negativity of having to draw them with the positive effect of the visit to the National Gallery.

She was right. Simon was delighted with the drawing.

'My sweet, sweet girl! This is exquisite. Adorable. Just like you.'

'Oh, you predictable gorgeous bloke you.'

She put her arms around him and gave a squeeze, then lifted her face to be kissed. He obliged, affectionately.

'So, what else have you been up to today?'

'A few quick sketches at my life group. Visit to the National Gallery. Started a large oil painting.'

She regretted admitting to the last the minute the words were out of her mouth.

'Large oil painting? May I see it?'

'Okay, but it's not finished. It's on the easel.'

Simon walked into the small back bedroom that did service as a studio and had a good look.

'Gosh, it's big isn't it. Must've taken ages. What's it supposed to be?'

Victoria resisted the temptation to scream like a banshee and gouge his eyes out with the sharp end of a paintbrush.

'Just an abstract, darling.'

'Right. It's very good. Thick. Impasto? That's the word, isn't it. Must use a lot of paint, something like that.'

'Yes, it does.'

'Tricky to sell, I would imagine. From the posting point of view. Packaging. You'd need specialist couriers. Very expensive.'

'Yeah.'

'Worry about that when it happens, eh?'

'Yep. So what are we doing tonight?'

'Beethoven.'

'What, the film? Never! With the big slobbery dog?'

Victoria remembered seeing it as a small child with her Mum. Her mood brightened immediately with the happy memory.

'No, silly – the composer. A violin and piano recital at the Wigmore Hall. The Spring Sonata and the Kreutzer Sonata, plus a token piece of twentieth century music that we shall be forced to sit through. Never mind. It's a good programme otherwise.'

'Cool. Just need to go to the bog and then I'll be ready.'

Victoria retreated to the bathroom and made a face in the mirror that said: "I hate chamber music recitals and would sooner be out clubbing," before returning to the living room with a more appropriate expression in place.

'I haven't been to the Wigmore in ages. This'll be fun.'

Chapter Six

London heaved with early autumn tourists. It was hot, smelly, noisy – and Victoria was loving it. She'd forgiven Simon for the figurines, for asking about her painting, and for proposing to take her to a classical music recital rather than a corny old film, and she'd managed to exorcise the intensity of Spain. She was home, in her favourite city. The peeling plane trees and stink of diesel from the buses, and the grease from burger bars mingled with the aroma of Italian coffee all compelled her to squeeze Simon's hand with delight and stand on tiptoes to plant a kiss on his cheek.

He didn't say anything, but he squeezed her hand back and looked so happy that nothing else mattered in the world. She adored this man, despite, or perhaps because of all his foibles and awkwardness, and his old-fashioned gravity.

Entering the Wigmore Hall meant stepping back to an age of style and elegance just a few hundred yards behind the questionable qualities of contemporary Oxford Street. The décor never failed to give Victoria a thrill, regardless of the music about to be forced upon her. She took her seat, glad to know that if the recital bored her, which it undoubtedly would, she could at least spend her time gazing at the art nouveau murals and drift away in their colours.

Simon bought a programme and handed it to her with a flourish. She'd just started to read it when he plucked at her elbow and whispered: 'Just spotted an acquaintance of mine down there near the front. We'll have to go and have a chat in the interval.'

'Oh? Who is it?'

'John Stephenson. Another antiques dealer, I'm afraid, but highly respected in the trade, and a most interesting fellow.'

'Oh, fuck it. Fuck it, fuck it, fuck it.'

'Victoria – shush!'

A couple in the row in front of them turned round and frowned. Victoria looked straight ahead, carefully not to meet anyone's eye.

'Sorry, it's just that he's – well, he's –'

'He's what? Likely to be another boring old fart?'

'No, silly, nothing like that. Thing is, I sort of know him. He used to be – or maybe still is, I'm not really sure – married to a friend of mine.'

'Really? You mean Emma? "Used to be?" Are you saying that they're splitting up?'

'Yep.'

'Wonder why. I only met her once. Very pretty girl, I thought.'

'Yes, pretty *and* intelligent – art history graduate.'

'Ah, that explains it. I always wondered how a highbrow like John came to marry a sweet giggly thing like her. Didn't realise she had brains too.'

Victoria punched him gently on the arm.

'You know when we met on the train? And I told you I'd been to Durham to see a friend who was going through a divorce? A man who slapped her around?'

'Yes, I remember, but that's absurd – it can't be.'

'Can't be what?'

'Can't be the same people. The John Stephenson I know would never hurt a fly. Charming fellow. You'd like him. What a strange coincidence.'

'Coincidence? Nothing of the sort. Can't be that many John Stephensons who are antiques dealers and married to people called Emma, can there? It's got to be the same bloke.'

'I suppose so. Maybe you're right, but darling, don't forget: you've only heard one side of the story. I've known John for a very long time. Regardless of what Emma may have said to you, I can guarantee that John would never be violent. It's not in his nature. He's far too civilised. Too controlled.'

'Well, there you go.'

'What do you mean?'

'Controlled. People like that are the worst. Bottling stuff up, you know? Then *kapow!* It all blows and you'd better not be anywhere near when that happens. Emma was caught in the full force of the explosion. I've no idea what set it off, but she wouldn't lie, not to me. We were at uni together. Three whole years sharing digs. And anyway, I saw the bruises. Look, do we really have to talk to him? I'd far sooner not.'

'No, of course we don't have to if it's going to upset you, but if he sees us, I'm sure he'll want to come over and say hello.'

'Yeah, I suppose. Just don't expect me to be enthusiastic with the small talk, okay?'

'Okay. Now, settle down and read the programme. I'll be asking questions later.'

'No you won't, cheeky.'

Victoria turned her attention back to the programme and read the notes on Lutosławski's Partita, which was to be the first piece. A few minutes later, the musicians entered the stage to polite applause. A young man sat down at the piano and adjusted the stool – *a nervous habit, surely*, thought Victoria. Wouldn't he have made sure it was at the right height earlier? The violinist, who looked about fourteen, made some minor adjustments to her tuning, took a deep breath and stood very still. After a few seconds, she nodded to her accompanist, and they began.

The music was fascinating; wild and lyrical with a perfect balance of tension. The two musicians sometimes played together, and sometimes went off on their own journeys, travelling to places where tonalities were new and strange, before returning home again. Victoria was mesmerised. This was something special. The piece ended, and she applauded with enthusiasm.

'Thank God that's over,' muttered Simon. 'Dreadful bloody row.'

Yes, that was to be expected. He didn't understand abstract art, so how was he going to understand that sort of music? Victoria didn't mind too much, but it was a shame. He'd brought her to a concert she'd expected to hate, but instead she was inspired – and he was bored. Perhaps the next piece would bring them together. She looked at the programme. Beethoven's "Spring Sonata". Could be good, could be tedious. She wasn't sure she liked Beethoven.

The piano started with a rippling figure, then the violin entered with a gentle melody, and they were off. Five minutes later Victoria stifled a yawn. How long was this piece? Best part of half an hour at a guess. Oh well. Time to examine the murals and read the rest of the programme. It didn't have much to say about this piece, but was fascinating on the Kreutzer Sonata that was to follow after the interval. It had apparently inspired Tolstoy to write a novella full of "jealousy, animal lust, abstinence and murder". Victoria looked up from the programme and squinted at the neat black hair of the man in the front row who she presumed was John, though it was hard to tell from this angle. Was he a man of animal lusts? Or was he an aesthete, someone who pursued beauty – art for art's sake? Would he kill for art? Would he hit an innocent woman in frustration? Was

Emma really so innocent? Would this bloody Beethoven sonata never end? Victoria tried not to look at her watch too often, for fear of upsetting Simon, whose eyes had a softly unfocused look, and whose lips were open in an expression of quiet rapture.

Quiet rapture. Could there be such a thing? Victoria wondered how John's face looked at the moment. There was a "ping" as the violinist accidentally caught the E string with her bow hand. Victoria imagined a look of sneering disgust on John's face. He wouldn't be impressed. Oh no. Perfectionist John would want explanations and apologies. He'd want to take the young violinist over his knee and give her a good spanking. Victoria just stifled her giggle. Of course he wouldn't. She looked at her watch. José, where are you? I'm bored.

Here, sweetheart. Spanking? This is what you want? You should have said.

No, no, of course not. Not at all. Not from you, anyway.

Not me? But I think this Simon, this simple boyfriend – he will not be interested in such things.

How do you know? He might have a wonderfully perverse streak that he's been too shy to show me.

I think not.

No, neither do I. Nice thought though.

Yes. Come ... let us "think" together.

Yes, let's.

Victoria indulged herself in an erotic daydream that lasted until the end of the sonata. The applause brought her back to reality. Simon turned to her.

'Now *that* was music. Exquisite! Beautifully played too, don't you think?'

'Yes, very ... umm ...'

He wasn't listening, luckily.

'What would you like – coffee? Something a bit stronger?'

'Pint of bitter?'

'Darling!'

'Sorry, wasn't being serious. Yes, coffee would be lovely. Thanks.'

They joined the press of people who were chatting away extolling the virtues of Beethoven and conveniently forgetting that another composer had featured in the recital; one whom Victoria had decided to explore further. She'd have to download that Partita and listen to it while painting; see what happened.

The coffee was strong, and the instant caffeine-kick an unexpected pleasure for the habitual tea drinker. She was sipping it decorously from a tiny cup, extending her finger just so and enjoying the contrast with her usual over-sized mugs, when she heard a familiar voice behind her.

'Simon – how are you?'

She turned and was faced with John Stephenson's Adam's apple. She'd forgotten how tall he was. No, he wasn't that tall. She was short. Her own fault for never wearing heels. She felt like an insignificant gnome beside the two men.

Simon held out his hand to shake John's. Oh how bloody old fashioned. Victoria wanted to kick him, remind him that this John person was a violent bastard, and the normal rules of civilised behaviour did not apply.

Simon failed to read her thoughts, and spoke with perfect politeness. 'John – good to see you. I believe you know Victoria?'

'Yes of course. Victoria?'

She met his eyes briefly as he nodded at her and raised an eyebrow as if to say: you're the last person in the world I want to talk to right now, but you're with my friend so I'm honour bound to greet you. Just don't expect me to shake your hand.

Fair enough. She wasn't at all keen to touch a man who'd hit her friend. She managed to mutter his name without spitting, and just – only just – stopped herself from asking after Emma. And then the bastard reached out and took her hand after all. Shit! How had he managed that? It was a brief, gentle touch, and then it was over, thank God.

Simon, who had apparently seen nothing untoward in the exchange, asked John what he was doing in London and John replied with guff about searching out a particular maker's furniture at a sale, and questioning its provenance. Victoria realised that she was not only a gnome, but an invisible gnome, so she made a tactical exit, muttering something about powdering her nose. She didn't think either of them noticed her disappearing off to the ladies. The temptation to leave the building altogether was strong, but she didn't want to embarrass Simon. She stayed in the loo until a notice came over the tannoy that the performance was about to start again.

46

Simon was already seated.

'You all right?' he asked.

'Yes, fine. Sorry I was so long.'

'No problem. I understand. But I really can't believe all that stuff about Emma, you know. John's a gentleman. No question.'

'If you say so.'

'Victoria!'

'What?'

'Never mind. They're about to start again.'

They applauded the return to the platform of the two musicians and settled back to listen to the music. During the course of the sonata, Victoria made up her mind not to pursue the matter of John and Emma with Simon. They'd only row about it, each taking the side of their own particular friend, both in a state of ignorance as neither of them knew any of the details. She spent the next half hour or so making up imaginary conversations with Emma, trying to sort out what had really happened. At the end of the sonata, while the audience was exploding in rapturous applause for a piece she'd barely heard, she was no further forward. She glanced at Simon's profile and realised that he was genuinely moved by this music, and even if she couldn't understand it, that was no different to him not understanding her art. His enthusiasm and his love of the Beethoven clearly equalled her passion for those mysterious four thousand year old cup and ring marked stones in the Durham Museum of Archaeology, or a square of canvas painted blue; pure blue, with nothing else to sully the perfection that she'd once seen at Tate Modern.

Maybe the two of them weren't so different after all.

They hardly spoke on the way back to Victoria's flat, but it was a comfortable silence, and they held hands all the way except when the crush of people prevented contact. Victoria was glad not to be in Emma's situation, glad not to be loving a creepy and completely unsuitable man, unable to make the relationship work on any level. Okay, so Simon was unsuitable superficially, but the fondness she felt for him tonight was a tangible thing that enveloped them both like a blanket.

Back at her the flat, still wordlessly, they moved into the bedroom as if it were the most natural thing in the world and something that they did all the time. Victoria put her arms round

Simon's neck and kissed him deep and long, and then at last they were on the bed and making love and the closeness and long-sought intimacy drove all other thoughts from her mind.

Chapter Seven

The miniature paintings of St Paul's Cathedral were selling well. Each one took half an hour or so to paint and cost only a few pennies to produce. Postage and packing came to under a pound. There was a small fee to list them on eBay, but Victoria was still making a profit of nearly £25 on each one. If she produced two or three of these a day she could make enough money to pay the rent and most of the bills – and she was producing nearer six. For a little variety, she also did Tower Bridge and the Houses of Parliament. This left little time for anything else, especially as on Simon's advice she was redecorating the flat. He'd persuaded her to paint the walls white to give a neutral background for her artwork and his porcelain, more and more of which was finding its way into her life. She'd been dubious about the lack of colour at first, but was now enjoying the extra light and illusion of space.

Simon stayed over at weekends and still came round most weekday evenings for a few hours, but for much of the time he stayed in his flat, completing paperwork connected with his business. Victoria never went to his house. After a few early visits full of terror at the thought of accidentally breaking his ornaments, she'd always managed to find some excuse to invite him round to her place instead. The arrangement worked well for them both.

One Monday morning in late August a picture postcard dropped onto Victoria's doormat. The photograph on the front was an interior view of an arched doorway in a medieval building. The door was open a crack and sunlight was streaming in. Victoria turned the card over and read the message.

My sweet, I think you forget me, but now my sleepy princess will awaken because I visit you this weekend. I fly to Heathrow and arrive at Paddington at 7:30pm on Friday. Meet me.
Besitos, José

Oh blimey. He had to be joking. Victoria shivered. José and Simon together in the flat? Three in a bed? She giggled, tried to imagine the scene, and laughed out loud. Catching sight of her face in the mirror, she was surprised to see a broad grin. Must be mad. Did she really like living dangerously? These last few weeks had been blissful and serene. Why this sudden desire to stir things up? No, that was a silly reaction. José was an acquaintance from Spain who was visiting London at the weekend, and was going to pop round and say hello – maybe they'd go out for a drink, do a bit of sightseeing – that sort of thing. Or maybe he and Simon would shake hands, find they had nothing to talk about, and José would make his excuses and leave, to find some sweet little tourist to entertain him. Except that Victoria wanted him all to herself. Couldn't Simon be persuaded to visit an antiques fair in Cheltenham, or something? Inverness? Bermuda? No, not a chance, not at such short notice. This was going to be tricky, true, but it might also be fun, and could perhaps inspire her to produce art that had more integrity than the current crop of banal miniatures.

Telling Simon later that day that she had a – dark and handsome – Spanish friend – lover – visiting at the weekend proved no problem at all. He wasn't jealous. Why should he be? It wouldn't have occurred to him that she'd slept with José. After all, she'd only been in Spain for a week. That was hardly time to form a relationship in Simon's world.

'Do you know where your friend is staying?' he asked.

'No, he didn't say.' Probably thinks he's staying here. Fat chance.

'I hope he's got something fixed up. He'll be lucky to find anywhere if he hasn't.'

'That's true, but there's always my sofa if he's stuck.' No there isn't. Naughty Victoria. You know what he'll expect if you invite him to stay. And that is simply Not Going To Happen. Okay? Okay.

'Hmm. I'm not sure about that. How well do you know this man?'

Better than you think. 'Yeah, see what you mean. A week's holiday isn't very long to know someone properly, is it. Tell you what, I'll only offer him my sofa if he's absolutely stuck.'

Simon looked doubtful. 'He could always stay in my spare room, I suppose.'

'That's kind of you, darling. I'll suggest it if he starts looking longingly at my soft furnishings.' No I won't. If he stays with you, the two of you will start comparing notes, and where does that leave me? Doesn't bear thinking about. 'I'm sure he'll have booked somewhere. He's not stupid.'

'Good. I look forward to meeting him.'

'Why?'

'Why? Because I don't know any of your friends. It's odd, that. We've hardly met any of each other's circle, have we? Except for our one mutual acquaintance.'

'Mutual? Oh, you mean John. Yes. José is very different to John.'

'Not an antiques dealer, I take it?'

'No, he's in wine production I think. Not sure exactly what he does. He didn't say.'

'Well, I look forward to meeting him.'

'You just said that.'

'Did I?'

Simon looked intensely at his fingernails and Victoria realised he was jealous after all. Well, well, well. The thought cheered her up immensely, there being nothing like a little green monster to spice up a relationship.

'So – where are we going tonight?' she asked.

'Guatemala, I thought.'

'That's different. Bit far though, wouldn't you say?'

Simon put his arms round her and kissed the top of her head.

'I've discovered a little Guatemalan restaurant in Finsbury Park. Quiet and authentic. Just the thing for a midweek meal out. Fancy it?'

'Yeah, why not. Won't be a moment.'

Victoria extricated herself from his embrace and slipped into the bedroom. She ran a brush through her hair, wincing as it caught on the day's tangles, and checked her teeth for errant pieces of greenery. All looked fine. Guatemala today, Paddington Friday – only Friday would not bring a cuddly teddy bear from Peru with a jar of marmalade, but a cuddly Spaniard from Galicia with a roving eye. She grinned at the mirror, but the grin was almost a leer. Crikey. Control yourself, Victoria. Sensible face. Now.

Friday arrived with cooler weather and butterflies in Victoria's stomach. She hadn't decided on any plan of action regarding José. The anxiety was getting to her so much that for the first time in weeks she couldn't settle to her tried and tested London miniatures. Instead, she found a tube of sepia gouache and a sheet of corrugated cardboard and painted trees full of rooks' nests and a river in spate with wild grasses bending over on its banks. Dark clouds and lowering hills framed the scene. She had no idea where the image had come from. Certainly not sunny Spain, and not Simon's world of porcelain perfection, either. She put the picture to one side, not sure what to make of it, but knowing the act of painting had been cathartic.

Simon called round at half past six, and they set off towards Paddington station. Victoria attempted to keep up a conversation, asking him how his day had been, but failed to hear a word of his answer. He in turn asked her about her day, and she told him about the picture, but could tell from his eyes that he was reading the advertising hoardings, and not listening to her detailed description. Pity. For once she was attempting to tell him the "story" of a painting, and he wasn't hearing it. By the time the train arrived, Victoria hadn't the faintest idea of what they'd been talking about, but knew they'd somehow managed to keep the conversation going.

She looked along the platform. People were alighting from the train with determination, most marching towards the exit at high speed. A few embraced friends or relatives who had arrived to greet them. Would José be there? Where was he? What did he even look like? Victoria panicked. She couldn't remember. How absurd. But then suddenly he was there – he stepped down from the train, caught sight of her and waved. She was relieved that he hadn't blown a kiss. He was smaller than she remembered, but she was so used to Simon's height now that most people appeared small.

'Your friend I presume,' said Simon.

'Yes – come on – let's see if he needs any help with his things.'

'I forgot to ask – does he speak English? Because I don't have a word of Spanish.'

'Not to worry. Neither do I. His English is fine.'

Good enough to talk me into bed. Shut up, Victoria! Concentrate, or you'll say something out loud that you'll regret. This is a casual friend whom you're introducing to your boyfriend. That's all.

She led Simon towards José's approaching figure, trying to keep a false grin off her face, horribly aware of her racing pulse. Would Simon be able to feel it through her hand? Hopefully not. Her palm had started sweating, but there was nothing she could do about it. She pulled away from Simon's grip and wiped her hand on her jeans.

José's face broke into a laughing smile and he called out: 'Vicki! My lovely girl! At last I see you again!' He dropped his bags, grabbed her with both arms and pulled her away from Simon with rough force before enveloping her in a bear hug and planting a passionate kiss on her lips that turned her legs to jelly. Yes! Her dark Spanish lover had come back to her!

Except that it didn't happen like that. The daydream had been fleeting and delectable, but the reality was sobering and sensible.

'Hola Vicki!'

'José! Good to see you again. I'd like you to meet my boyfriend, Simon.'

Simon stepped forward and proffered his hand. 'José? How do you do. Any friend of Victoria's ...'

They shook hands and José was all charm and friendliness. A few more words of meaningless introduction, and they were walking back through the station, all smiles and relaxation. José and Simon were soon deep in conversation, talking with alacrity about nothing at all of any interest. Victoria walked behind them, giving a little skip every now and again to keep up with their pace. Dammit, why did this always happen with José? Thoughtless creep. He always walked too fast for her. Always. Any minute now he'd probably sprint off down Euston Road and she'd never catch him, and if he took Simon with him – which was looking more than likely – then that would be that. She'd be all alone, and it wasn't fair, because he was *her* friend, not Simon's.

Victoria hadn't expected to feel so left out. Her boyfriend and her ex-almost-boyfriend were getting on too well. She recognised the technique José was using to put Simon at his ease so expertly. It was a practised seduction. All that worry for nothing; all that anticipation, the stress, the concerns that they'd hate each other and have nothing in common. She thought back longingly to her picture, desperately wanting the wild landscape and the rooks calling from the treetops; a river in spate and dark clouds rolling in across northern hills.

José turned round at last.

'Hey, slowcoach! Come.' He held out a hand. The smile was genuine, it wasn't a command, it was a friendly invitation. She didn't take the hand, having seen a quick look of concern on Simon's face, but was soon drawn back into their company as effortlessly as if there had never been any doubt that this was where she belonged.

Chapter Eight

Back at Victoria's flat, José undid his backpack and pulled out a bottle of wine. He instinctively homed in on the cupboard that housed Victoria's wine glasses and took out the three largest, filling them to roughly halfway. He lifted one, swirled the wine around and inhaled deeply, and then handed the others to Simon and Victoria.

'Let us drink a toast,' he said: 'to friends old and new.'

'Cheers,' said Simon, and they all clinked their glasses together and drank.

José looked around the flat and squinted at one of the few abstract paintings that Victoria still had displayed. He shook his head.

'I think you are missing Spain. You paint your walls white, and this is good, but you will never manage to bring Spanish light into this Northern city. You must return to my country for that – to the light and the colour of Galicia.'

'Err, yes, perhaps I will one day, but I was thinking of going to Wales next year.'

She wasn't at all, but the idea had sprung into her head as an escape hatch, and the more she thought about it, the more she liked it.

'Wales?' said Simon. 'First I've heard about it.'

'Yeah, to do some painting. Thought I'd rent a cottage in the spring – during school term time, so it would be cheap and not too busy.'

'I see. So you wouldn't want me along then, if you're working?' Simon looked worried.

'I think perhaps she has a secret lover in Wales, and doesn't want either of us along,' said José, unhelpfully. 'So, Simon. These pieces. They are valuable I think.'

José had picked up one of the hated figurines, and Simon's face lit up.

'You know porcelain?'

'A little. I know beautiful things.'

José caught Victoria's eye, but Simon chose not to notice. Instead, he launched into a discussion of the finer points of collecting Sèvres, which José, to Victoria's surprise, listened to intently, interpolating occasional comments which proved he really was listening and not simply being polite. Victoria didn't know what to make of it. If José had wanted to chat up Simon, he couldn't have picked a better subject, but neither of them were gay, so what was he playing at? Trouble-making? More likely just flirting because he couldn't help himself. It was both amusing and embarrassing to watch. Simon was so easily charmed.

Victoria ignored them both, and concentrated on the wine. She sipped it, savouring the warmth, and thought about the idea of a working holiday in Wales. Could be good. Mountains, rocks, solitude – yes, that would do nicely. It would be a relief to get away from London. There was the trip to Alnwick coming up, of course, but that was likely to be something of a trial. There'd be the formal dinner, having to be polite to all the John Stephensons, and then another heart-to-heart with Emma – which could be fraught or fun, depending on her mood. Not an ideal sounding weekend away, despite the attraction of walking with her friend on the beach at Bamburgh, in the cool, grey, North Sea light. Now, *that* was a thought. The light. Must take lots of photos. Excellent source material. Might not be much time for much sketching, but photos were always useful.

She took another slurp of wine, which was fragrant and delectable – of course, how could it not be – and smiled as José re-filled her glass.

A few hours later, she realised she'd barely said a word all evening. Simon and José had talked non-stop about porcelain, wines, Spanish history and politics, the state of the railways, and goodness knows what else. Victoria was pleasantly tipsy, and happy to be an observer from the corner of the sofa.

The two men made an unlikely pair – tall and elegant Simon, with his perfect profile and immaculate manners, and livewire José, with his energy and charm and ability to captivate his audience. Victoria took mental notes, and played a game of giving each of them a certain number of points for factors in their favour, before removing points for random annoyances – like the way José was ignoring her, and Simon's old-fashioned leather brogues. She closed her eyes and let the conversation wash over her. If Simon started to dress less like his grandfather, and José paid her attentions in the considerate way Simon did, would that improve them? Or would they still not be quite right? How about: Simon's height with José's colouring; Simon's good manners, with José's charisma. Yes, that could work. She must suggest it. Get them to meld themselves together into one person – with two heads and four legs – which would be useful for galloping across beaches, but not much else. Although, perhaps she could ride the two of them across the aforementioned beaches? Two of everything though ... the mind boggled. She chuckled at the thought.

José noticed. 'Sweetness, I think I've heard that laugh before.' The wink he gave her was dangerous.

Simon stopped talking and looked embarrassed.

Careful, Victoria. Careful. 'Oh, sorry, I was miles away,' she said, almost too casually.

'I think you were in Spain' said José.

'No. Tate Modern.' Her mind had leapt there unexpectedly, so it was a truthful enough answer.

'You go there to meet your lovers?'

'My *what*?'

'The paintings that you love. I remember you talk to me about the way paintings speak to you, touch you, get under your beautiful skin.'

'Chrissake, José.'

She was cross and drunk, and he was sitting there oh so smugly and twisting her words, making her feel stupid and embarrassed, just like he always did. It was no good. She wanted him out of the flat before either of them said anything that couldn't be unsaid.

'Right, boys, time for you to leave. I need some sleep.'

Simon leapt to his feet.

'Yes of course darling. I'm so sorry – here we are, chatting away – most inconsiderate. I have to get home anyway – early start tomorrow. José? Where are you staying?'

'Here, of course – if Victoria will have me?'

'Sorry, don't have a spare room.'

'Ah, I think that you are teasing.'

'No, I'm not. Simon?' She looked at him anxiously.

He nodded and turned to José. 'I'm sorry José, but Victoria's flat is far too small for overnight visitors. You should have booked a hotel, but if you're stuck, you can stay at my place tonight, and then sort something out in the morning.'

'Ah, I am the foolish one. I did not realise. But you are such a gentleman, Simon. It will be my very great pleasure to stay with you tonight. I thank you so much.'

The last comment was made in a tone that would have melted Victoria had it been addressed to her. She wondered what it was doing to Simon. He appeared not to have noticed.

'Right. We'll get going then.'

Victoria could hardly bid her guests farewell from the corner of the sofa, so rose to her feet as slowly as she could to cover any unsteadiness. She lurched over to Simon and gave him an affectionate hug and a warmer kiss than usual, wishing she could stay holding onto him, but José was waiting in the wings for his goodnight kiss, and panic, panic, panic – was he going to be all Spanish and passionate? Was the evening going to end in catastrophe?

But José had already moved to the door. He wasn't going to kiss her after all, and she was disappointed. He waved, gave her a charming smile and said: 'Goodnight my beautiful lady, and may your sweet dreams be filled with the memory of *La Playa de las Catedrales*.'

Oh, you clever man. You avoid a scene, but promise to inhabit my dreams. Very well. Now off with you. I don't mind dreaming about you, but that's all.

An hour later, Victoria was still sitting on the sofa, lost in pleasant thoughts of Spanish beaches and the sea and that quality of light that might, just might, draw her back to Spain one day. The second wine bottle was empty and she was thinking of going to bed, when the doorbell rang. She checked her watch. Five past midnight. No way was she answering the door this late. She ignored it, but it rang again, twice, and then her mobile went off and there was an incoming text from José which read: *Open your door Vicki, please, it's cold out here. I need your warmth.*

What the hell? When he'd left with Simon, they'd been the best of friends. Why had he come back? What could have happened? More to the point, should she let him in? Christ, no. No, no, no. She knew how that would end, and was on the verge of texting back the single word: 'NO', when it occurred to her that if she did, he'd know she was still up and would keep trying. Better to ignore him. The bell rang again, twice. Then he hammered on the door. A dog started barking. He'd wake everyone in the street if he carried on. She'd have to let him in. No, she wouldn't. Oh hell. She didn't know what to do. She curled up on the sofa and hugged her knees willing him to go away, but the bell kept ringing.

Sit it out. Come on, Victoria, you can do this. If Simon's changed his mind about having José stay, for whatever reason, then you certainly don't want to be offering a shoulder for him to cry on until you know what's happened. Just wait. He'll go. And if he doesn't, you can always call the police. It's not a problem.

Another text came in: *My tears fall. Loneliness consumes me. I miss my beautiful Vicki. I need her so much. There are things I must tell her. Betrayals. I have made discoveries. Simon is not to be trusted. Please, my sweet. Open your door. Let me in. Let us speak, let us find comfort in each other's arms. I love you so much.*

Okay, that was clear enough. José was up to his old tricks of manipulation and seduction. She would switch her phone to silent, and leave it in the kitchen. Simon might have his faults, but at least he was trustworthy. No doubt she'd find out in the morning from him what had gone wrong, but in the meantime, José could get lost. The memories of their perfunctory lovemaking in Spain came flooding back and made her wince. She was not – absolutely not – going to go through that again. She felt sick. Too much wine mingled with fear and revulsion. Not a good mix.

If only she could stop shaking. This was silly – the door was locked and he couldn't get in – but still she trembled.

She missed Simon desperately, and wished she was with him now, but there was no way she could escape from her flat without José seeing her, and anyway it was too late. Simon wouldn't take kindly to being woken up at this time. And what if ... what if José had said terrible things about her and *that* was why Simon had kicked him out? What if he was now thinking that there must be some truth in whatever he'd been told? What if? There were too many what ifs. It was no good. She couldn't do anything now. Had to sleep.

The doorbell rang over and over again. Victoria stumbled into the bathroom and put the shower on so that she couldn't hear it. She undressed quickly and stood in the hot water, scrubbing herself vigorously to rub away the memory of José, but he wouldn't go. It was as if he'd seeped into every pore. She wished she'd never met him. Never gone to Spain. Never met Simon even. Never met anyone. Just lived in a small cave up a mountain as a hermit with a small piece of ochre to scratch out pictures on the wall.

Sometimes art was all that mattered.

Holding that thought, she turned off the shower, dried herself swiftly and got into bed. She snuggled under the duvet and thought of earth colours and caves, and of someone – she didn't know who – but someone kind and warm who held her close.

Chapter Nine

Victoria woke the next morning with a slight hangover and a suspicion that there was something she should be worried about. It only took a few seconds to remember. José. Simon. Text messages, doorbells. Oh, buggery hell. She tried to will herself back to sleep, but it didn't work. Her mind had woken up and was buzzing.

The mobile in the kitchen would be filled with messages. She didn't want to look at it. Had it not been for the inconvenience of living without a phone, she'd have put it in the bin without further ado, other than maybe smashing it to bits with a hammer.

On the other hand ... it was no good. She had to know. She shambled into the kitchen and checked for texts. That was odd. Apart from a few final bleats from José last night, there was nothing. Why? Why hadn't he texted her all through the night to swear undying love, promising her the world if only she'd let him back into her flat, her heart, her bed? The bed was probably the reason. He wasn't stupid. He'd have realised there was not the slightest chance of them sleeping together. What about Simon though? That was the greater concern. Why hadn't he texted? Because he never did. Yes of course, that would be the reason. It wouldn't have occurred to him. Bastard. No, not a bastard. A dear sweet man who loved her more than she deserved.

Satisfied with her explanation, she shuffled back into her bedroom and got dressed. It was a grey day, but Simon would be coming over in the afternoon and they could go for a walk in the park or along the South Bank. Something simple. There had been vague plans to take José round the sights, but that wasn't going to happen now. It had better not. Christ! What if he turned up? What if they both turned up at the same time? She had visions of challenges to duels, or more likely an ugly little scene of bare knuckle fighting on the landing. Simon had the advantage of height, but José would undoubtedly have the experience. Bloody hell. Last thing she needed. Wouldn't happen. Couldn't.

She pulled a brush through her hair, wincing at the tangles, trying to put Simon and José out of her mind. It was early – only seven-thirty – and she had the whole morning free. She could put on some music, start a new canvas and see what happened. It would have to be an abstract. No good trying to paint any postcard potboilers today. She needed to get back to basics. There was a large primed canvas ready and waiting – she pictured herself squeezing copious amounts of paint onto it, and setting to work with a palette knife. It was a good thought. The picture would probably end up as mud, but then again, it might not.

A couple of hours and a pint of tea later, it was most certainly not mud. It was thought. Pure and simple. And if Simon had asked her what she meant by that, she'd have happily made something up – called it a thought of a river; a slate scree; the cry of a curlew; heather, stunted and windblown; a drowned village; an old sailing boat. That would do. If she threw all those images at him, he'd peer into the picture and try to find them and not be too worried when he couldn't.

At half past ten the doorbell rang. She listened for her mobile, anxiously. If she didn't answer the door, and it was José, he'd text. If it was Simon, he wouldn't. Nothing happened. The bell rang again. Still no incoming text, but José would ring the bell at least two or three times before trying to contact her any other way. She couldn't leave it much longer, because Simon – if it were Simon – would go away, and that would be a disaster, as he'd probably think she was in here with José, and then it would all be over and that absolutely, categorically mustn't happen.

Could it be the postman? No. Too early.

Her pulse was racing. She had to answer the door. Simon would never forgive her if she didn't, but if it was José, he would push his way in, and small though he was, he was wiry and strong, and she was terrified of him. The thought came as a surprise. She hadn't realised.

It could be Geraldine from next door. She sometimes ran out of milk.

Victoria fixed a picture of Geraldine firmly in her mind, and went to open the door. If it was José, it was her own bloody fault, and she'd have to face the consequences.

It was Simon.

'Oh, thank God!' she said, but instead of the usual kiss, he pushed past her and strode into the living room.

'Is he here?'

'No, of course not. He came round later last night, but I wouldn't let him in. Wouldn't talk to him. I didn't know what had happened – I was so worried. And afraid.'

'Afraid? He's supposed to be your friend. Why were you afraid?'

'He's not my friend. Never was my friend. He's just – someone. Someone I met on holiday in Spain, who latched onto me.'

'Or you latched onto him.'

'No. Yes. I don't know. He was there and it was hot and sunny, and he offered to show me places, and I thought he was fun. Then. But he's not, is he.'

'Not even remotely.'

'You were getting on fine with him last night okay. Talking for hours. Porcelain, and wine and everything.'

Simon didn't answer. He picked up one of the figurines and put it back down again with a look of disgust on his face.

'Simon – what happened? Please?'

'You sure you didn't let him in?'

'Positive. I wouldn't. You have to believe me.'

He put his hands in his jacket pockets and walked over to the window. With his back to her, he began speaking, quietly and carefully.

'Okay. I want to believe you. But –'

'But?'

'It isn't easy.'

She longed for him to turn round, to face her. This was horrible. She was excluded and helpless. She felt a lump in her throat. Don't cry. Please don't cry. Just listen. At least it's Simon and not José. Everything will be all right if you just listen.

After a silence that lasted too long, Simon spoke, quietly and unemotionally.

'We walked back to my place. Talked of this and that. He suggested another drink. I poured us a couple of whiskies. Then he started talking about you.'

'Oh.'

'About what you'd been like in Spain. With him. He didn't go into any details. Just talked of – of passion. Said you were a passionate woman. Said I was a lucky man.'

Victoria blushed. Stupid reaction, but she held onto the fact that José hadn't gone into any details. Maybe Simon would think the "passionate" referred to her conversation, the way she expressed herself, her art. No, don't kid yourself Victoria. He'd know full well what José meant.

Simon turned round to face her.

'How long were you in Spain? You told me it was a week. Must have been far longer for your ... relationship ... to progress that far. Why did you lie?'

Oh, cripes. What to say? Admit to jumping into bed at the first opportunity, or lie and say she'd been there much longer? Impossible decision. Needed hours to think over. She kept quiet, reminding herself to listen to everything he had to say. That was all that mattered at the moment. Give herself time. She looked up at him and was shocked by the sadness in his face. This relationship was too bloody one-sided. Simon mattered to her, of course, but that look in his face – did she really matter to him so much more?

He gave a shudder.

'But never mind that. I want to know, but I have no right to ask, no right at all. I realise that. It all happened before I even met you. That's why I didn't pursue the matter with him, and I'm not going to pursue it with you.'

He paused, stared intently at the carpet, and continued: 'I didn't kick him out because of what he said about you, though in retrospect, I should have. It's appalling that I didn't. Blame jealousy, or whatever, but I ... something in me wanted to hear what he had to say.'

Victoria swallowed. She wanted to know too, but there was no way she was going to ask directly. She found her voice.

'Then if you didn't kick him out for that, why did you?'

'He – what's the phrase? He "came on" to me. Yes. I think that's it.'

'Cripes!'

'Victoria.'

'Yes?'

'I don't like your taste in friends.'

'No,' she gulped, tears prickling in her eyes: 'neither do I. He's horrible. Disgusting. Vile. I wish I'd never met him.'

'At least we agree on that.' He exhaled, shut his eyes, and then drew a deep breath. 'Come on. Let's get out of here. Catch a train to somewhere. Go for a long walk. Anywhere. So long as we're out of London for the day. Away from it all. And do stop snivelling.'

At last he smiled, and everything was going to be all right, but then the blasted doorbell rang.

'Oh, shit! I'm not answering that. No, no, no! You can't make me!'

'I don't intend to.'

Victoria ran into the kitchen, grabbed her mobile and threw it into bin, pushing it down beneath cabbage leaves and tea bags.

'Just in case,' she said, as she came back into the living room.

The bell rang again.

'Do you want me to answer it?' he asked.

Victoria nodded. 'Please.'

She walked over to a bookcase and took out a slim volume on the works of Oskar Kokoschka, tried to read the description of one of his paintings but failed to take in a single word. She heard Simon walk into the hallway and open the door. She tried not to listen any further, but couldn't avoid the murmur of words. Softly spoken – that was good, wasn't it? Not that Simon would have shouted, but still. After a few minutes, the door was closed and Simon came back in.

'Jehovah's Witnesses.'

'Thank God!'

He laughed. 'A highly apt response. They'd be delighted, but I'm afraid I sent them packing. Come on. Let's get out of here before anyone else calls.'

Chapter Ten

Binning the phone had been a masterstroke. The next couple of weeks passed peacefully, with no texts possible, and just one postcard from José which Victoria shredded having read the message. She didn't tell Simon about it, remembering John's comment about "open wounds". Some things don't heal. José's name was never spoken, so she wasn't about to say, "Oh, by the way, I received a charming postcard from José today, in which he wrote of his broken heart, how much he misses me, and how he longs for me to return to Spain to comfort him."

There was a fragility to Simon these days. He needed the psychological equivalent of what Victoria's mother used to call "strengthening medicine", but the Alnwick trip was fast approaching and then he'd be amongst his cronies, able to talk antiques for the whole weekend, so that should do the trick. Victoria would tell Emma all the gory details of the José debacle, and she, in turn, would no doubt counter with horror stories about John's violent temper. Everyone would be happy. There was nothing like a bit of shared misery to lift the spirits.

She re-read the last email from Emma.

Hi – you killed your phone or something? Tried a few times, but I can't get through. Not to worry. The dreaded Alnwick dinner's in a couple of weeks, isn't it. *groan* What are your plans? You'll have to do the little woman in attendance thingy, of course, but I could pick you up on the Sunday and we could go down to the cottage and walk along the beach. It's littered with broken hearts right now, at least two of mine included. Maybe we can pick up some driftwood and knock together a sculpture or something. Decorate my back yard in the style of Derek Jarman. Might be fun. Or go for a ride. I can book ponies if you like. Can you get rid of Simon? I'm sure he's lovely, but we'll have to be sensible if he's around, and where's the fun in that? I'll drive you back to your hotel later. Simon can talk antiques all day and we can talk about the things that really matter – seaweed, sand in your pockets, rocks that look like a giants built them into great fortresses, but the sea stole them back, tried to break them, and couldn't, not really. What the hell am I talking about? I don't know. Cya. Emma. xxx

Having visited the beach at Bamburgh many times, and knowing something of the geology – thanks to an ex-boyfriend in the university rambling club – Victoria knew exactly what Emma was talking about. It was great to be back on the same wavelength after the difficulties in Durham.

The Alnwick "do" would require a posh frock. Victoria lived in jeans and assorted tops – old shirts of Simon's covered in paint, a few jumpers with the threads pulling out, plus one smartish pair of black trousers for "best". The trial by dinner would require something more if she were to have the courage to walk between the rows of armour, pikes and broadswords, instruments of torture, and goodness knows what else that decorated the castle – quite apart from the assorted antiques dealers. She might even need a proper haircut. No. That was going too far. A trim of her fringe with a new pair of scissors would do. No it wouldn't. Don't be daft. Should she buy a lipstick? She was still using one from her student days which was probably crawling with bacteria by now. It was all such a pain. Why couldn't she go in a stripy t-shirt and a big floppy hat and be introduced as Simon's wildly exciting Bohemian artist girlfriend? Because he'd be embarrassed, that's why.

A trip to Knightsbridge was the answer. She could look at the dresses in Harrods, laugh herself silly at the prices and styles, pop over to the Serpentine Gallery to restore her sanity, and then find some backstreet shop with antique cocktail dresses – except that they'd probably be even more expensive. Christ, how could this be so difficult? What did other women do? Were they born knowing how to dress? No, probably not, unless they were French.

When Simon came round on Saturday morning, she asked him straight out.

'What should I wear for the Alnwick dinner?'

'Whatever you like, darling.'

'Victorian swimsuit and straw boater?'

'No, I don't think – ah, you're not being serious. What's the problem? Wear whatever you ladies customarily wear upon such occasions.'

'Aarrgghh!'

'Good grief! Whatever is the matter?'

'Oh nothing, nothing at all. Just don't complain if I turn up in a

66

polka-dotted summer frock when everyone else is in something so simple and black that they pass out with colour overload when I make my grand entry.'

'Well there you go. You answered your own question. Simple and black. See? You knew all along.'

She stared at Simon, trying her hardest to do a hurt puppy expression in the hope that he'd take the hint and give her some money to buy something decent. He didn't notice, which meant that if she shamed him by turning up in something ghastly it would be All His Fault and he'd be the one to suffer.

Last chance.

'Come with me? Help me choose something?' Pay for it. 'Please?'

Simon gave the standard "bloke asked to go clothes shopping with girlfriend" look of horror, but allowed himself to be persuaded. That was the advantage of boyfriends of relatively short standing. They were still eager to please and could be manipulated.

She had an evil thought: 'Tell you what, why don't we do the shopping and then pop into the Maria Lassnig exhibition at the Serpentine?'

He'd hate it. Octogenarian Viennese feminist artist with a penchant for nude self-portraits? Yeah, just his cup of tea –not. Anyone for Sèvres? Ha!

'Yes, of course. Haven't been to that gallery for ages. I believe the Lassnig exhibition has had excellent reviews.'

'Thanks darling.'

She kissed him swiftly on the lips and moved away before the kiss could turn into anything else. 'Now?'

'What?'

'Go shopping now?'

'Umm … yes, why not?'

'Good. C'mon then.'

After dragging Simon round several department stores and half a dozen boutiques, Victoria gave up on black and chose purple instead. To hell with the antique wives. She was an artist. She didn't "do" little black cocktail dresses. The chosen outfit was a retro affair of crushed velvet. Looking at herself in the mirror in the changing room, she knew she needed to be taller to make the dress look properly slinky, but it was good enough. She would buy some heels. Nothing too monstrous, as she'd have to be in them for hours, but she knew what she wanted; soft black leather and long pointy toes, of the sort that would once upon a time have had her mother complaining that nobody could possibly have feet that shape, and how did she walk up stairs? Simon would most likely say the same. Good grief – was she dating her mother?

'Come on, Mum,' she muttered as she dragged Simon out of the last shop and towards Hyde Park. The sound of the traffic conveniently covered her words. Once in the park, they passed the usual oddities – a man in a rowing machine on wheels, doing about two miles an hour; another skiing along the tarmac and not managing much more. What was wrong with a bicycle? With roller blades? No matter – the sun was blazing down, Simon had just spent a ridiculous amount of money on her, and she was going to have a long natter with Emma in just a few weeks time. And see John Stephenson. Possibly. Possibly not. Be disappointing if he wasn't there, after all this anxiety. A waste of weeks of being a stress-head.

They entered the gallery and were faced with a vast canvas of a naked elderly woman, legs akimbo, brandishing two guns; one pointed at her head and the other aimed straight at the visitor. The picture was as "in your face" as it was possible to be. Victoria risked a peek at Simon, and came close to snorting with laughter at his entirely predictable shocked expression.

The painting was glorious – wicked and funny and shocking and uplifting and life-affirming all at the same time. Victoria knew she was going to love this exhibition. Simon was going to hate it. Success! That would teach him. Teach him what? Who cares.

Painting after painting showed the artist with a wry, cheeky expression, unashamedly displaying flaccid breasts and mottled thighs. Other paintings depicted a fat naked man in various poses, a woman sitting on the toilet bathing her husband in the bath and much, much more, all produced with a verve and energy that took Victoria's breath away. Many of the paintings were so fresh they looked almost unfinished, with their swathes of bare canvas surrounding explosions of colour and life. This was what mattered; not which frock to wear to a convention of antiques and their wives.

Victoria looked out of one of the vast windows across the

parkland. Families with young children were heading in all innocence for the gallery, no doubt having spotted the "free entry" sign. She wondered how the parents would explain that first painting to their curious offspring. Would they have the sense to say you don't explain paintings? Probably not. They'd fumble for words then try to distract the kids with bribes – offers of ice cream that would enable a quick exit.

There was a flash of red – roses? Pelargoniums? Blood spatters from distressed tourists who'd cut their wrists having realised how little they understood contemporary art? It didn't matter. The light reflected her mood, bouncing off the lake and the distant glinting gold of Prince Albert, as he sat imperiously in his memorial with a pigeon shitting on his head.

Simon tapped her on the shoulder.

'I've had enough. Going outside. See you there.'

He turned and left.

What was wrong with the man? Had he no life in him at all?

Victoria walked slowly back to the entrance in his wake, catching the artist's eye in each painting as she went. She liked to think that they winked at each other; that they had a laugh at the men in their lives, and then shot themselves through the head in despair at how useless – how utterly bloody useless – they all were.

She caught up with Simon on the lawn outside the gallery. He was stretched out on the ground, squinting at the sun, and sat up as she approached.

'Sorry darling, not really my thing.'

'Yeah, so I gathered.'

'Cross with me?'

'No. Course not.'

She managed to smile at him, and found that actually she wasn't. Not much.

On the way home, she stopped off at a craft shop and bought a small bag of clay. She had an urge to make a figurine – something totally hideous; an anti-Sèvres figure. Crude. Ugly. Full of venom. Medusa-like, so that anyone looking upon it would be turned to stone, or at least frozen with horror for a moment or two.

The following Monday, when Simon had gone to work, she unwrapped the clay, cut off a good sized chunk, and spent ten minutes slamming it down onto the table and kneading and working it until it was ready to be moulded to shape. Muscular arms. Well developed chest, but sagging and old. A head on a withered neck. Sunken eyes and cheeks. A long pointed tongue flickering out of its pinched mouth. Flaring uneven nostrils. Horns instead of hair – a dozen of them, curling out in all directions.

An hour later she smiled at the homunculus, satisfied with her work. He'd need hollowing out to help with drying, but that would have to wait, as he was too soft to work at the moment. Quite what she was going to do with him, she had no idea, but she already knew that he would become at the very least, a drawing, a painting, an inspiration. His ugliness was refreshing – even comforting.

Simon was too perfect. She needed ugliness in her life. Danger. Violence? God, no. Not that. Just ... something.

Chapter Eleven

Victoria had packed the purple dress with care, along with a new pair of pointy black boots. Her hair had been professionally cut for once, on Simon's insistence, and she'd bought a new lipstick. She'd now worked herself up into such a frenzy of anticipation that Simon had to tell her to stop being so manic. This had much the same effect as a mother slapping a child to stop it crying. Victoria seethed for a while, wanted to strangle him, and then affected a total lack of interest in the proceedings just to spite him.

Simon had bought the railway tickets a while ago, but only now blithely informed her that they would be breaking the train journey at Durham so that he could, "see a man about some porcelain".

'Wow. Excitement,' said Victoria. 'Do you suppose I can go up and see his etchings while you're fondling his figurines?'

'Victoria!'

As it turned out, the elderly gentleman who owned the figurines really did possess a collection of etchings, smuggled out of Poland by a great uncle during the war. Victoria was impressed, and enjoyed a happy half hour examining them. Simon spent the time closeted with fine porcelain and emerged looking smug with a neatly tied box tucked under his arm. The old man came out beaming, clutching a cheque. Their pleasure was infections, and Victoria relaxed. She was back in the North, and despite being a Londoner, this felt like a homecoming, thanks to the years at the university.

They had a couple of hours to kill before the next train that would stop at Alnmouth, so Victoria suggested they visit the Botanical Gardens. Simon had never been, but Victoria knew the place well, and wanted to see if it had changed much since her student days.

The gardens were in all their late summer glory. The great gunnera leaves looked on the point of collapse, ready to fall into a rotting mass on the ground. Insects were taking advantage of the weather to gather all the pollen they could, or eat each other, depending on preference, before the colder weather set in. Students lay around on the grass, leafing through copious notes or sticking their tongues down each other's throats.

Simon and Victoria visited the glass houses first, pausing to pull faces at the koi carp in the ornamental pond. Then it was through the rainforests – press the button on the wall to make it rain – before emerging at last in the formal gardens. Victoria led the way along the well-remembered bamboo pathway, through the woodland, and over the brook to the meadow beyond. Here the heat was intense. Flowers reached out to the sun, their petals stretched in open invitation, their nectar seeping and oozing, as bees, drunk and delirious, staggered from bloom to bloom.

Victoria turned to Simon in the midst of this fecundity, suddenly desperate to feel his hot mouth on hers, but he had walked by unseeing, frowning into the distance, thoughts no doubt on porcelain rather than the glories all around. Victoria stuck out her tongue at his back and dawdled after him up the bank, but she was soon distracted by the abundance of colour surrounding her. Crouching down, she touched a scarlet flower, marvelling at the dusty pollen that fell onto her fingers, followed by petals – one, two, three. *He loves me, he loves me not, he loves me.* The pods, newly exposed by the fallen petals, were fat and green, ready to burst open and scatter their seeds. One sprang open with a ping when she stroked it and out popped a mass of pale brown specks onto the path. She looked up to call Simon, but he had walked on too far and she'd have to shout, so she didn't. Why was he so blind? What was wrong with the man?

Moments later, as though he'd heard her silent plea after all, Simon turned and came walking back towards her, brushing past the meadow grasses and treading on flowers with random destructiveness. Didn't he care? Didn't he notice anything? Would he even notice if she were pregnant, Victoria wondered? Probably not. What if she popped out babies, with a ping, ping, ping, scattering them all around? No, he'd be busy dusting a piece of porcelain – prioritising the things that really mattered. Best not become pregnant then. He'd make a crap father anyway. Too sensible. Too fond of his precious ornaments. No toddler would have a chance. Smash, bang, wallop. Dreadful thought.

'We should be getting back,' said Simon when he was near enough not to have to shout. 'I'll burn in this sun. Didn't think to bring any sun block and this hat doesn't give anywhere near enough protection.'

72

She examined his flushed cheeks and the bright pink patch at the end of his nose. Revolting.

'Yeah, you're probably right. Hey, listen – did you hear that chirrup? Look, there he is, on that leaf. Did you used to catch them?'

'Catch what?'

'Grasshoppers, silly. Look. Let me show you. I learnt this years ago, when I was small – used to be hundreds of them on the Downs. And skylarks – do you remember the song of the skylark?'

He frowned, as if trying to recall, but didn't answer.

Victoria knelt down among the flowering grasses and cupped her hands over the grasshopper, excluding all light. It stopped chirruping. She opened her hands to make a small gap, and the insect jumped up and onto her hand, where it stood rubbing its hind legs together.

'There! See? Doesn't know it's sitting on a giant. It'll stay there and enjoy the sunshine, quite oblivious to my presence.'

Simon looked down. 'Ugly little bug, isn't it. I thought grasshoppers were slim and green. That thing's fat and brown.'

'Maybe it's a cricket. Does it matter?'

Simon glanced at his watch and then stared across the meadow, thoughts clearly elsewhere.

'It's gone three. Come on. We need to go or we'll miss our train.' He sneezed. 'Damn. Bloody pollen. It's all over my trousers too. Look.'

'Oh, poor you. What a catastrophe. Smudge of yellow on your turn-ups. End-of-the-world scenario. Do you want me to call the emergency services?'

'Come on. Get up. We have to go.'

He offered her his hand with such an ill grace that she could hardly bear to take it, and when she did, it made her shudder – so soft and white – a hand which had obviously never dug a garden or thrown clay on a wheel. Elegant hands, yes, with long fingers, perfectly manicured nails – yet they turned her stomach.

She allowed herself to be pulled to her feet, but snatched her hand back as soon as she could and walked on ahead, over the bridge and up the hill towards the entrance.

Simon followed slowly, swearing under his breath with almost every step as he slipped on the steep grassy bank due to the slick leather soles of his shoes.

Carrying a holdall wouldn't be helping matters. Victoria knew she should offer to help with the bags as they contained her clothes as well as his – but she didn't. Let him work. Let him sweat. Let him struggle and suffer and be punished for not being perfect enough, or for being too perfect, or whatever it was that was wrong with him.

'Damn!' he cried out, loud enough to make her stop. 'Victoria! Give me a hand would you? Turned my blasted ankle.'

And that was all it took. She couldn't bear him to be in pain. Her mood flipped back to where she wanted it to be – the place where she loved him to bits, and he was hurt and she'd been horrible and it wasn't his fault that he didn't know about grasshoppers and skylarks – that was simply something that had been missed out of his childhood, and she shouldn't blame him and be cross.

She ran back down the slope, knelt down and flung her arms round him, knocking his silly hat off in the process, then snuggled into his chest and whispered: 'I'm sorry. Sorry, sorry, sorry.'

He picked up the hat and carefully placed it back on his head before responding.

'Hey, it's okay, you didn't push me over. I slipped. Should've been more careful. My fault, not yours.'

'No, it's mine. I've been horrible, so you fell over. Here, let me take the bags.'

'Sure you can manage?'

'Yes, of course. Now, get up and lean on me. We need to conquer the slope before your ankle really starts to hurt.'

'It hurts now.'

'I know, but if it's a sprain, it'll hurt far more in an hour or so.'

'Thanks for being so cheerful.'

Victoria forced a smile. 'It's what I'm here for. To cheer you up.'

He nodded with deep seriousness and looked as if he was about to say something profound, then yelped with pain again as he tried to stand.

'Do you want me to phone for help?' Victoria asked, somewhat at a loss.

'You can't. You threw away your phone.'

'Oh fuckit. So I did.'

'So now what do we do? Any thoughts?'

'I know – I'll pop back up to the entrance. They've got

wheelchairs. I'll bring one down and then wheel you up.'

'What, a wheelchair on a steep grassy slope? All eleven stone of me? You'll never manage.'

She sat down on the grass next to him. 'You know, this is the most absurd situation. Here we are, sat on a lawn, completely stuck, with people walking past us, not realising that we are in the midst of a catastrophe, a crisis of monumental proportions. We'll still be here when they lock up the gardens for the night, and then we'll have to sleep under the stars. Ooh, we can make love in the moonlight. That'll be good. Never done it before in these gardens.'

'*These* gardens? What, you mean you've done it in others?'

'Now, I never said that, did I.'

'Okay. You didn't say, and I won't ask.'

'Thanks.' She kissed him on the cheek. 'You're sweet.'

'I know. You don't deserve anyone as nice as me.'

'That's probably true.'

'Let's give it another go,' said Simon. 'The ankle doesn't feel too bad. I don't think it's a full-blown sprain. You stand up first, put your feet against mine, give me your hands, and we'll both pull – that way, either we'll both collapse, or I'll actually manage to stand up.'

They tried, and it worked. Simon put some weight gingerly on the foot and managed to cope with a minimal sharp intake of breath. They set off in slow motion up the bank towards the entrance, Simon leaning heavily on Victoria.

'Hang on,' said Victoria, when they were halfway there, 'I threw my phone away, but what about yours?'

'Ah, wondered when you'd spot that.'

'So why –'

He thought for a moment. 'I suppose I was interested to find out what you'd do in a crisis. How you'd cope.'

'Why did you want to know that?'

'Because I've a feeling we're heading for one.'

'Really? Shit. What sort of a crisis? Financial? Some problem with the business? Political? I'm crap when it comes to politics, I'm afraid.'

'No, my love. Emotional.'

'Cripes.'

'Yes. Cripes indeed.'

They carried on staggering up the bank in silence for a few minutes, but then they stopped. Victoria had to know.

'Why though? What makes you say that?'

'Oh, things.'

'What things?'

He suddenly sounded tired. 'The way you snap at me. The way you often look at me as if you despise me, as if you can't bear to touch me. The way you think I'm blind and deaf and insensitive as that slug you just squashed.'

'Shit.'

'The way you say "shit" all the time.' He laughed. 'Okay, too much seriousness, but darling – I really do see things you know. Maybe not the same things that you see, and maybe I'm not the man you want me to be, but – is this working? You and me as a couple? I'm not sure.'

'Of course it's working. We're a brilliant couple. You're just grumpy because your ankle hurts'

If she hadn't been supporting him and carrying the bags, Victoria would have run off into the bushes to be sick. Oh dear God, was she really so stupid? Thinking she could carry on with her snide comments and revulsion and he wouldn't even notice? How long had she been doing it? Practically since day one, most likely – and he was right – she snapped at him all the time, thinking it didn't matter, that he was too self-absorbed to notice – or no, not even thinking that. Not thinking anything. Just snapping. Bitching. Being nasty.

Being unhappy.

Maybe he was right, and they needed a crisis to clarify matters. She looked around, vaguely hoping to see a serpent in this garden of Eden, who might, in his boundless wisdom, either swallow her whole and put an end to her problems, or explain to her what she should do, but there was no snake in the grass – not even a slow worm. Was a desire to be swallowed by a serpent indicative of shame, or a wish to escape? She had no idea.

They carried on in silence up the hill, lost in their own thoughts. Once back at the entrance, Simon used his phone to call a taxi to take them to the station.

Later, on the train, Victoria wanted to cry. Simon had taken off his hat and she held onto it, needing the comfort of its closeness and familiarity. Had she blown this whole relationship apart? And if she hadn't, should she?

She rested her head on his shoulder and drifted into a wistful daydream where they were making love in the sunshine, lying on soft turf, while a skylark sang overhead and grasshoppers chirruped. Forty-five minutes later the train pulled into Alnmouth. She retrieved the bags feeling refreshed and ready to fight for her man, though who or what she was supposed to be fighting, she had no idea.

Chapter Twelve

On the way to the hotel they stopped at a chemist's to buy an elastic bandage and a supply of painkillers, before moving along the seafront at a snail's pace to their destination. Victoria didn't feel like telling Simon he was being a "brave little soldier", as despite her best intentions she was annoyed with him for being in pain. Once in their room, she fed him a couple of ibuprofen and strapped his ankle tightly.

'How's it feeling?'

'Nasty. Hang on. I'll try to stand. *Fuck.*'

'Cripes. Must be bad. You never swear.'

'It's okay. I'll manage.'

'Sure?'

'Yes. Could use a drink though.'

'Let's see what we've got.' Victoria opened various cupboard doors and sniffed uncertainly. 'Doesn't seem to be any sort of a mini-bar. I can offer you tea, coffee, various herbals, milk substitutes, and a vast array of sweeteners. Looks like we'll have to go down to the bar proper. Maybe we should've bought a walking stick.'

'And a Zimmer frame? No thanks. I'll lean on you.'

'Fine.'

It wasn't fine. Victoria wanted to shout at Simon that she wasn't a prop to support his crippled body – which wasn't fair, but any desire to be fair had evaporated. He wasn't the only one who needed a drink.

They hobbled down to the bar, finding their way by following the murmuring of earnest discussions about crackle glaze and French polish. Victoria surveyed the sea of grey men trying to look casual in jeans or inappropriate combat trousers, along with their colourless silent companions.

'Oh, dear God. Are they *all* antiques?'

'Looks like it,' said Simon, cheerfully, before gasping.

'Still hurting?'

'Of course it is. Like blazes. I'll have to sit down. Can you get the drinks?'

'No, I'm only a girl.'

'But –'

'Yes of course I can get the bloody drinks. What do you want? Gin and tonic? Double?'

'Please. Thanks darling. Here.' He fumbled in his wallet.

'No, you're okay. I'll get these.'

As she moved towards the bar, one voice cut through the general chatter. It wasn't loud, it wasn't especially distinctive, but it was familiar and the words made Victoria freeze.

'Ah, you must mean Simon Tovey,' it said. 'We could ask him, but I can't stand the fellow.'

Victoria scanned the crowd, trying to pick out the speaker.

Another voice answered the first.

'Why? Whatever's the matter with him? Thought you and he were bosom pals?'

'Of course, but that doesn't stop him being younger, taller and better looking than me.'

The group chuckled, though whether in agreement or not, Victoria couldn't tell. She spotted them at last. A bunch of identikit antiques much like any other, except that one stood out because of his jet black hair. John-bloody-Stephenson. Christalmighty. Yeah, well she knew he would be here. Just didn't need him at the moment. Not even slightly. She gave him what she hoped was a baleful look to show him that she'd heard what he'd said, but he wasn't looking in her direction so didn't notice. She turned with dignity to the bar and was served immediately – one of her few skills, she thought ruefully. Hopeless with most aspects of dealing with boyfriends, but could always get them a drink. She returned to Simon with the doubles.

'Ever felt like taking a cup of acid and pouring it over someone's head?' she asked, placing the drinks on the table with exaggerated care.

'No, of course not. Someone annoyed you, love?'

'You could say that.'

'Want to tell me?'

'No. Don't want to talk about it, just want to pour vitriol onto his flesh so that it pours through his chest and leaves a great gaping sizzling hole.'

'Nice. Now, come on, own up. Who is the poor unfortunate upon whom you wish to vent your spleen? Not me I hope.'

'Heavens, no. John-bloody-Stephenson, that's who.'

Simon looked down at his drink with concentration and wiped some drops of condensation off the side of the glass in a slow sweeping motion with his thumb.

'I take it you've had another encounter with your bête noire. Is he at the bar?'

'No, just over there with a crowd of smug Chesterfield suites. They were talking about you and I overheard. Couldn't help it. Heard your name. You know how it is.'

Simon whistled through his teeth.

'Yes, familiar names always stand out, but it's not like John to say anything derogatory about me or anyone, I wouldn't have thought.' He arranged the beer mats on the table into an equilateral triangle. 'I know I shouldn't ask, but ... what did he say?'

'Oh, something stupid, not insulting at all – complimentary if anything – it was just the tone and the way they were laughing, and – oh, I don't know. It got to me.'

'You let John get to you too much. Forget him.'

'Difficult, especially as I've arranged to see Emma, who will no doubt take great pleasure in dissecting all his failings and laying them out on a slab for me to see.'

'Yes, that's true, but don't let her –'

'Don't let her what?'

'You know.'

'No, I don't know. Don't let her influence me too much? Is that what you're saying? We've been through all that before.'

Simon didn't reply. They sipped their drinks awkwardly to fill the space where there was no conversation.

An infuriating pop song came over the speakers. *And I will love you 4 evah evah evah evah evah* or some such crapulous rubbish. Will you? Victoria wondered, watching Simon's long fingers stroking his glass. And do I even want you to? The thought of *evah* made her blood curdle, her toes bend backwards and her hair split into a million strands a micron wide. She took a slurp of gin. Doubles? These were triples at least. This stuff was strong. *4 evah evah evah evah evah evah evah evah evah evah.* Chrissake. It was unbearable.

Simon didn't appear to have noticed the music. What was he hearing? Brahms symphonies? Some Schubert Lieder? Ride of the Valkyries?

Victoria gulped down some more gin. She'd have to say something. This was stupid. They were supposed to be having fun.

'So, what time's this blasted dinner tomorrow?'

'Eight.'

'And what are we going to do until then?'

Simon looked guilty. 'I need to catch up with some old friends. Discuss business.'

'Oh. And just what am I supposed to do? Knit a chest of drawers? Crochet a porcelain tiger?'

'Darling!'

'It's okay. Was hoping we might do something together. Be a couple. You know.'

Simon winced.

Victoria scowled. 'You all right?'

'I just kicked the table and jarred my ankle again. It'll pass.'

'Walking about and sight-seeing is not an option then. It doesn't matter – you might as well hobnob with the antiques. I'll give Emma a bell and see if she's free. I could spend the day in Bamburgh tomorrow instead of Sunday and keep out of your hair. Get back here sixish to get changed, and then we could get a taxi up to the castle. That sound okay?'

Simon looked unforgivably pleased. 'I think that's an excellent idea.'

'Yeah, you would,' said Victoria, more viciously than she'd intended.

'Darling!'

'Do you realise how often you say "darling" like that? Am I so shocking? So bloody embarrassing to your delicate sensibilities? Christ, I'm sick of it. Just don't fuckin' "darling" me again.'

Simon flushed and looked the other way. After a few moments uncomfortable silence, he finished his drink and struggled to his feet.

'I'm going to bed. You coming?'

'No. Gonna stay here and chat up some antiques. Might get lucky, you never know. You go. Don't mind me.'

She smiled to take the sting out of the words, but her nastiness hung there between them as an impenetrable barrier.

'Goodnight,' he said formally, stooping to kiss her on the cheek.

''Night. Oh, hang on – can you lend me some cash?'

'For you to get even more drunk? No. Goodnight.'

'Suit yourself.'

'I will.'

And with that he was gone.

Victoria looked down at Simon's half empty glass and considered drinking the contents, but the thought of getting bladdered on her own didn't appeal. She wanted to talk to someone. Shouldn't have been such a bitch with Simon. Damn. What was that all about? Stupid, stupid girl. Always pressing that bloody self-destruct button. It was no good; she shouldn't sit here moping – she should find someone. Anyone. John Stephenson? Yes, why not. He was the only person here with whom she could claim any sort of an acquaintance, and at least he wouldn't call her "darling".

She squeezed her way through the crowded bar until she reached his group. They were talking about art. That was good. It would mean an opening – possibly.

'It's a pity,' John was saying, indicating a print on the wall. 'That was an illustration in a perfectly decent book once. Now look at it. Torn out, mounted in a hideous gilt frame, and allowed to wither.'

'Wither?' one of his friends asked. 'Left on the shelf you mean? Poor spinster print, dwindling away in an anonymous bar? Yes, see what you mean. Good print though. Quality.'

'No, not especially,' replied John. 'Ordinary. Hello, Victoria.'

The group of tongue-and-groove tallboys turned round to see who John had addressed.

Victoria felt like spitting back a sarcastic comment, but none came to mind. Ordinary? She was anything but ordinary, and although she sort of knew he was talking about the print, it was still an insult. If only she could switch her quick wit on she'd be able to manage a great riposte, but she couldn't, and he looked sad. Why was he sad? Everyone else was smiling and looking interested.

John shrugged, and turned back to his companions.

Okay, ignore me, thought Victoria. No, hang on – he said hello and I ignored him. Christ, what is the matter with me!

'Hi, John!' She flashed what she hoped was a lovely smile, but knowing her luck and the gin it was probably more of a grimace. It didn't matter as he wasn't even looking. She turned to examine the print they'd been discussing. Yes, John was right – it was dull. It might work in the context of its original book, but it was no Doré, no Birkett Foster.

'True,' said John.

'What?'

'You were frowning at the print, and I'd swear you were mouthing something about it not being a Doré or Birkett Foster.'

'Cripes. You're good.'

He smiled, and the sadness left his eyes briefly.

'It's not a potato print either,' he said, gently.

Okay, that did it.

'What the hell do you mean by that?'

He chuckled and turned away, leaving her seething and confused. There was something so *knowing* about John. No wonder Emma had always felt out of her depth. He was much too quick. How did he know about her potato prints? He couldn't. Had Emma told him? No, they weren't communicating. Were they? Shit. She felt tears come to her eyes. Must be the gin. She missed those prints. Should never have sold them. Maybe she could do some more. Not here though; not now. At home. Back in London, in her flat, on her own.

Bed. Definitely time to go to bed. She slipped away without saying goodbye, though she had the distinct impression of eyes following her as she left.

On the landing leading to the bedroom was another print. This one was different; a battlefield rather than the customary hunting scene or ruined castle. It was also torn out of a book, but not a Victorian one; this was later – not the Boer war as she'd first thought, but the trenches of the First World War. Fog plumed through bullet holes, and a soldier looked up to the sky in despair and hope. What was he looking for? Victoria peered closer. The artist had given the soldier a look in his eyes as if he knew it was too late – however much he longed for relief, there would be no rescue, no new dawn. The engraver was teasing with his marks, his hints of possibilities.

Victoria's own hopes were fading. She'd had such high hopes of Simon after the tattered crow with the missing feathers that was José, but all she could hear as she lurched down the corridor towards the bedroom was the whine of destruction, of shells falling out of the sky onto mangled and bleeding soldiers. Would she be able to staunch the flow of affection that was haemorrhaging out of her relationship with Simon? Unlikely. She didn't even know how to tie a tourniquet. She'd never known anything remotely useful, other than how to get a drink at a bar, and in retrospect, that was a mixed blessing.

She crept into the bedroom. Simon was asleep. Already? He must be exhausted. She glanced at her watch. Half past ten. Okay, not all that late, but reasonable. She lay down beside him and wondered at the pain that stabbed at her, not from any manky old springs in the bed, though goodness knows there were plenty, but the pain of frustration; not of wanting Simon – he was there for the taking – but the desire for a fresh, clean sheet of heavyweight cartridge paper in order to make a potato print. What sort of a life was she going to lead if she was prepared to forsake the man who loved her for a piece of paper and a potato, sliced in half and whittled into a simple form, that could repeat, and repeat, and repeat, in green and gold and black, each repetition subtly different. God, she missed her potato prints. Should never have sold them.

She lay back and felt need boring into her flesh, chomping and clawing at her, while in the distance she thought she could just hear the call of rooks – or was it seagulls? No, martins. Just martins.

Falling into a fitful sleep, she woke once or twice trying to grasp a fleeting dream where a curlew flew high over the moors and called to her with a quite different voice, but there was snow in the air and her sight was obscured.

Chapter Thirteen

Victoria woke early with a thick head. Simon was still asleep, so she slipped out of bed and nestled behind the curtains on the window seat. The sea view was obscured by a thick mist that rolled by in waves. What did they call it round here? Sea fret? Haar? She'd been away too long. A pair of terns flew over with a keening cry, making her think of curlews and old wine.

Simon stirred.

'Whassa time?'

'Early. Go back to sleep. I'm going to walk down to the front and get some air. Clear my head.'

'Mmf.'

He turned over in bed, pulled the covers up to his chin, and appeared to have fallen back to sleep within seconds.

Victoria pulled on her jeans and a t-shirt, grabbed a jacket, and crept out of the room.

A few people were already down on the front walking their dogs. A lone golfer stood like a statue on the links peering through the mist. Victoria took the path past the harbour master's house and through the waves of marram grass down to the beach. The sea sounded very close and intimate, though she could barely see it.

She thought of another beach, another time; *La Playa de las Catedrales* – a turning point and a place for decisions. Wrong ones, as it turned out. Would she fare any better here, where the tiny white shells of Spain had been replaced by coal-blackened sand, and where a cool sun lurked beyond her senses? She hesitated, wondering if it was wise to continue. Yes, she needed to know. She walked up the estuary over the shifting sands. Choices, choices, choices. She'd rejected José's shallow passion, no question of that, but what was she to do with Simon's porcelain charm? She looked out across the grey of the sea and an estuary that snaked away from her into the mist.

She shaded her eyes and squinted, searching with some trepidation for a memory of José. He was nowhere to be seen. She shivered. This was England, not Spain, after all, but that was okay as she wasn't anxious to be with him or anyone just yet; not while there was a beach of dark sand to explore. She bent down and scooped up a handful, enjoying the way it gritted against her palm. Sitting back on her haunches, she closed her eyes and thought about yesterday's journey, and the disastrous evening that had followed tainted by just a little too much alcohol and the apparently omniscient John Stephenson. Her long-gone Spanish lover would have been amused and would have revelled in her discomfort, egging her on as she morphed from total cow to drunken idiot. Only he hadn't been there. That was odd. Not so long ago, he would have been in her head, telling her what to say and do, but now he'd disappeared completely. Someone had frightened him away. Simon? No, Simon wouldn't frighten anyone. Who then? Or what?

She stood up, brushed the damp sand off her jeans and continued up the estuary. The haar was clearing in patches. A chance sunbeam lit up a winding stream, turning it into a silver snake that sparkled through the coal-blackened sand on its way to join the River Aln.

There was a timeless shape ahead of her – a curved and elegant form with twin masts. Victoria approached the beached boat, skirting round pools of water left by the receding tide, wondering if she could jump into one and end up in a completely different world, like the children in *The Magician's Nephew*. She reached the yacht and read the name: *Marean*. The navy and umber paint was weathered but tough, and the furled sail was maroon, with deeper reds nestling in its folds. Victoria knew she wanted – needed – to paint it, all of it; the haar and the boat with its small rusting companion that sat in the sand not twenty yards away. When, though? When would she have the opportunity? And how had she managed to come away without any paints? Call yourself an artist, Victoria? No matter. Emma would have some. She would be able to paint later today, if not this boat, then at least she could escape with Emma and paint the sea or the castle at Bamburgh instead. There were so many places whose story cried out to be painted, but this boat – this was special. She would have to return.

She stepped back and studied *Marean* with an artist's eye as the haar swept by and a tern flew over the sand spit where its companions roosted each night. Her eyes followed the serpentine windings of the river back down to the sea, where she could imagine she heard *Marean* calling with a seagull's cry. She never heard that sound in London – certainly not when she was with Simon. He'd led her into a world devoid of mist; a world of precision and careful colours to be dusted on a daily basis to in order to retain their delicate perfection.

The mist finally cleared and the sun sent glints of expectation into the sea which roared in its usual way, no longer mysterious.

It was time for breakfast. Victoria headed back to the hotel, her mind full of pictures waiting to be painted: of light hidden behind charcoal, pierced by one red spot, malign and threatening. Yes, she needed that threat, along with candyfloss clouds swirling like egg white in water, their dark streaks ready to pounce and bind them tight.

Simon was still asleep. There was safety for him in slumber. He probably relished the times when he didn't have to argue with her, or try to understand her compulsions. She looked down on him with a confused mix of doubt and affection.

He stirred, opened one eye, and smiled.

'Hello. Nice walk?'

'You've been asleep for ages.'

'No I haven't. Awake most of the night. You were snoring.'

'What, with my little nose? Come off it.'

'What's the time?'

The conversation was prosaic after her inspiration of just minutes earlier. He might be in Alnmouth physically, but his soul was in a cardboard box surrounded by small pieces of polystyrene, all wrapped up in a carrier bag. It was no good. She couldn't do small talk. She needed to rouse him, somehow.

'Time for temptation, for salmon skies. You want some?'

'I want some bacon and eggs. Mushrooms maybe. Not salmon.'

'Idiot. Come on. Try. Remember a beach, a holiday, ages ago. Pink candy floss.'

'No thanks.'

'But doesn't it take you back? Seagulls? Have you no memories? Were you never a child?'

'Where?'

'What do you mean, where? Christalmighty. Did you never go to the beach as a boy? Not even a skeletal cobwebby seaside? A circle? Like stirring milk into lukewarm tea?'

'My dear, I haven't the faintest idea what you're talking about, and neither have you. Can't you try to be normal for once? Please? For me?'

He looked tired and miserable, so instead of spitting with frustration, Victoria tried to consider the question seriously. Normal? What did that even mean? Boring? Dull? Conventional? No, she refused to be normal. She went back to the window seat and looked out to sea.

'Look, there's a tadpole.'

'No, there can't be. That's the sea.'

'In the sky, silly, not the sea. It's gone now. You missed it, didn't see it weaving its way through the eye sockets up there at the top where you never thought to look. More fool you.'

'Victoria. Please stop.'

'Why? Why won't you ever join me? Why do you have to stay in your bone china teapot, never venturing out in case you crack and shatter into a million shards of normality? You're tempted, I'm sure you must be, or you wouldn't still be with me, would you? Come on. It's safe, I promise you it's safe. You've got nothing to lose.'

'Nothing to lose? No, that's true, but only because there's nothing left.'

'What do you mean, "nothing left"?'

'Nothing. Nothing at all. Victoria, it was fun while it lasted, I suppose.'

'Are you –?'

'Breaking up with you? Yes, I think perhaps I am. Somewhat abruptly, I know, but I'm hungry and we'll miss breakfast if we don't get a move on.'

'You *what*?'

'Breakfast. Eggs, bacon, and appearances, the latter being the key ingredient, and the only thing we've got left, it seems.'

'Oh God. You don't expect me to play the obedient girlfriend do you? Be all sweet and attentive, when really I want to smash your head to pieces like one of your bloody figurines?'

'You don't want to do that. You don't feel strongly enough about me to be violent.'

She stopped abruptly and considered his unexpected statement. Maybe he was right.

'Shit. Why couldn't you have always shown so much insight?'

To her surprise, Simon laughed, and she couldn't help giggling a little herself. Whatever else happened now, there would be no more porcelain. She wouldn't have to pretend to like the blasted stuff any more.

'I hate Sèvres. Bloody hate it!'

'I know. It's obvious. Can't say I'm too grabbed with your paintings either. I never know what they're supposed to be saying.'

'You bastard,' she said, with more affection than she'd used towards him in ages.

She constructed a scenario where she threw a pillow at him, and he threw it back. Pillow fight? Yes, why not. She could jump onto the bed and launch an attack and oops ... that wasn't supposed to happen, she would think seconds later when they were kissing each other and he was pulling off her jeans and the sheer relief of having expressed her hatred of Sèvres at long last meant she was game for anything – absolutely anything, and so was he.

Except that he wasn't and neither was she. It didn't happen. He had criticised her art and it was all over.

'Bollocks,' said Victoria, under her breath.

'Can't we at least try to be civilised?'

'No. Why the fuck should we.'

'Because this dinner matters to me, and I thought I mattered to you.'

'Oh yeah?'

'Yes, and I think I still do. You don't really want to embarrass me in front of my friends.'

'You reckon? And I suppose you think you know me, so you're safe?'

'Yes, I do.'

'Idiot.'

'Victoria, please. One weekend. Is that too much to ask? One weekend of relative normality. Then you can go and decapitate chickens and make splatter paintings, or whatever you want, and never see me again.'

'Normality, eh? You ask for normality when the world has turned orange and the joints of my fingers have snapped apart?'

'My point exactly. If you could stop talking surreal nonsense like that, we might have a chance.'

'It isn't nonsense. I say the things I see, without being bound by convention, but you're too dense and uptight to follow. There's nothing wrong with what I say. It's you. You're too stupid for words.'

'I'm not stupid.'

'You can't see it, can you?'

'Can't see what?'

'A creature with a tail trailing spikes of apricot. It's flying away, leaving bubbles behind. There's a ship, heavy laden in burnt umber and Prussian blue – Marean is her name. She's down by the estuary if you don't believe me – she lurches onto my finger, snaps off one more joint and it hurts. Don't you see? Can you really not see?'

The tears started to fall as she sat wringing her hand. She looked up at him, wishing that she could make him understand.

'You never could trace my name in yellow, could you? Perhaps I should board the ship, follow the creature whose grin isn't fixed after all, but mobile and shaped like a tree.'

She stroked the wooden mouldings round the sash window, felt the curves and found some tactile comfort. The swirls in her paintings would engulf her some time, but not today, not now. A fly's faint buzzing reminded her of her own frailty; her inability to explain her passion in everyday words. She could only do it through her art, which Simon would never understand, and if he didn't understand her art, how could he ever understand her? He thought he knew her. Nobody knew her.

'I think you need to see a doctor,' said Simon, quietly.

'No, I need breakfast. So do you. See you down there.'

She jumped off the window seat and left the room at high speed, slamming the door behind her. In the corridor, she ran into John.

'And you can fuck off too!' she shouted, before hurtling down the stairs and out onto the terrace, gasping for air.

Half a dozen martins appeared from nowhere and made swift circles in the air, their high-pitched cries drawing her sorrow away, making it bearable. She sat on a bench listening to the swallows and the sea. Had she really just sworn at John? Shit. Yes, she had. She giggled. Never mind. He was big. He'd cope. But Simon ... oh God. Why couldn't she behave like an adult when she was round him? Why did she have to spout such gibberish? He was right. He mattered to her. This was an important weekend for him. She should grow up and behave before she blew the relationship sky high – if she hadn't already.

He was too good for her. That was the problem. Maybe she was better off with an absolute sod like José; a bully who treated her like dirt.

She looked out to sea and for the first time in a long while allowed herself to remember Spain properly.

Chapter Fourteen

It was the fourth day of her Spanish holiday. Just the fourth? Victoria felt as if she had been here for four weeks, not four days. She stroked the peeling paint, noting how the door felt warm under her fingertips, despite its mantle of creepers which should have given some respite from the baking heat. She swore as a sliver of paint slipped under a nail – yet more damage to add to the sunburn, the blisters, and the embarrassment of a holiday romance which made her skin creep if she thought too hard about it. Easy solution – don't think. A drop of sweat trickled down her sun-burnt cheek. Maybe there would be a cool square beyond the door; a place to sit in the shade by a fountain and sketch the architecture.

She turned to José, who watched her through narrowed eyes.

'Can we go inside?' said Victoria. 'If we knock, will anyone answer? Show us around?'

'No, my sweet. We will not seek entry now. I choose my times of admittance with great care. You will learn this later tonight, I think.'

Great. She wanted to kick José where it hurt and reply: you should be so lucky, mate – but she couldn't – didn't have the nerve. How long had she known him now? Three days? And already took her sexual compliance for granted? Cripes.

The door though – that was something special – but she could see no way through if José refused to co-operate.

She tried again.

'Is it your house? Your family's?'

'The house belongs to my family, yes. For many lifetimes.'

'And?'

'And that is all. Come. We will eat now. There is a bar. I know the owner.'

Yes, of course you do, you know everyone and everything, dammit.

José held out his hand and Victoria went to him meekly and infuriatingly, well aware that she had been beguiled by a crooked smile and dark, slightly bloodshot eyes. Sad or what.

The meal was light, fragrant and delicious, and José's friend in the bar a charmer. Of course. How could he be otherwise? Victoria switched off all her critical faculties and followed where José led, drinking red wine from over-sized glasses and licking her lips far too much.

During the subsequent lovemaking in her hotel bedroom she couldn't help being distracted by the dappled light on the bed. She went through the expected actions dutifully, but her mind had snapped into fine artist mode as she considered how to put into practice the advanced colour theory necessary to produce convincing shadows. José didn't notice a thing, and left shortly afterwards, apparently satisfied. They were to meet the next day on the beach, where Victoria hoped to be able retain a little more self-possession.

She sat on the bed staring at the impression left by their bodies, wishing she'd brought at least a small set of watercolours. She hadn't even packed any oil pastels. Pencils and pens were all very well, but she needed something more than cross-hatching to take her mind off José tonight. In frustration, she went to bed early. She expected an erotic dream at the very least, but instead, enjoyed a confused adventure where she chased coat hangers and shopping trolleys down a mountainside before ending up in a ditch.

The next morning, much refreshed, Victoria took a taxi to the *Playa de las Catedrales* in good time to explore its geology before any romantic distractions intervened. There was an arch – a doorway – beneath the cliffs. She stroked it with both hands to feel its mineral certainty and overlay the memory of the other door. This one was natural; part of a rocky formation on the beach, not a deliberately mysterious barrier that might or might not be anything to do with José's family. She was alone this time too, so gaining entry would not be a problem, unless sea sprites were abroad. Unlikely. It was too hot. Horribly hot. She stopped and slapped on some more sun block, wincing as it hit the parts of her neck that were already on fire.

The shade beneath the arch tempted her. Victoria lowered her head to avoid cracking her skull, but halfway through she hesitated. The cool darkness of the caves to her left beckoned, in stark contrast to the searing light on the beach to her right. Decision time: did she want to retreat into manky old bladderwrack and green slime, or push through to pulsating heat and tiny white shells? No contest, despite the threat of sunburn. She hadn't come to Spain to lurk in the shadows – plenty of those back home – and besides, she had a date, agreed to last night under the influence of too many olives – she would do anything for a dish of olives – too much red wine and too little sense.

On the other side of the arch, the sun beat down with the unexpected smell of warm dog. Victoria shaded her eyes and squinted, searching for José. He was nowhere to be seen, but that was okay because it was early and she wasn't anxious to be with him yet – not while there were flecks of colour in the sand to be explored. She knelt down and scooped up a handful, enjoying the way the grains trickled through her fingers and refused to be held. Satisfied, she stood up, shook the sand from her shorts, and squinted along the beach. The beach shimmered, so she put out one foot carefully, worried that the heat would burn her feet through the rope soles of her sandals – but no, it was safe, so she inched away from the safety of the walls of rock and into the absolute bleached clarity of the beach. Turning back briefly, she was tempted again to return to the shade, find the sketchpad that lurked in the depths of her bag, and immerse herself in her one great passion – but the greater passion must make way for the lesser today. A few photographs would suffice. She could work them up later, back home.

A distant figure called.

'Hola! Vicki!'

The adrenaline flowed and she steeled herself to be deluded once again. As she walked forward, a blue pebble caught her eye. She picked it up and put it in her pocket to join the others as a talisman, a safeguard against both José's lies and her own. When she looked up again, he had disappeared. She shaded her eyes and scanned the beach.

'Vicki!'

The voice sounded much closer now, but where was he? How had he become invisible? She felt too exposed out here on the sands, so hurried back, ashamed, to the cliffs, where she laid her hands on the warm rocks like a benediction before creeping round the edge to peer into the caves. Perhaps he had sought the intimacy of darkness for a meeting. One cave was enormous and irresistible, but he couldn't be in there – his voice would have echoed. She had an urge to explore, so followed a stream, trailing her fingers along the damp walls until they narrowed in on her and she could go no further. With the comfort of stone all around, she turned back towards the light.

José was standing at the entrance to the cave, against the sun.

94

She couldn't tell from his silhouette whether he was looking towards her or away. A piece of seaweed between them caught the light. Its translucence was unexpected. Seaweed shouldn't look like a giant apple leaf made of jelly. Victoria watched, wondering if it would fold in upon itself. There was slight movement, but not enough. She grew tired of waiting. It would take – what – an hour to fold over completely? By which time the tide would be in, most likely.

She guessed José had positioned himself carefully for effect. What an arrogant sod – but not to worry – he was undoubtedly attractive in silhouette and she was on holiday for only a few more days, so could put up with his vanity easily enough. The pose was both graceful and virile; almost a Michelangelo's David. She committed it to memory, regretting that she couldn't get out her sketchbook now and draw him, but he only had so much patience where her art was concerned.

'Hi there, handsome!' she called.

There was a moment's silence before he turned with practised weariness.

'What are you doing? Foolish girl!'

Charming. Typical. Not, hi Vicki, I've found you at last! How I've missed you!

'Come out of the cave,' he said. 'There is a monumental tide rising. You will drown. I know this place. It is not safe.'

A "monumental" tide? Ah, but that was part of the problem – his accent and the way he used words; the way they wormed their way under her skin every time. She steeled herself, waiting for more words to intrigue and charm her.

José made a small gesture with his hands and Victoria's heart lurched.

'Come now. Don't be fractious.'

Fractious? Absurd. But still she came at his bidding, skipping like a six year old, delighted when his face broke into a smile.

'It is dangerous, a lone girl to be walking along the sand, hiding in caves. Nobody say this to you?'

He spoke with dangerous intimacy, but she didn't answer. She liked to be alone on the beach. She didn't want this man, and suddenly hated his presence. Couldn't a great wave roar up the beach and drown him? Now? Please?

He frowned. 'Next time you wait for me. Yes? *Yes?*'

'Yes.'

Lies, lies, lies. If she'd waited for him, he wouldn't have come. She knew this instinctively.

'You need me to defend you. Yes?'

'Yes. Thank you.'

Thank you? For what? Chrissake, from whom did she need defending? Greasy tourists reeking of factor fifteen? Children dripping with ice cream? Nuns with eyes cast down but hoping for heaven, following the trail to Santiago?

She could have slept in the cave and been safe enough – apart from the "monumental" tide, of course. Okay. Maybe he was right. The waves were rushing in between the rocks, undercutting and splashing their shattered roots, frail as wafers. How could they survive this continual battering? They couldn't. As she watched, a flake of grey rock slipped away to be pounded into sand. How long would it take for the whole cliff face to be eroded? Hundreds of thousands of years, most likely. She yearned to stand there and watch and wait; to learn each stratum intimately so she could bid it farewell with due ceremony as it fell into the sea. All very well, but José was waiting, and his patience would last moments, not millennia.

She walked up to him and took both his hands; did a little bob as if to curtsey.

'Here I am, my suicidal king.'

'Your what? I am not suicidal, I think.'

She noticed that he didn't deny kingship.

'I know you're not, but you remind me of a picture I once drew of the King of Hearts: high cheekbones, deep eyes, wide mouth. Hands crossed over the hilt of his sword, ermine draped over his shoulders. A face of sorrows, the shadows cross-hatched and lonely.'

'You are mad and I do not know what you are saying. Is he handsome, this king?'

'Oh yes. Very.'

'Good. Then I will be your king. Come now. We are wet.'

'What? Shit!'

A wave sloshed over her sandals and she jumped back, letting go of his hands.

'We must run,' he said, before sprinting off across the sands faster than she could follow. She trudged after him, enjoying the sensation of warm water on her feet and grit between her toes.

96

She stopped for a moment. The sun still beat down in painful waves. If she closed her eyes and looked through the lids she could see bursts of pink foam on a scarlet red sea. The breakers crashed in threes, always threes, always in the same place, probably due to rocks under the water, but whatever the reason, there was something exciting about the rhythmic pounding.

'Hey! You are slow! Come! Run!'

She ignored him – didn't even look in his direction. Crimson sky, scarlet sea, and white horizon; this was something that mattered. Could she paint it? No, not paint. This would lend itself to printing. A lino cut. That would work. A series perhaps, in different colours for the different moods of the day. Pillar box red for midday, but blues for later, dusky brown-blues.

José was too bright, too sugar pink. He'd laugh if she told him, and would defy her to find anything remotely pink about either his physique or his persona. She rehearsed the conversation in her mind.

So, José – if not pink, how do you see yourself?

She imagined the look of studied concentration on his face as he considered the question. No, that went nowhere. He wouldn't consider it. He'd ridicule it, brush it aside as not being worthy of an answer.

You silly girl, I am not pink. I am the crimson soul of this land, the gold of its desert landscape, the blue of its mountains, the grey-green of its olive groves.

No. Not even that. He didn't understand anything about colour. He'd never talk about it. Only her imaginary Spanish lover spoke of such things. José was altogether more prosaic, and yet he managed to surprise her just often enough. There were deep lines from his nose down the side of his mouth. They reminded her of someone. An actor perhaps? Who was it? Someone, someone, someone … no. The memory was gone. Pity.

José stood motionless a long way ahead, and again she didn't know if he was facing towards her or away, but something about him drew her. Something primeval – basic – biological imperative? Cripes, no! What a thought. Little Josés running around in nappies. Stop it, Victoria! No, tonight she'd respond in ways that might surprise him, show him that although she seemed on the surface to be the archetypal cool collected Englishwoman, underneath … except that was a load of old bollocks. All the other little English tourists no doubt thought precisely the same thing. Next week, she would be replaced by another awestruck simpleton, and José's offhand seduction would start all over again with someone else.

She shook her head. None of it mattered, as next week she would be safely back home, able to utilise him as her muse with impunity. That was why she'd come to Spain in the first place, wasn't it? For inspiration? He'd certainly provided that. She was ready now. She would tie him to canvas with paint and sculpt his arrogance in pink plasticine; wind his form in chicken wire and pour molten wax into his clay shell. That would teach him.

Chapter Fifteen

The memory had been sweet, and the recalling cathartic. Was it enough to help her face Simon? He'd said something about breakfast. That sounded reasonable, but first she'd phone Emma and see if her planned escape was possible.

All was fine. Emma would pick her up in an hour's time. She had plenty of art materials if Victoria wanted to borrow any. Good. Sorted. Now for breakfast.

She found Simon on the dining room terrace, drinking coffee and reading the paper. Either he'd already finished his bacon and eggs, or he hadn't had any. Victoria suspected the latter. She joined him and smiled at the waiter who asked what she'd like to drink.

'Tea please. Thank you.'

Simon sipped his coffee and said nothing.

'Emma's picking me up in an hour,' said Victoria: 'so I'll be out of your way all day. Probably do some painting on the beach. The weather's lovely, and Emma says she can lend me materials. I'll be back sixish, as we arranged. I'm dying to try on that purple dress. Been a scruff for far too long. I have the sweetest little shoes to match. Wait till you see. Real heels and everything. At least three inches.'

For once, the small talk wasn't a problem. Was this because she felt as if she were talking to a stranger? No, not a stranger, but someone to whom she was attached by a long thin thread, rather than a solid chain. The thread was still there, albeit badly frayed. Had it already snapped? No, of course not. Simon would come round. Everything would be all right.

'I know I have no right to ask this,' said Simon, putting his cup down with care: 'but are you able to give me any sort of guarantee that you won't misbehave at the dinner tonight? That you won't drink?'

This mattered. Oh, this mattered. She could get snappish and sarcastic, or she could be dutiful and kind, or – there had to be another way.

'I need to talk to Emma; to sort out my thoughts and feelings. If, when I come back, I don't feel it would be wise to come with you because I know it would only cause embarrassment, then I won't. Fair enough?'

'I suppose that will have to do. May wisdom prevail. For once.'

'Simon, you're never sarcastic. What's got into you?'

'Disappointment? Disillusion? Desperation?'

He wiped his mouth on his napkin and stood up.

'I'll see you later then, or not, depending on what nonsense Emma puts into your head.'

He walked out as the waiter arrived with Victoria's tea. She busied herself placing the cup and saucer exactly where she wanted them so that she didn't have to look at Simon's retreating back. That piece of thread had better have plenty of elastic woven into its core, or she was in trouble.

She was in trouble anyway. She lifted her head and looked around the dining room, half expecting to see John Stephenson, but he wasn't there. Probably avoiding her. No. Why should he? She took a sip of piping hot 'Yorkshire' tea. Delicious. The solution to all possible problems, at least in the short term.

Emma turned up at the appointed time, all smiles.

'So, wheh do I get to meet the gorgeous Simon?'

'You don't. He's with the other antiques. And –'

'And?'

'I rather think he's just chucked me. Temporarily, at least. Things are certainly very awkward.'

'Bloody hell, Vic. You don't keep hold of them very long, do you. That Spaniard only lasted a week, as I recall, and as for those lads in the uni rambling club – series of one night stands, wasn't it?'

'It was not! Brian lasted at least a fortnight.'

'*Mea culpa*, so he did. I'd forgotten him. The little chap with glasses?'

'No, that was Rob.'

'Happy days, eh?'

'God yes. Wasn't life simple.'

'In retrospect, of course.'

They climbed into Emma's elderly hatchback and headed north along the narrow coast road to Bamburgh, reminiscing about past boyfriends and avoiding any further mention of Simon. Time enough

100

for all of that later. Victoria was aware of a certain numbness regarding the last twenty-four hours, and was making the most of it. Apart from swearing at John, she considered she'd been relatively calm, but she doubted the mood would last.

An hour later she was happily ensconced on the beach with easel, paints, brushes, a multi-coloured rag, and all other necessities. The open case beside her exuded the comforting aromas of turpentine and linseed, though today she would have to stick to the acrylics due to the limited time available. The castle profile was familiar from a thousand postcards, so the "known" image would need to be overlaid with today's reality. She concentrated hard and stared at stone walls until they started to turn purple. Did she dare paint the castle purple? No. She hated the colour. That dress ... On the other hand, it would confuse the Simons of this world, so it might be worth it. She imagined the conversation.

'Why have you painted the castle purple?'

'Because that's what colour it was, stoopid.'

'It can't have been. It's sandstone. Can't possibly be purple.'

'Can.'

'No, not possible.'

''Tis too. Look at colours long enough and you start to see what's really there.'

'That's rubbish, Victoria, and you know it.'

'You calling me stupid?'

'No, it was you who just called me "stoopid", if you recall.'

That was the way conversations had tended to go recently: Simon resigned to the fact that she wouldn't let him win an argument, and Victoria abusive and childish. Colours really did change, but you needed to learn to see the change and that was hard to explain to someone who'd never experienced such a thing. Recently she'd had no desire to try.

Okay, so not purple. How about ... she looked again at the selection of paints. Bollocks to Simon, she was going to paint it vermillion. That would do for starters. Get the forms in, at any rate. Worry about the detail later. Shadows. Yes. Deep dark shadows. Somewhere to hide her feelings where Simon would never find them. Somewhere to lurk and watch and wait.

'What's that?' piped up a small voice

Cripes. Kids. Whoever invented kids should be shot.

'It's paint.'

'What you painting?'

She pointed vaguely in front of her, and started sweeping the brush across the canvas, trying to ignore the child.

It refused to be ignored. 'Why you doing it like that?'

'Like what?'

'You're supposed to draw the outline in black first. With a ruler to get it right. Then you colour it in, but you mustn't go over the lines or you'll get wrong of Miss.'

'Your name isn't "Simon" by any chance?'

'No, I'm Shaun Aran Teasdale.'

'Bugger off, Shaun Aran Teasdale.'

'Eee! You said a rude word.'

Victoria put down her paintbrush.

'Now listen, Shaun. "Miss" has got it all wrong. You have to go over the lines or you'll shrivel up inside and become a sad little loser who discovers he's a Simon after all. Believe me. You have to break the rules.'

Shaun looked uncertain. 'I'll get wrong of me Mam.'

'Oh, I give up.'

The boy twisted his mouth as if trying to think of something interesting to say, which was more than Simon ever did these days – then he turned and hopped away.

Men. Useless, the lot of them. She opened a tube of Naples yellow and scrubbed the colour all over the sky, then blocked in some ochre forms in the foreground, only just resisting the temptation to outline them in black. More scarlet scumbled over the castle walls and she was starting to realise her vision; her knowledge of how this particular castle existed on this particular day.

Half an hour later she had more or less finished, which was a good thing as the sea had come in unexpectedly and was lapping at her feet. Yet another monumental tide – it seemed she was fated to be chased by the wretched things. She balanced the canvas on a nearby rock, folded up the easel and packed the paints away. Acrylics dried almost instantly in the sun, so there was little risk of bits of seaweed or sand getting stuck in the painting – not that that would've mattered. Might be a good effect. Another time. Now she needed to talk.

She looked up and saw Emma approaching at a run and wondered at her second sight before realising it was most likely local knowledge of tides.

'Here, I'll help you with these,' said Emma.

'Thanks.'

'You've had your morning of therapeutic painting, so now I reckon it's about time we set the worlds to rights.'

'Yep.'

'Good picture. I've never thought of the castle like that before, but it works. It bloody works. How did you know it would look like that today? I would never have realised; never have had that degree of insight.'

'Emma, will you marry me?'

'Hehe! Know what you mean. Men – they never understand anything, do they?'

They walked along the sand-dunes and headed in the direction of the Emma's cottage.

'This Simon of yours,' said Emma.

'Not mine any more. Or only slightly.'

'Never mind that. Tell me about him. Which one is he?'

'Which what?'

'You remember how we used to categorise blokes at uni? Greek God or marsh wiggle?'

'Yes, of course. Greek God, definitely.'

'I need specifics. Compare him to John.'

'You sure?'

'Yes.'

'Okay. Well, he's younger, fairer, taller, and he's ... he has fewer lines. Yes.'

'Come on Vic. Stop being loyal. Try to think aesthetically. You're an artist, aren't you?'

'Okay, but are you sure you want this?'

'Yes. I'm curious. Don't mind how you answer. I'm trying to see John objectively. This should help. If Simon's made of marble, which is more or less how you've described him then is John more, I dunno, oak? No, that doesn't sound right.'

'Heavens no, John's not oaken. Not remotely wooden. Too

whippy and slight, from what I've seen.'

'True, he's certainly not Entish – but I was thinking more of the crevices and crevasses.'

'How do you mean?'

'His wrinkles. Those deep lines that run down from the side of his nose. Though I suppose that's from smoking as much as anything.'

'John smokes?' said Victoria, surprised.

'Yep. Used to, anyway.'

'Doesn't look like a smoker. Doesn't smell like one, either.'

'Must've given up, then. Given up me, given up ciggies, given up kittens, given up breathing, given up life I hope. That would help.'

'Emma!'

'Okay, okay. I'll be sensible.'

'Good – not that I was, this morning, when I told him to "fuck off" for no good reason other than bad temper on my part.'

'Bloody hell, Vic, you didn't did you? I would never have dared. Wanted to often enough, and I certainly have in my imagination, but to say the words out loud? Maybe I should've done.'

'Couldn't have done any harm. I didn't get struck by lightning or anything, though I was moving at high speed, which probably helped.'

'Outrunning lightning is a handy trick. Oh, but it's so hard. I've always thought I should let go of my spitefulness, rather than give in to it, but maybe I should let it out a bit more. John's a great target, but I've tended kept such things to myself; internalised it all.'

'Not necessarily the best way. Certainly not what I'd do. You should hear the horrible things I've said to Simon's face.'

'Really? I thought he was Mr Perfection, his only flaw being that he's chucked you. How could you possibly be horrid to him?'

'That's just it, though. He's Mr Bloody Too Good to be True. Except that he isn't: he didn't see the flowers at the Botanic Gardens, didn't see the swelling seed pods and didn't understand the grasshopper. He didn't know what I was getting at in the slightest. I forgave him of course, but still.'

'Can't say I've ever understood a grasshopper either. Are you turning into Dr Doolittle or something?'

'Heh. Perhaps.'

104

They looked across at the rocks.

'A similar thing happened to me once,' said Emma. 'Remember Toby?'

'Adonis?'

'Yeah, that was the guy. I tried to tell him about these rocks, about what they meant to me, but he didn't understand; he just saw rocks – a beach. Seaside. Didn't see what I was trying to say at all. I was opening my heart, baring my soul, and he never even noticed. It broke my heart.' She turned to Victoria. 'He wasn't right for me. Sounds like Simon's not right for you, in much the same way.'

'Chrissake, Emma, I know he's not bloody right for me. He's all wrong – totally wrong – but José was the opposite of Simon, and he was as wrong as is possible as well. How can they both be so wrong when they're so very different? I must be overlooking something. Maybe I should change tack altogether. You sure you won't marry me?'

Emma giggled. 'Nope. Sorry. Not that way inclined.'

'Me neither. Pity. Would solve a lot of problems though, wouldn't it.'

'You reckon? I don't think so. Love affairs don't depend on gender to be problematic.'

'What a cheering thought.'

'Well, it's true, isn't it?'

'I suppose. All this fresh air's making me hungry,' said Victoria. 'Any chance of a cup of tea and a sandwich?'

'Absolutely. Tea shop or back at the cottage?'

'Cottage. I need to dump this canvas. Let's go back along the beach and pick up some driftwood. We were going to make a sculpture for your back yard, remember?'

'Yeah.' Emma looked about idly.

'What about John, though,' said Victoria. 'Did he understand about – oh, rocks and grasshoppers and things? Toby clearly didn't, but John, being that much older – I dunno.'

'You know, I've really no idea. I never got close enough to him to find out. He used to take me up to Cow Green reservoir, high up on the moors, and the place clearly meant something to him – something spiritual – but I was too shy to ask him what it was. He tried to tell me, I think, but I was embarrassed. I didn't want to see that side of him for fear that he'd want to see that side of me, and it was too soon – far too soon for me to open up to him like that.'

'Emma, that's tragic. I mean seriously, really tragic. Why did you marry him if you weren't close?'

'I thought it was just a matter of time. I thought we'd grow together.'

'And you grew apart instead?'

'Yes.' She shivered. 'More than apart. Remember how we used to talk about the string that held couples together? Very Jane Eyre, but it's true. The binding that tied me and John together was under massive tension, right from the start, but elasticated like a bungee rope, because we bounced miles apart, coming back together again to collide and bounce back off again. Those were the bruises you saw.'

'Emma, they were real.'

'Of course they were. I used to walk into doors a lot. Bungee jumping can be most disorientating.'

'And John?'

'His bruises were invisible, but I'm sure he must have had them too. I don't know. Shallow creature that I am, I think I'll recover quicker than he will.'

'You're not shallow.'

'Thank you. If we were that way inclined, I'd give you a great big snog right now.'

'No. You'd die of embarrassment.'

'Wouldn't. This whole gender thing –'

'Not that. Look. Elderly couple with dog. Aren't they your neighbours?'

'Oops – so they are. That was a narrow escape.' Emma waved at them. 'Hi there!' She turned back to Victoria. 'Deaf as posts. Don't think they heard. Look, driftwood. That's a good piece.' She picked it up.

'Yuck. What's that? It's got a slimy thing on it,' said Victoria.

'This is the seaside. Of course there are slimy things. It'll dry off.'

'Okay. Look, there's another good one. Some more over there. That'll be enough. I want that sandwich.'

Chapter Sixteen

They returned to the cottage, ate sandwiches, drank tea, and went over the same ground again and again. Victoria wasn't sure in retrospect that they made any headway, other than to clarify the fact that Emma might as well learn spitefulness as a means of coping with heartache, and Victoria had put her foot in it as regards Simon, who hadn't deserved any of the treatment she'd dished out. By five o'clock she knew she was going to support him at the dinner that evening, and absolutely, categorically, would not drink too much. Nothing at all might be the best plan. She wasn't going to apologise to John for swearing at him, but that could hardly matter. Simon was the one who counted.

They wrapped up the painting and loaded it into the back of Emma's car.

'So, you're sure?' said Emma.

'Yes. I'm going to placate the Greek God.'

'How far?'

'To Alnwick Castle and back again.'

'You know what I mean.'

'Yeah. It's tricky, isn't it. I'm feeling all conciliatory at the moment, but he might have talked to John for all I know, and hardened his heart against the foul-mouthed trollop I appear to have become.'

'Unlikely. John's not the type to invite confidences of that nature. I think you'll go to the dinner, be bored out of your brain – as I always was at such events – then you'll come back to the hotel and wonder why you bothered. You and Simon will have an almighty row, and you'll storm off back down to London tomorrow, where you'll produce ferociously good artwork that will make your name. That'll show him.'

'Good plan. I can certainly put up with one boring dinner for the sake of fame and fortune. How about you? What do you suppose you'll do now?'

'I'm taking up that post at the Laing. I'll need to find somewhere to rent in Newcastle, but there's plenty of student-type accommodation going for a song in Fenham, and I can more than offset the cost by letting the cottage out. People always want holiday lets in Bamburgh, whatever the season. As far as John's concerned, I ...'

Her voice petered out.

'You're divorcing him and need never see him again.'

'I know. And I can't bear it. You have no idea.'

Emma started the car and they set off, driving in silence. Rain fell from a clear blue sky as sun and wind played weather games together, creating colours to confound any watching artists.

'I wish I knew how to help,' said Victoria, eventually. 'Now that I've met John a few times, I can see how he could get under your skin. He certainly annoys the hell out of me. He's so bloody all-knowing. I never understood before why you married him, but I'm starting to get it now. He has a certain something. Man of mystery, but with too much insight. I can see how you might fall for him on the rebound from your glorious but prosaic Toby.'

'Thanks. It helps that you understand. I wish I knew how to help you with Simon, though. The only thing I can suggest is that you be honest with him. Seems to me like you've been playing a game of trying to please – you know, admiring his porcelain, stuff like that – and it's backfired horribly.'

'Yes, but the problem is: when I'm honest, he sees the real me.'

'And what's wrong with that?'

'People don't like the real me. I'm not very nice.'

'Fair enough,' said Emma, chuckling. 'You're horrible. I'm the nice one. But look where it got me?'

'Hmm.'

They carried on in a companionable silence, broken only by the faint rasping of worn out wheel bearings whenever they turned left.

'Good luck,' said Emma as they arrived at the hotel half an hour later. 'Enjoy the dinner. Food'll be all right. Company's the problem at these events. And oh my God, the speeches ...'

'Oh, I'll cope I've no doubt, so long as Simon deigns to take me in the first place. Thanks Emma. For everything.'

'No problem. Any time.'

Victoria carried the painting up to the room and braced herself to face Simon's anger or spite or derision or anything else. He was sitting in the window seat, leafing through a catalogue.

'Hello,' she said, quietly.

He looked up, unsmiling, and waited for her to continue.

'I'd like to come tonight, if I may. I'll behave myself.'

He didn't reply.

Victoria leaned the picture up against the wall. 'Did you have a good day? Networking, or whatever you were doing? We had fun in Bamburgh. Weather's not so great now, but it was sunny this morning. I got a painting done. The castle. You won't like the colours, I'm afraid. There was this kid, who tried to tell me how to paint. His name was Shaun Aran Teasdale. He ... oh, never mind. The tide came in, and I had to stop. Then we picked up driftwood and ate sandwiches. Me and Emma, that is, not me and Shaun. Look, are you happy for me to come or not? I'll need to have a shower and stuff if I'm coming. Wash my hair. You know.'

Simon looked back down at his catalogue.

'Yes, wash your hair. It's a mess.'

'Jeez ... you really know how to charm a girl. Okay. I'll get ready.'

Victoria stomped into the bathroom, eyes stinging. This was going to be harder than she'd thought. She turned on the shower, stripped off quickly, and got under the furious stream of water, exhilarating in the way it battered her flesh. The heat made her wince, but she needed the excess of sensation. If he was going to be a cold fish, so be it. She didn't have to be an ice maiden. No, she was going to take Emma's advice, and just be herself.

She stepped out of the shower and dried herself roughly on the towel before walking out naked into the bedroom. Simon never looked up once from his catalogue, though he must have been aware of her presence, glowing with heat, just a few feet away.

'Clean undies, I think,' she said, rummaging through her bag. 'Big knicks or thong? What do you think?' She held up both for him to look at.

'Victoria, it's over,' said Simon, so softly that Victoria could barely hear. He stared out of the window, his fingers all the time wandering over the pages, reading the words of the catalogue as if they were in Braille.

'Fuck you then. No, no, I don't mean that! Sorry! I said I'll behave, and I will. Promise.'

She chose the big knicks. They'd provide her with some comfort, if nothing else this evening.

Outside, the rain thrummed and splattered. Had they brought an umbrella? Victoria couldn't remember, and had visions of splots of rain ruining the purple dress. The wind sobbed against the window and buffeted it with random howls. There was a picture to be painted in all of this; something to capture the mood – but not now. She would hold onto the memory and use it later. Yes, of course. That was the answer. Transform these experiences, however painful, into works of art. Remember all of this: remember each sensation, live it through and grasp it tightly, embrace it, then commit it to canvas; make something of it all, use it.

Relieved with the sense of purpose the thought had given her, she had no problem slipping into the purple dress without trying to impress Simon; could enjoy the feeling of crushed velvet on her flesh, the texture and the silky slipperiness of the underskirt. As she was getting dressed, she could hear the rain easing off as the wind pushed the clouds away. She caught glimpses of specks of birds wheeling across the sky. There was a distinct chill in the air now, but it was a natural chill, not an emotional one. Simon's coldness was just a front anyway. He was a sweet man, a warm man. He'd thaw. She just needed to be patient. And if he didn't, she could always paint icebergs.

Chapter Seventeen

Ten chilly minutes later, the taxi arrived to take them to the castle for the dinner. The wind gusted, rattling the badly-maintained sash windows. It was spitting with rain again. Victoria regretted not wearing a jacket, but knew better than to try Simon's patience by suggesting she ran back inside to get a cagoule to wear over the purple dress.

As they drove out of the village and along the narrow roads, Victoria avoided touching Simon or instigating any other form of communication. Instead, she stared at the stillness in the distance where telegraph wires converged at a point above another taxi travelling some way in front of them, giving an illusion of immobility beneath heavy clouds. The car in front might have John in it. Maybe he'd get struck with lightning. Except that he couldn't. Not in a car. The one safe place, so they said – acting like a Faraday cage or something.

They reached their destination and ran across to the castle entrance over the drizzle-damp gravel. The wind sent flurries of needle-sharp raindrops in a swirl around them, but once inside, they were greeted by an unexpected wave of warmth and a sea of smartness, the grey antiques and their jeans having been magically transformed into a picture of elegance. Victoria looked up at Simon. Gods, but he was handsome. That dinner jacket was so *right* on him. Perhaps the evening wouldn't be the washout she was expecting after all. She looked around the entrance hall, which was decorated from floor to ceiling with weapons: swords, armour, pikes, and other weapons whose names she was glad not to know. All very handy, no doubt, but shivery-weird, especially when she noticed a string quartet tucked away at the top of a staircase and heard Bach, swiftly followed by Cole Porter. Yes, there would be plenty of material here for a whole series of surreal artworks. She smiled, took Simon's arm, and walked with him into the throng.

He switched on his charm and greeted everyone they passed by name, introducing her with a gracious: 'I don't think you've met Victoria.' They all smiled, shook her hand, introduced her to their wives and partners, and then ignored her. She grinned inanely at the wives and partners, who grinned inanely back. This was a most strange way to pass one's time at a social event. She wished Emma were by her side to pass judgement on everyone; to dissect their foibles and whisper, *look at her with the knitting needles in her hair!* or *antique arms alert!* as a woman with flabby wrinkled arms and an abundance of wilting orchids pinned to her bosom marched past. She began to suspect the whole evening would pass without her saying anything to anyone other than a polite 'Hello'. She needed a drink. No she didn't. Wouldn't. Mustn't.

A waiter came by with a tray and she picked up a glass of orange juice and sipped it decorously. Oh. Not orange juice, then. Definitely Bucks fizz. The real thing, too – she could taste more than a hint of Cointreau. Okay Victoria. Take it easy. Tiny, tiny sips. Don't be tempted by another glass. Don't worry that you haven't eaten anything since that sandwich in Bamburgh hours ago.

She looked around for John, but couldn't see him. Couldn't have been him in that taxi in front after all. She was disappointed, but then heard his unmistakeable voice behind her.

'... a fine pair of Louis quinze-style marquise bergères ...'

Oh lord. What were they, then? "Bergères" sounded like shepherds, but they were probably armchairs or elephants, so she was glad not to be part of the conversation.

'Simon, Victoria. There you are.'

'John.' Simon shook his hand.

Victoria waited for some sarcastic comment, but it seemed she was going to be ignored after the initial greeting, so that was okay. Boring though. She took another sip of her drink. No, slow down Victoria. You're here to support Simon, remember? She looked up at his profile. It really was perfect, no question. Easy to love and honour, if not necessarily obey, a perfect profile on aesthetic grounds if nothing else. Look at all the adoration heaped upon Michelangelo's David, despite his enormous hands and tiny appendage. Simon, by comparison, was perfectly proportioned. That had to count for something to an artist.

No it didn't. What was more interesting to draw: a perfectly planed plank, or a piece of driftwood?

John was driftwood. No, that was rubbish. If anything, he looked even smarter in his dinner jacket than Simon did. The dark hair helped, and the slighter frame. So, if not driftwood, what? A piece of his own serpentine furniture, probably. Elegant, and that little bit different.

'What do you think, Victoria?' said John.

Shit. She hadn't been listening to a word. She could simper and say something silly and girlish, or she could take Emma's advice and be honest.

'Sorry John, no idea. I was miles away.'

She downed the rest of her drink in one and smiled brilliantly. She hoped it was brilliantly – couldn't be a drunken grin yet, not after just one glass. Where was that waiter?

John raised one eyebrow and went back to talking to Simon. Victoria switched off from the conversation again and concentrated on holding her breath. That drink had been fizzy. Hiccups would be embarrassing, and rule number one tonight had been don't embarrass Simon. Rule number two should be, if you do embarrass Simon, then do it with a vengeance. No, that wasn't fair. Be good Victoria. For Emma's sake, if not your own.

She somehow survived the rest of the champagne reception while the string quartet played a medley of Handel, Irving Berlin and the Beatles. Then it was off to the dining hall for trial by dinner. The tables were set with a selection of wine glasses and far too much cutlery per person, but she'd get through all of this somehow. Had to. Shame she only had a little clutch bag with her. If she'd had something larger, she could have brought a small sketch pad and a few pencils. Even a biro and the back of an envelope. She had a tiny pen in her bag, but she couldn't draw on the napkins as they weren't paper but linen. God, she hated posh dinners.

She sat down, and Simon immediately poured her a glass of water.

'That is *all* you're drinking from now on.'

'Yes, okay, keep your wotsit on. I didn't know that orange stuff was alcoholic. Honest. I'll be good. Promise.'

She sipped at her water. Water? Tasted of posh lemonade. She looked at the jug and saw a variety of sliced citrus fruits floating in it. Fair enough. It was tasty, and at least it wasn't fizzy.

Conversation soon flowed; the men talking shop and the women talking about nothing at all as far as Victoria could tell. They made mouth noises and smiled a lot, but that was about it. She refused to join in. Nobody seemed bothered. Simon would be relieved.

Bamburgh beach felt a very long way away. She should have brought Shaun Aran Teasdale with her. They could have laughed at all the weird cutlery and peculiar courses that were served one after another. She could have encouraged him to get wrong of his Mam and the waiters and the antiques and everyone else. They could have had some fun.

The meal was followed by coffee that could have been just a smidgen hotter, and endless dull speeches. Emma had been right about those. Victoria excused herself and slipped out to the ladies. Relief! She sat in the cubicle, breathing in the mingled scents of expensive air freshener, pot pourri and vim. The wash basins were ornate, with irresistibly elegant taps. She splashed some cold water on her face, looked up at her reflection, and raised her eyebrows in surprise. The new hair do was fabulous. The dress was exquisite. She looked amazing. How the hell had she managed that? Gawd knows.

More to the point, how were any of the antiques out there resisting her charms? Because she'd refused to communicate with any of them and their wives had steered them away from any such communication, most likely. Okay, time to change things. The evening might not be such a washout if ... but no. There was that stupid promise. The one that said she was going to behave.

She wondered if Simon had noticed how beautiful she looked tonight. He hadn't said anything, but she remembered his words in the gardens – was that only yesterday? It felt much longer ago. He'd told her that yes, he did notice things. She only assumed he didn't; had always assumed he didn't.

Okay, so let's assume he had noticed. What now? Use that knowledge? For him or against him though – that was the question.

Let the next five minutes decide the answer one way or the other.

She left the ladies and walked back into the dining room, aware of the sway of her hips in the dress as she moved. Head held high, she made her way to the table and sat down again, smiling sweetly at the other couples. Some of the men brightened immediately. Was that all it took? Brief eye contact and a smile? So it would seem.

The speeches were over at last, and everyone moved into another room. Victoria thought for one horrible moment they were going to be old-fashioned with the men moving off somewhere else to drink brandy and play snooker or something, but they didn't; there was brandy, certainly, emphatically refused by Victoria, but at least she didn't have to let go of Simon's arm and go and make polite conversation about knitting chandeliers with the wives.

'Oh, what a lovely chair! I want it!' said Victoria, making a beeline for an old leather armchair, shiny with use. She sat down, and it was hard as wood. 'Gosh, that's spooky. Reminds me of my old dentist's waiting room. I wonder what happened to the chair when old Mr Caygill retired. Maybe it's lying abandoned and derelict, crumbling but somehow softened, waiting for sharp knives to slash its flesh; for cigarette burns or worse. I can remember what that feels like. I pity that chair.'

'Victoria, what *are* you on about?' said Simon.

'The chair, silly.'

'Are you sure you just had the one drink?'

'Quite sure. This is me. The normal me. I talk like this.'

'No you don't.'

'True, I haven't round you, not much. Last time I did, I seem to recall you told me to see a doctor.'

'Hmm.'

'But it's who I am, Simon. Emma suggested that I be totally honest and straightforward with you, and that's what I'm trying to do. She thought all that trying to please you was where I'd gone wrong.'

'Please me? *That* was trying to please me? Good God. What else did your silly friend say.'

'She's not silly. She has a first in art history, and is taking up a post at the Laing shortly.'

'So she's educated. Doesn't mean she isn't an airhead in some ways. No, sorry. That's not fair. I suppose it's the thought of you dissecting our relationship with your friend that's upsetting me.'

'Did you ... did you do the same with John today? Talk about me?'

'Yes, very briefly. He thinks we're totally unsuited, though he didn't say why.'

'Oh, great. And I suppose as the almighty John is always right, you'll take his words as gospel.'

'It doesn't matter whether I think he's right or not, Victoria. We've split up. Remember?'

Above the murmuring voices, Victoria suddenly heard John laugh. What was so bloody amusing? No, he was far away across the room; he wouldn't have heard her words. That psychic ability of his was all in her head, not his.

Yes, they had split up, and that "Let's still be friends" thing that people – civilised people – somehow did, was not an option. John was right. They were entirely unsuited. Simon would be better off with Emma. Now there's a thought. Pair up Simon and Emma, which would leave the way clear for her to go after John. Christ no. Go after an acknowledged wife beater? Shit. Okay, so take up with José again. Oh God. Why was she so bloody useless at relationships? What the hell was the matter with her?

'Yes, you're right,' she said. 'We have split up. So there's no need for me to sit around with you like a demure little thing. I'm going to go and get a drink. Goodbye, Simon.'

And with that, she made what she hoped was a dramatic exit. Of course she wasn't going to get a drink. She wasn't that much of a cow. Instead, she made her way out of the labyrinthine castle and phoned for a taxi. It arrived within ten minutes, and she was back in the hotel not long after. She took off the purple dress with care, packed it away in the holdall, and slipped on a long t-shirt. Then she turned the lights out and went and sat on the window seat.

Heavy rain sobbed against the sash window. Ruination lay beneath a thrum of insistent water. The wind howled across the sea as her hopes slipped away. She heard waves breaking in the distance. A seagull screamed as the seventh wave crashed and shocked her eyes open. She hadn't realised how tired she was. She shivered. It was definitely time for bed. She covered herself up with the thin duvet and listened to the sounds of the sea-swell, which rocked her to sleep eventually, as the terns roosted on the sand spit and one lone gull flew out to sea, keening for its lost mate.

Chapter Eighteen

Over the following weeks, Victoria continued to attend her weekly studio session, and managed a decent façade of cheerfulness when there, but otherwise she was bereft and found it increasingly difficult to paint anything. She needed inspiration, so started taking the train down into Kent and going for long country rambles in an attempt to fill the hole in her life where Simon used to be. It ought to be within her capabilities to replace him with something that couldn't reject her and walk away. Autumn had finally edged summer away, and she spent hours with her sketchbook rambling through woodland, across sticky ploughed fields and up and down rolling hills looking for plants and berries to inspire new artwork. On one occasion she came across a group of spindle trees with their strange fruits, tinted with autumn departures and loss. She broke off a small branch and took it back to the flat, where for some unaccountable reason it made her cry, so she threw it away. Another time she went for a walk through some woods where sweet plump chestnuts littered the floor, bursting out of their prickly green cases. She gathered up handfuls, stuffed them in her pockets and took them home to boil and peel them and eat with cabbage. There were far too many, of course. One person can only eat so many chestnuts. She froze the leftovers; sad little brain-like creatures that invited careful drawing, but she couldn't be bothered.

She knew she ought to email Emma. They'd hardly been in touch at all since Bamburgh. Emma had written once to say "sorry" that things hadn't worked out with Simon, and Victoria had replied with a generic "that's life", but that was it. No further communication.

Did she dare email Simon? No. Of course not. Don't. Really don't.

She switched on her computer. The wi-fi connection that she "borrowed" from a neighbour often played up so she'd become almost immune to the "signal strength: no signal" message. Almost, but not quite. Tonight, she stared at a blue screen while a small yellow gizmo wandered back and forth, searching for a wireless connection, pretending all that was required was a password, easily typed with a line of asterisks – but the computer wasn't fooled.

Everyone was too far away, out of range; they didn't intend to answer her.

Connect. Please connect. Please. Connect. Please. She held her breath: *signal strength: no signal. status: acquiring network address. condition red.* Or was it green – everyone else was connected, but not Victoria. Ah, Simon, don't you want to see my hidden icons any more? Don't you? *A network cable is unplugged.* What? I know! I know dammit. I know.

Another day, another walk. Early morning sun streaked through the woodland, leaving dappled patterns on the ground that left Victoria despairing of ever capturing their movement. She had tubes and tubes of earth colours, but the clay that formed their pigments was dead, and this was life. She left the woods even more subdued than normal, passing rows of suburban gardens littered with leaves that mocked her supposed talent as an artist. How could she capture all this life, when she was barely living? Blue tits flitted through close-knit shrubbery, seeking insects, full of unaccountable need and energy. A pink rosebud remained in one garden, hanging onto the summer, untouched yet by any ground frost. It made her want to cry. Everything made her want to cry nowadays.

The softly persistent rain matched her mood. A pair of jackdaws crossed the road with all the time in the world. Victoria followed.

Someone's voice, a woman's: 'I slammed on the brakes – she just walked out in front of me!'

Who? What? Are those sirens? Why? Tarmac. Lying down. Is that blood? My blood? Too much blood.

'It wasn't my fault! I didn't see her!'

People. Looking down at her. Where were the jackdaws? Were they all right? A contraption. Steel. Paramedics sliding it under her. Then nothing. Nothing. Nothing. A trolley. An injection into her thigh. Another. 'For the pain.' What pain? That thing, that agony? That boulder lying on her legs? How can an injection do anything about that? 'We'll get you to theatre soon. Is there someone we can call?' Yes. Call Simon. Please call Simon. No. Don't. Please. Signal, no signal. Condition red. A network cable is unplugged. Unplugged. Dead.

She stood facing a wall; dry sepia stones rough, rough tones. She needed to glaze over that lot. Smooth it out. The castle was red, not sepia. It wore a purple dress. Then another time: a passageway, grey rocks, wet pavement, reflections, lighting a way out, a crack, an escape. Why?

Voices.

'She's coming round.'

'Best get a move on then.'

Victoria opened her eyes a crack, still half in her dream. Two people in white were bolting together some sort of a contraption over her bed. That couldn't be right. Scaffolding? What? One bird, then hundreds weaved across the sullen skies, beckoned away by migration and a sweet chestnut harvest that meant scalded fingers, and that *hurt*, it hurt, the flavour of autumn. She was a permanent spider outside Tate Modern, sat in the centre of a scaffolding web – for how much longer?

Ah! How can anything hurt so much?

She tried to open her eyes again.

'Hello, Victoria,' said one of the nurses. 'Nearly finished now. You'll soon be more comfortable.'

Comfortable? How could she possibly be comfortable? She looked down at her legs and saw a nightmare: a thick steel knitting needle stuck through her shin, pulleys and weights and impossible things that were funny in *Carry On* films, but impossible in reality; agonising in reality.

Oh, please, sleep, come back. Where's Simon? Why isn't he here? Because he chucked you, you idiot. Remember? No. Don't want to remember. Where's my Simon, my lovely boy. I'll learn to love his porcelain figurines, I promise I will, cross my heart. Need my Simon. Please. Sing me to sleep, Simon. Take this away. I don't want any of this – I want my Simon.

Another long sleep, broken by nurses taking blood pressure, doing checks, but tired, oh so tired, just go away, please go away, let me sleep.

Days, nights, all the same. How many? No idea. No fucking idea. Shit. How did this happen?

Then awake, properly awake, and a visitor. Familiar. Tesco's bags. Cynthia? Yes, of course, Cynthia from the life class.

'Hi,' said Cynthia, softly. 'Heard you'd had a spot of bother. Thought I'd better come and see how you are. We've all been so worried.'

'Cynthia – how did you know?'

'Mal told me – you know, Mal Unpronounceable, from the class. The good-looking boy. You were missing last week and he was concerned as you hadn't let anyone know. He asked around – called at your flat a few times. He has friends in the hospital, it seems, which is how he eventually located you. He came and visited, but you were asleep and he says he nearly passed out when he saw this contraption around you, so he had to leave in a hurry. Boys, eh? Not too clever when it comes to "real" things. Anyway, he told me where you were, and I said I'd pop in and see how you're doing.'

'Thanks, Cynthia. I sort of knew I should tell someone what had happened, but I didn't know who to tell. Couldn't think straight. Concussion, or something.'

'That's all right, dear. I don't think you're up to doing much at the moment, but I can keep popping in, and I can sort out the necessaries for you – change of jim-jams, you know, that sort of thing.'

'Oh, thank you so much. I didn't know what I was going to do.'

'Now don't you cry, luvvie. It'll be all right. They'll fix your legs and things and you'll be out of here in no time. Is there anyone I should tell right away? Boyfriend? Someone like that?'

Simon. Please tell Simon. I need him. No. Don't tell him.

'No. There's nobody. Not now. Just Emma, and she's three hundred miles way.'

'Okay. Maybe when you're feeling a bit better, eh? Can I get you anything else? Magazine? Anything like that?'

'Maybe something with pictures. I don't think I can read at the moment. My head feels weird.'

'Okay. I'll pick up some arty stuff for you. Best go now. You look like you need to sleep.'

'Cynthia – are you sure this is okay? Visiting me?'

'Of course it is, dear. Time's bound to be variable, depending on what day of the week it is, as I have to fit in with my classes, but I'll be here. Don't you worry.'

'Thank you.'

'No problem. I'll be off then. Leonardo needs his exercise.'

'Leonardo?'

'My Jack Russell.'

'Of course.'

She shut her eyes and tried to reconcile a small yappy dog with the greatest artist the world had ever known. It didn't work; it was mad, but then everything was mad, and Simon was never coming back. She wanted it to be over, finished, just as Emma had wanted John to push her down that bank next to the Cathedral.

Such a desire was becoming increasingly comprehensible.

Chapter Nineteen

As Victoria's head cleared, the pain increased. She was given to understand that she had suffered a severe concussion, had smashed her right femur and torn ligaments in her left knee. She wasn't told that this would require weeks in traction: hideous weeks full of bedpans and sick bowls and pneumonia and eventually total institutionalisation, though that knowledge would creep up on her as time passed. Her days revolved around a fixed number of events: mealtimes, surgeons trailing students in their wake, tepid cups of tea, changed dressings, bed baths, and Cynthia's visits. Mal popped his head round the door once, but had to retreat quickly, and didn't visit again. Cynthia kept Victoria supplied with everything she needed – news of Leonardo, supplies of toiletries, and of course, company. They talked mostly about art. Cynthia's course was going well, and she was full of enthusiasm. She visited exhibitions and brought catalogues back for Victoria to browse.

Victoria wrote a brief note to Emma, and received a long and worried letter back, with a promise to visit once she was settled into her new job and was able to take a few days off. She didn't mention Simon or John, which was a relief.

The nights were the worst. Once the pneumonia – a common side-effect of immobility following broken limbs, they told her – abated and her temperature dropped, she stopped having hallucinatory dreams, but deep sleep was hard to find and as a result she had far too much thinking time. She learnt the names of the nurses – knew which ones were friendly and which were closet sadists, which would leave her sat on a bedpan indefinitely, and which would smile and greet her as if she were human. A lady with a miniature mobile library in a trolley came round the ward regularly, so Victoria tried losing herself in books, but her eyes couldn't follow the words for more than a few moments – the doctor explained this was due to the concussion, and would improve – but it meant much of the time was spent staring at the metal cage around her bed, trying to remember the events of the summer. Her memory felt unreliable. Had she really done that? Said that? She tried inventing scenarios where the outcome was quite different, but it never worked; never had any authenticity.

The surgeon told her bones take at least six weeks to knit. He didn't tell her that she would be there far longer, though it became obvious as time passed. Ten weeks later, she was still lying immobilized in the same bed in the same position in the same ward when a tall fair man in a dark suit walked in at visiting time. He looked like a young Greek God. Victoria closed her eyes, opened them again, and he was still there, only nearer: then he was sitting down in the chair next to her bed and handing her a small box of expensive chocolates.

She took them wordlessly, gulped, sniffed, rubbed her eyes, looked into his, looked down again and swallowed hard.

'Hi.' She managed to get the word out without her voice cracking.

'Hi.'

'You took your time.'

'I know. Sorry about that. Only heard yesterday.'

'Who told you?'

'John. He'd heard from Emma. I happened to bump into him the other day at a sale. He asked after you. Assumed I knew, naturally enough.'

'Ah.'

'Why didn't you let me know? You could've written. No, sorry. I'm not here to nag you. No reason why you should let me know, not after the way I treated you.'

'You? Treated me? I was the one who behaved like a drunken fishwife.'

'Not your fault they spiked your alcohol with alcohol.'

'Heh. No. Oh God, Simon, I've missed you so much.'

'Yes. It's been ... weird.'

'Weird?'

'I haven't known what to do with myself. Arrive home from work and sit there thinking I should be doing something. Start getting ready to come round to your place. Realise I can't. Flick channels on the telly, endlessly. Try to fill my time in at weekends. Go to sales I needn't attend. Buy pieces I know I won't be able to sell.'

'You're still by yourself then? After all this time? Must be nearly three months.'

'Getting on for that, yes.'

'How've you been?'

He didn't answer. Victoria reached out and took his hand and he leaned over and kissed her sweetly on the lips and then passionately – except of course it didn't happen like that. If she'd reached over to take his hand, she'd have fallen out of bed, no doubt taking the scaffolding with her. His hands were out of reach. Perfectly manicured as ever. Untouchable.

She didn't know what to say, but she needed to keep the conversation going somehow; needed to see his mouth move and know it was him, that he was really here, so she said the first thing that came into her head.

'How's John?'

'Gloomy. This divorce is proving tougher on him than I expected. I thought he was perking up when we were at Bamburgh as he seemed to have more life about him that weekend, but I don't know – something's eating away at him. I was watching him in the salesroom the other day. He was stroking a finely carved piece of mahogany with what looked like affection, but then he backed off in disgust and wiped his fingers as if he'd touched something unmentionable.'

'Yeah, I can imagine. Emma told me a little about his relationship with chairs and things.'

'Bit like me and porcelain?' He grinned.

'No, I don't think you're as obsessive as he is.'

'You're probably right. He's at the top of the business because of his obsessions; the way he pursues the piece he wants until he gets it. It's made him a very successful man. Far richer than I'll ever be, though of course it means that when he loses a piece, it hits him doubly hard. Hence his problems with Emma, I suppose. I wonder what really went wrong there. I know you told me he hit her, but ... okay. I still can't reconcile that fact with the John I know, but I do believe you. Really.'

They sat in silence together for a while, Simon frowning slightly, Victoria watched his face, loving every fleeting expression that came and went.

People were starting to move. Visiting time was over.

'Will you come and see me again?'

'Do you want me to?'

'Please. For the chocolates, if nothing else.'

'Okay. Later this week perhaps.' He stood up. 'Bye then.'

124

He still didn't touch her.
''Bye.'
And then he was gone.

Chapter Twenty

Simon kept his promise. He visited every couple of days, usually in the evenings. One time he coincided with Cynthia, who, much to Victoria's surprise, lost the power of speech in his presence. Bubbly Cynthia, with all her confidence? Victoria asked her about it the next time she visited.

'Well, he's so bloody good looking, isn't he. I thought I was sitting next to a film star. I'd love to draw him. What a profile! I suppose you must have sketchbooks full of him.'

'No, funnily enough I haven't. I sketched a couple of porcelain figurines for him once, but that was as close as I ever got to a portrait.'

'How strange. I don't mean that you've never drawn him, but that you would think he was anything like porcelain.'

'Well, he is. Have you looked at his hands?'

'Oh yes, you bet.'

'Cynthia!'

'Sorry, but I see a lovely pair of hands like that and I can't help imagining you know what. No – naughty Cynthia – he's your fella. I'm much too old anyway. Don't know what I was thinking.'

'Not sure that he is my fella anyway. He was, a few months ago, but he chucked me before the accident. Now when he visits, it's pleasant, and I think he's genuinely missed me, but is he my "fella"? Don't know. Really don't know.'

'He wouldn't keep visiting you if he didn't care.'

'True, but I think he's bored on his own. I'm something to do.'

'Oh, Victoria! But okay, if you say so.' Cynthia fumbled in her bag, took out a small mirror and checked her lipstick. 'He *is* very good looking.'

'I know, but looks aren't everything.'

'Of course not, but he's soft-spoken, gentlemanly, charming, considerate –'

'Yeah, yeah, I know.'

'So what's the problem?'

Victoria thought for a moment.

'Sometimes I dream, and it's not of him.'

'Oh. That's awkward. Who is it?'

'I'm not sure. I wish I knew, because the dreams are a bit … umm …'

'Ooh, lucky you! And you've no idea who you're dreaming about? What does he look like?'

'That's the weird thing. I don't know – dark or fair, tall or short – I really have no idea.'

'Maybe he's the side-effect of the diamorphine?'

'Can't be. They haven't given me anything stronger than paracetamol in weeks.'

'Oh well. I don't know, dear. Maybe the man in your dreams is your mind's way of coping with the trauma. A useful distraction. After all, breaking up with a gorgeous bloke, quickly followed by getting smashed up in a road accident, *does* count as traumatic.'

'True enough. How's Leonardo?'

'Up to his usual tricks.'

'Oh goody. Do tell.'

They slipped back into the usual topic of conversation. When Cynthia left, Victoria slept immediately. The early weeks in the hospital, when sleep had been so hard to find, had now been replaced by long periods of excessive lassitude. She assumed it was another of her body's coping mechanisms, and didn't fight it, but she spent virtually all day and night asleep nowadays and was worried about what would happen when she was released from hospital. The sentence would be drawing to a close soon. They were talking about taking down the scaffolding, removing the cast from her left leg now that the knee was pretty much healed, and putting a full length cast on her right leg so that she could start to regain her mobility. The thought was terrifying. Once they unchained her from the safety of her cage, she would have to go back to her old life with all its problems. What would happen about shopping? How could she possibly go to a supermarket or even the corner shop after being immobile for all these weeks? Then there were the stairs to her flat – all three flights of them. Impossible! She'd have no muscle tone at all. She'd never make it. They'd find her curled up at the bottom of the stairs in despair. Except that she wouldn't be curled up, not with a full length plaster cast. She'd be straight – rigid – as if rigor mortis had already set in. Which it would shortly anyway, because it was late autumn now and the bottom of the stairs to her flat could get bitterly cold.

No, she'd have to stay here in the warm where people cared for her and brought her meals and a bowl of warm water morning and night so that she could wash; and patted her back and her bum with talcum powder to stop her getting bed sores, and all was fine and safe.

She had a boyfriend in here. Would she still have one when she got out? She didn't know, and that was the most terrifying thought of them all. Simon visited every other evening now, like clockwork. He was always kind. Always brought her a little gift. Always smiled.

Life was perfect. This must be what they meant by people getting institutionalised. Scary stuff.

Simon was due that evening. Usually he was one of the first visitors in, but Victoria looked in vain for his tall form to come striding across the floor. Instead, ten minutes after all the other visitors had arrived, a slight and altogether darker figure appeared.

'Oh, fucking hell!' said Victoria.

'And hello to you too, Victoria,' said John. 'Simon sends his apologies. A client insisted on seeing him tonight and wouldn't be put off. Simon also apologised profusely for putting you and me through this. He realised you might not be exactly overjoyed to see me, but at the same time thought the personal touch was better than a phone call and he didn't want to leave you pining for a visitor who never came.'

'Yes, I suppose. Sorry John. Shouldn't have sworn at you. Always seem to be doing that. It's kind of you to come.'

'Yes, it is. You could try to look pleased.'

'Oh, fuck off.'

'Ah, you're so predictable – which is nice in its way, I suppose, so I'll forgive you. Now then. What does one do? I'm not used to hospital visiting. Do I ask you how you're feeling, and then listen while you give me a tedious description of your day, full of pills and pessaries and bodily functions?'

'You don't have to stay.'

'I know I don't, but Simon will interrogate me later on, and I'd like to be able to give a decent account of my visit. Simon's my friend. He deserves –'

John looked at Victoria and frowned.

128

'What, a decent girlfriend? Instead of a harridan?'

'I don't think you're a harridan, despite your best attempts to appear that way whenever we meet. I actually find you refreshingly forthright. You never go out of your way to be polite to me, and that's unusual. I've been told that some people find me intimidating, so they behave in an unpleasantly obsequious manner as a result. Maybe it's my money which impresses – which incidentally, does not amount to anything like as much as people imagine. Or it won't once Emma's finished collecting what she considers to be her share.'

'Her "share"? After the way you've treated her, I hope she takes you for every penny you've got, you tight-fisted arsehole.'

'That's venomous, even for you. I wonder what my little Emma's been saying.'

'She's not "your" little Emma any more, luckily for her.' Victoria took some deep breaths to calm herself down. 'Emma's one of my oldest friends, and you've made her very unhappy.'

'I think you'll find it's she who's made herself unhappy.'

Victoria gasped, but couldn't think of a suitable riposte.

'And of course,' continued John: 'I could counter by saying that Simon's one of *my* oldest friends, and you've made *him* unhappy.'

'He's not unhappy.'

'That's a matter of opinion, but to be fair, perhaps he's marginally more cheerful now than he was in Bamburgh. Having a part-time girlfriend who stays in one place with pleasing predictability must suit him, but what happens when you come out of hospital?'

'That's none of your business.'

'I rather think it is. He's my friend.'

'Then don't try to break up his relationship with me.'

'And what sort of a relationship is that? No, don't answer. Perhaps I should go. Or to use your own delightful phraseology, I suppose I should "fuck off"'.

Victoria laughed despite herself.

'Christ, I am awful sometimes, aren't I'.

'Absolutely despicable. But you're a good artist.'

'Really?'

'Oh yes.'

'Be serious. Have you ever seen anything of mine?'

'Yes. That pair of potato prints, which now have pride of place in my study.'

'Aha! So that was you. I always wondered who'd bought them.'

'I saw them and I liked them so I bid for them and bought them. That's the way I do business.'

'I know,' said Victoria, under her breath.

'They're unusual. Shouldn't have any grace about them, given the technique, but they do. They're bold and intricate at the same time – each one subtly different, showing unexpected facets of the same object. Potatoes, yes, but also beginnings which display unexpected transformations. They make me stop and ponder. It's a rare piece of artwork that has that effect on me nowadays.'

Victoria was about to make some sarcastic remark, but was caught by his expression. He looked the same as he had in Tate Modern. Desperately sad. Oh, Emma. What have you done to this man?

John looked at his watch.

'Time's up. I've done my duty, and will be able to report back to Simon that we discussed art, if only for about twenty seconds, but I needn't tell him that. He'll be back in to see you on Thursday. Good bye, Victoria.'

He held out his hand and she automatically took it. His palm was warm and there were dark hairs on the back of his hand. She tried to hate them, tried to force herself to remember Emma's bruises, but couldn't. She enjoyed the contact.

''Bye, John. And thank you.'

'I'm not sure what for, but you're welcome.'

And with that, he left.

Chapter Twenty-one

A team of junior surgeons duly arrived to dismantle the scaffolding. They attacked it with glee, as if it they were playing with a Meccano set. Victoria's leg quivered helplessly as the weights that had aligned the broken bones were removed. Then the porter took over, and she nearly vomited due to an attack of vertigo when her bed was wheeled across the ward and down to theatre. She hadn't expected so much dizziness, but that was due no doubt to three months of being stuck in the same position. Things didn't improve once they arrived in theatre. She'd expected some sort of an anaesthetic, but instead, a cack-handed student doctor unscrewed the knitting needle from her shin without any warning, turning it the wrong way at first. He was admonished and tried again, with more success the second time. Victoria watched horrified as a glob of blood and goo plopped out of the hole left behind. A nurse quickly mopped up the mess and applied a dressing. A more experienced surgeon then constructed a full plaster cast, together with a sort of hinge arrangement around her knee. She was wheeled back to the ward to be told that she'd missed tea, and that Cynthia had come and gone. Great.

Sleep that night was difficult. Now that she was no longer tied to the bed, Victoria at last had the option to turn over. She knew she used to sleep on her side, but couldn't work out how to do it with the heavy cast, or where her other leg should go. Turning onto her front was comfortable for a while, but it hurt her foot. A concerned nurse came over to see what the problem was. Victoria said she was fine, and resigned herself to lying on her back – at least she was flat. After three months of sitting up, she enjoyed the novelty.

The next morning a physiotherapist came round with a pair of crutches to help her stand up. The blood drained from her head, but she managed to remain upright, and even took a few shuffling steps.

Once back in bed, the fears returned. They said they were going to send her home as soon as she could manage stairs. She didn't want to manage stairs. Could she pretend? No. They wouldn't let her stay here indefinitely. She had to start living again some time.

'Now that's an improvement,' said Cynthia brightly later that afternoon. 'I'll have to tell Mal you're safe to visit now that the ironmongery's gone.'

'He'll have to be quick. They're kicking me out in a few days.'

'Oh, that's wonderful!'

'No, it isn't. Cynthia, I'm scared.'

'Why? I can get your shopping in for you, and you've got your young man to come round and look after you when he gets in from work. You'll be fine. I'll sort out a table easel for you and make sure all your sketching materials are within reach. Probably best to avoid painting at first, because of all that to-ing and fro-ing you'd have to do cleaning stuff. Pen and ink would be ideal. Nothing to carry. Have you got enough suitable paper? Not to worry if you haven't, I can always bring you in supplies.'

'Thanks. I'll be all right, I suppose.'

'Of course you will. When you're a bit more mobile, you can start back at the studio. They've all missed you down there. And of course you can do lots more of those little picture postcard thingies you were doing. I can take them down the Post Office for you.'

'I won't be doing any more of them.'

'Why not?'

'They're not "real". They don't have any grace about them.'

'Grace? Heavens. Well no, I suppose they don't, but they're not supposed to, are they?'

'Cynthia, it's not proper art. It's not what I should be doing. I'm better than that.'

'I know you are, but you've still got to earn a living and pay the rent on that little flat of yours. Perhaps you should move in with the lovely Simon. Be a kept woman.'

'Christ, no!'

'Why? What's wrong with being a kept woman? I am.'

'Really?'

'You don't suppose the few pounds I make from modelling pays all my bills do you? Or my college fees?'

'I'd never really thought about it. What are you, some rich man's mistress? Or do you have a wealthy landowner husband in the country who sends you regular cheques so that you can live out your dreams in the city?'

'Neither. My partner's a head teacher and we live in Twickenham. We're comfortably off.'

'Well I never. He'll be on a good salary then?'

'Yes, not bad at all.'

'You've never talked about him.'

'Haven't I? Leonardo brought us together.'

'I might have guessed.' Victoria chuckled and settled back to listen to one of Cynthia's increasingly unlikely tales about her little dog. She'd miss these chats, and hoped her friend meant what she'd said about doing bits of shopping for her. That way they'd keep in touch once she was out of hospital. She didn't want to be alone in the flat with just evening visits from Simon to keep her company.

Simon ... what was she going to do about him? When he came through the door at visiting time, she loved him to bits, but often by the end of the visit she often couldn't wait for him to go, and sometimes came close to flinching when he kissed her goodbye.

I told you that you do not love this man.

Chrissake, José! Where did you appear from?

That special place in your heart you reserved for me long ago, where I have nestled, keeping you safe from this cold fish whom you name Simon.

Yeah, right. Now you can bugger off. But thank you – you've actually helped. I'd forgotten what a sod you were and how sweet Simon was, how forgiving and how – oh, how wonderful after that ghastly visit of yours. He is fantastic. I don't know how I could have forgotten that.

You see? So I have my uses.

'And there was Leonardo, barking at Peter,' said Cynthia: 'and – Victoria, have you heard a word I just said? You've got a smile on your face that suggests you've been miles away, in a far more interesting place.'

'Sorry Cynthia! You're absolutely right about me and Simon. He's a lovely man, and I'd be mad to let him slip away. It's not going to be easy though. He did chuck me, after all, and he's never said we're officially back "on", so to speak. What's the matter? You've gone all quiet.'

'You're going to hate me for this, Victoria.'

'For what?'

Cynthia looked out of the window.

'Cynthia? What is it?'

'Simon's lovely, but … okay, let me be blunt. If you were given a choice between doing art – and I'm not talking about your postcards, but proper art – and living with Simon, which would you choose?'

'Art, obviously. But it's not a question of either/or, is it?'

'Isn't it?'

'I thought you were just telling me to move in with him?'

'That was me talking without thinking. Obviously it would be convenient, and he's a beautiful young man, but is he right for you? Does whatever it is you feel for him even begin to compare with the passion you feel for your art?'

'It's different.'

'Completely different?'

'Yes.'

'Exactly,' said Cynthia, nodding her head. 'It shouldn't be so very different,' she added. 'You should feel as if losing him would be the equivalent of having your hands chopped off so that you couldn't paint any more. But it's not, is it?'

'Oh come on, Cynthia. Nobody feels that sort of passion for their partner, do they? Not outside films and books and things.'

'That's the way I feel about my Peter.'

'Then you're the exception.'

'No, I think I'm lucky, but I don't think I'm exceptional. Victoria – be kind to Simon. He could be a good friend to you, but I'm not sure he's an ideal lover. Hey! Don't cry! I'm sorry, didn't mean to upset you. Really. It's just –'

'Oh, fuckit, fuckit, fuckit. Sorry. What the hell am I going to do? You're right, of course you're bloody right. Shit. Bollocks.'

'Victoria!'

'It's just reaction. I'm scared, I'm tired, I don't know what to do with my life, I don't know if I can do anything as an artist at all, and I miss my mum. She would have looked after me, but she can't, she's long gone, and that's that. Do you know how long I've been in this bloody hospital? How much art I've done? Three little sketches. That's all. Why wasn't I sitting here over the past weeks doing a series of studies of hospital life to be worked up into something interesting? Something that would give an insight into what this place is really like, getting underneath the routines to the horrors lurking below? Why? Because I'm not really an artist. I'm kidding myself.'

'Bollocks, if I may borrow one of your expressions. You've not done any of that because you've had a nasty blow to the head so have been suffering concussion and post-traumatic stress, or whatever. Wait till you get back to the flat. The work will pour out. You'll produce wonderful, wonderful art.'

'I hope you're right. Because if I can't do that, then I can't do anything, and I might as well get John to push me off a cliff.'

'John? Don't you mean Simon?'

'No, John. I think he's a better cliff-pusher than Simon. Simon would just say, "Darling, don't worry, you'll feel better soon," whereas John would snarl, "Go on – fall, drown, smash yourself to bits. Produce something *real*, instead of this perpetual sham."'

'Heavens! There's a bit of transference, if ever I heard it.'

'What do you mean?'

'Sounds to me like you're putting words into this John's mouth that you really mean yourself.'

'Oh, I do that all the time. Used to a lot with José, anyway. It's a dangerous habit in some ways.'

'I should say. You could build up a vivid picture of someone in your mind based on the words that you've put into their head, and then find out in actual fact that they're a completely different person.'

'Tell me about it! That's more or less what did happen with José.'

'So don't do it with this John, whoever he is. Listen to the words, and accept them as your own. And now I have to go. Look, don't worry about leaving here. I really will help, and Simon will too unless you're too horrible to him.'

'Yes, I know. Thanks, Cynthia! 'Bye for now.'

''Bye.'

Chapter Twenty-two

Victoria returned to her flat five days later, sick with nerves. The journey in the taxi was difficult, because despite the hinge in the cast, she could barely bend her right leg, and the left knee hadn't recovered sufficiently from having the ligaments fixed to have much useful movement either.

The taxi dumped her at the foot of her stairs, with a heavy bag borrowed from Cynthia containing her accumulated bits and pieces from hospital. There were three flights to be conquered. She reckoned it would take a good ten minutes. In the end, it was nearer an hour. She let herself into the flat, went straight to the kitchen to re-boot the boiler, and then to the bedroom where she lay down on the bed and sobbed helplessly. After half an hour, she'd sufficient recovered her composure to make a start on the pile of post that had arrived in her absence. The three bank statements made increasingly desperate reading. She was well into her overdraft thanks to the direct debit payments on her rent, plus various utility bills, with no income to offset the drain of funds. It hadn't occurred to her that this would happen. What an idiot.

Easy solution. All she needed was John to come round and buy up her entire stock of canvases for a few thousands, and she'd be laughing. Only that wasn't going to happen. She'd have to talk to Simon. He wouldn't be happy, but he might help, just might, if he'd come anywhere near to forgiving her.

And why should he? No reason. Her only hope was that despite everything, he still had feelings for her that had survived all the viciousness she'd thrown in his direction before the accident, and his feelings had maybe grown as he'd seen her lying helpless and dependent in hospital.

He came round later that evening. She showed him the statements and bills.

'This doesn't look good, Victoria.'

'I know. I'll have to look for somewhere cheaper. Can't go on like this.'

'And how do you intend to afford even somewhere cheaper?'

'I don't know. Housing benefit? Isn't there help for people like me?'

'Have you been paying any National Insurance contributions?'

'Ermm. I dunno.'

'Victoria! That means you probably haven't. Dammit, how did you get into such a mess?'

'I got run over. Remember?'

'Yes. And I suppose you expect me to bail you out.'

'Please? Pretty please?'

'Victoria, it's no good.'

'What do you mean?'

'I – oh, hell. I don't know. But you and I. This situation. I could pay all your bills, of course I could. I can afford it. But what sort of a position does that put you in?'

'Kept woman. I quite fancy the idea. Either you could pay the bills, and I stay here, or I could move in with you. What do you reckon? Could you cope with me over at your place? I'd be good. Promise.'

'No.'

'No? What do you mean?'

'I mean you need to sort this out for yourself, without attaching yourself limpet-like to me. You need to take responsibility.'

'What? How? Simon, I can't. I'm broken – hurt beyond repair.'

'That's not the impression I got from John. He said you and he had been talking about art. Sounded quite chummy. You never talk to me about art.'

'Oh for Chrissake. He bought a couple of my pictures. That's all. He liked them. So what. So bloody what.'

'Victoria, I'll be frank. I don't like your artwork. I don't understand it. Don't begin to understand it – so how am I supposed to understand you?'

'You don't need to understand me. Just love me. I'd snuggle up and give you a kiss at this point except that I'd probably kick your shin with my cast and give you some dreadful injury.' She giggled despite herself.

'My dear, it's not going to work. It can't work.'

'Then what am I supposed to do?'

'I don't know. Stand on your own two feet?'

'Look, you don't understand. This is serious. I have no money. I can't pay my rent.'

'I know. I can't help. Or rather, I can, but I'm not going to. I'm sorry.'

'Please Simon!'

'No. Goodbye, Victoria. Look after yourself.'

'I can't!'

'Then get John to look after you.'

'Oh, bollocks to John! I can't stand the man. Is this some stupid jealousy trip? Chrissake, Simon. I really. Cannot. Stand. John.'

'All right, fair enough. But I can. He's my friend.'

'I thought I was your friend.'

'Yes; enough for me to come and visit you in hospital, but no more than that. What I said in Bamburgh wasn't a spur of the moment decision. I thought you understood that. Goodbye, Victoria.'

He picked up his coat and left.

Victoria felt the tears welling up, and knew she was going to cry, but also knew there would be some relief mixed in with the sorrow. She would never have suggested going to live with Simon if she'd thought for one moment he'd agree. The idea was nightmarish.

He was still a blue meany not to give her any money. Oh, sod him. She'd survive. Somehow. She'd think about it tomorrow. For now, she was tired – bone-weary and helpless and needing hours of sleep: proper sleep without the disturbances of hospital clanks and wails and spillages and smells.

The next day Victoria caught sight of the piles of bank statements, panicked and set about painting a dozen postcard views of St Paul's cathedral from memory. They were virtually identical, but the buyers wouldn't care. She photographed them and posted them on an auction site, then wept a little before making a bowl of porridge – the best comfort food she knew. A couple of internet bids arrived within the hour, and two of the pictures were sold. She cried again with relief. Perhaps she could sort out her life after all, but oh, it was hard, so hard.

This was the new pattern of her life – hours spent churning out hollow and sad little pictures before trying to sell them. It was sheer drudgery, but it was a routine, and it made enough money to start paying back her debts and stop the electricity from being cut off. Cynthia popped round most days as she'd promised, but it was only for a few minutes to take orders for grocery shopping, and to pick up packs of cards to post.

After a week, Victoria decided she needed to get out or she'd go mad with boredom. She gingerly picked her way down the three flights of stairs and out onto the street. The sign above the bus stop reckoned the next bus was due in just a few minutes. She could wait.

The bus was horribly crowded. She had to stand, one hand holding her crutches, the other with white knuckles gripping a bar that might have been Simon's neck. In her mind she snapped it. How could he do this to her? At last someone stood up and offered her a seat. She sat down, squeezing her unbending leg in somehow, and took a book out of her bag, bending its spine back much too far. She stared round the bus and decided the other passengers were taking special care not to meet her eyes. She didn't blame them. A shudder and jerk later, the bus stopped outside the British Museum and she got out.

She couldn't face the museum itself, so hobbled along a street that could have been anywhere in the city. There was a smell of dust in the air. She hurried on, bewailing the absence of light today. Wasn't she allowed even a little sun? A thin grey trickle made it through the dull mist. She was cold. Wet. The wind got up, and the fine-blowing drizzle was followed by splots of heavy rain as the wind gusted round and dodged the taxis. Rain out on the moors was beautiful, but in the middle of the city it was all too horrible for words. She sobbed her way to a bus stop and was soon back at the mountainous stairs. After an age, she reached the third floor, where she collapsed onto her bed and cried.

After a while, all cried out, she looked through sore eyes around the place. Nobody had dusted the flat in weeks. Years, probably. There were cobwebs everywhere. In a corner of her room, she watched a spider rushing at a fly, caught in a dusty web. The fly struggled to free itself, just making it in time. The spider retreated and waited as if it had all the time in the world to wait and pounce and destroy. There would be no escape in the end. Death was inevitable.

Outside the window, a trio of seagulls was being mobbed by starlings. After a raucous squawking and beating of wings, they flew

139

away, as if they'd never been there. Victoria longed to fly after them, back up north to a misty estuary where a boat called *Marean* lay in the sand waiting for high tide so that she could float again.

A week later, Cynthia invited her to go for a drive, to get out of London.

'You're looking pale, Victoria. You need some fresh air. A trip.'

'I'm not sure I can afford the time. Need to get more cards done.'

'Come off it. You've been producing half a dozen a day for the last fortnight. Give yourself a break, woman!'

She agreed, in a daze, not really caring one way or another. Once in the car, she felt as if she were slipping into a dream. The motorway sped past through wet underpasses and out into the rain. She watched the chevrons flashing by, one, two three, and cars, more cars, flying past, under bridges and tall-stretched blue signposts, then grey, punctuated with vicious orange hissing lights. The car swept back into the rush, the tornado scream of another underpass, tunnelling deep beneath the ground, down, down, down, and the slick-slide of wet wipers roared, dreams streaked wet and dead in the foot well, the depths of the carpet, the wrappers that crinkled the water, the rust, the crunching seepage – wait for the screech – wait – too late! She woke with a jolt, expecting sirens, but no – they were still driving along the M25, calm and steady and perfectly safe, and it wasn't even raining.

They stopped at a country park. Victoria had no idea where it was. She didn't care. Leonardo ran round in swift circles. There were trees; there was grass. That was all.

On the way home, Victoria slept again, dreamlessly this time. Cynthia dropped her back at the flat.

'I can't come up – need to get back to make dinner. Are you going to be all right?'

'Yes, fine.'

'You sure? You've got a bit more colour in your cheeks, so that's good, but – oh, I don't know, Victoria. You seemed more cheerful in hospital when you were in all that pain. I worry, you know.'

'Don't. I'm okay. Really.'

'You need a holiday.'

'Can't afford one. Maybe in a few months' time. Might go up and see Emma.'

'Excellent idea! Good. I'll be off then. 'Bye!'

''Bye, Cynthia. And thanks.'

'Any time.'

She slept better that night and woke slightly refreshed. Getting out and walking had been good for her after all, despite the nightmares. She'd had the plaster cast removed a week previously, and was getting used to hobbling around with just a walking stick to help. Her left knee was still wobbly from damaged ligaments, but the surgeon had assured her that as her muscles developed the knee would become more stable, though it might be prone to arthritis later on. She'd worry about that when it happened. For now, the slight lurch in her guts when the knee bent sideways was the least of her problems.

Over the next few weeks, she took to going out at dusk and wandering through quiet places; through graveyards and alongside the older city churches. She hardly noticed the winos that inhabited such places, and didn't think they saw her at all. Sometimes she would sit on a bench in a cemetery and make up stories in her head that perhaps – one day – she could commit to paper as sketches, even paintings. She would have to start painting properly again soon if she was ever going to recover from this wretched depression she'd slipped into. Simon had thought she could do it on her own, without any outside help. Maybe he was right. Certainly she'd be stronger in the long term if she could pull herself out of this without any outside assistance, but oh, it was hard, and many days she was incapable of getting out of the flat at all. The postcard paintings kept her going. They were real. Tangible. They turned into cash. They paid bills. That would have to be enough for now.

Chapter Twenty-three

Another day, and another graveyard. Victoria sat on a bench, eyes squeezed shut, imagining she could still run as fast as she when charging round the field at school, feet pounding the grass, feeling as if with just a little more speed she could take off and fly. She opened her eyes. A carved angel stood a few feet away, facing the church with lichen-covered eyes, as if waiting for the brickwork to turn to dust. Victoria empathised, and stared at the statue, committing it to memory, until some movement from a couple a few yards away distracted her. They were sitting together on a bench in front of a large tomb. The man read a small red book with a frown on his face while the woman plucked the petals from a flower she'd probably pinched from a nearby grave. She looked bloody miserable. Victoria wasn't surprised. The man was revolting in the way he turned each page with care and stroked his fat white fingers across the paper. Was the woman hoping for death, before succumbing to the man's proposals? He looked vile enough for such a reaction and Victoria hated him, haphazardly and vehemently. She looked away again, making a few quick notes in her sketchbook to keep the memory fresh.

An old woman shuffled past Victoria's bench, her cheeks hollow with despair and forbidden knowledge. The silver-red buttons that lined up in ranks along the edge of her threadbare coat were done up in a haphazard order that left her rucked up and crumpled, looking as if any manner of angular cruelties were twisted around her body. Victoria stood up quickly and hurried past a man who had a look in his eyes which seemed to ask, why hurry, why even make the attempt? What's the point? In startling contrast, a girl passed by with light in her hair and joy in her pacing, swinging past the iron railings and the steely certainty of the laurel leaves. An old man shuffled past, carrying a tray of eggs. He moved slowly, hunched over his eggs, careful not to break any, taking one step at a time. Victoria imagined a malign ghost following close behind him with the sole intention of tripping him up and sending him flying past the last of the gravestones.

There were pictures here. Possibilities. Some were terrifying, but others could be attempted without causing too much distress, surely?

Victoria found another bench and sat down. She opened her sketchbook and roughed in an angel plus the old man with the eggs. The morning's dew evaporated in the sunshine as she drew. A late-flowering rose, the last in its bed to make the attempt, struggled against the gusting winds and bloomed half-heartedly, but at least it tried. T-shirted teenagers cut through the graveyard, walking by with bare flesh in the bitter cold. It started to rain, of course. It always rained when Victoria sat somewhere and tried to draw, but she supposed the slate grey skies wouldn't be allowed to turn to blue until they were fully drained.

She packed her sketchbook away and hurried back to the flat, glad of her increased mobility. She hadn't used the stick for several weeks. It meant people no longer stood up for her on the tube, but as she never went very far, she could always cope. The hours of pain in her legs after her frequent trips didn't bother her. They kept her focused. If there had been no pain, she would have retreated into dreams too much for safety.

A whining in the bathroom alerted her to the presence of a wasp. Where were all these wasps coming from? Shouldn't they be hibernating, or whatever it was wasps did? Maybe it was looking for a safe place to sleep. That was understandable, but didn't feel like helping anyone or anything.

'Sort it out yourself, you hopeless, thankless creature. Get thee gone! Avaunt! Stand on your own two – no, six – feet. At least you can fly. Think yourself lucky.'

She opened the window and shooed it out into the gusty grey weather. Two more postcards today, and then she could relax. She prepared the card and paints, and started sketching out the dome of St Paul's for the five hundredth time or however many it was by now. Apparently the number of people in the world happy to buy such trash was inexhaustible, but if ever they did stop bidding for these mini-masterpieces, she could always do Tower Bridge or the Houses of Parliament instead. While she painted she tried to let her thoughts wander elsewhere, away from the identikit pictures to memories of rambles up the Durham Dales during her student days: rough rock under her fingers which crumbled with age and weathering; and tiny bugs hidden in crevices safe from the wind which would flick them across the expanse of bracken if they left the safety of the rock. They'd probably survive, but a new home would have to be found. The rock and the weathering would not be the same away from the familiar white grasses; the cotton tufts, reeds and rushes, but they'd cope. How had she ever let the wind catch her and blow her here, to London, where the bugs were cockroaches and where concrete buildings cracked and disintegrated – where life was cropped short on dog-shit covered pavements? Why wasn't she still up north, where she could breathe?

The first postcard was finished. She put it to one side to dry and took another. Could she bear to do St Paul's again? Yes. But first she'd have to have a cup of tea.

She boiled the kettle, poured hot water into the brown-stained mug, squidged the teabag around for a few seconds, and threw it towards the over-full bin. She missed. Of course she missed. She picked it up off the floor, noting yet another brown splodge. One day she would wash all the marks away. Until then, they'd better stay there as an accusation that she was useless, hopeless, a pathetic creature who couldn't even keep her kitchen floor free of spent teabag stains, so how was she supposed to transform herself into a great artist? By painting with teabags? Actually, that wasn't such a bad idea. No. Throwing teabags at paper wasn't very clever, even though rumour had it that Leonardo da Vinci used to throw sponges full of paint at walls to work into designs.

She went back to the table with her tea, settled herself down, and started forming the dome of St Paul's yet again. She would fix this cathedral in colours whether it agreed or not: commit it to card, tie it down with tints that couldn't be erased … She put the paintbrush down. This was no good; this painting by numbers. This was not binding an image properly. For that, she needed sinews of couch grass, tearing the core of the image away until all that remained was a whisper, a hillside, the bleat of a sheep, a smidgen of smoke on the breeze, a sealed circle ending where once there was a flurry of sparks, a bonfire, divine conflagration, the howl of a dog in the dark.

She closed her eyes and leaned back in the chair, remembering bitter winds biting through her fleece, once warm, now useless on a day when frost invaded the air; a still morning, with bright sun – a simulacrum of summer. The wind chill on Hadrian's Wall would freeze any centurion's ears and nose on a day like this. How long had it been since she'd been to the Wall? Ages. Not since university days. Must go again. If you stood on the wall at Housesteads, you could see for miles, north and south, see countless possibilities while nearby there would be a blackbird, scoffing berries, completely unaware. Ah, memories. Maybe she ought to get out of the city permanently, as Cynthia was now starting to advise. She'd give it a few more weeks – get some more postcards done – then pack up a travelling paint box, go up north, and do some real work. Have a genuine February idyll. It was time.

She should paint Simon now – maybe as a porcelain figure; beautiful, but breakable.

Ah, breakable. Yes. What had she done? All that bleating about expecting him to pay her bills, expecting him to let her move in amongst his immaculate figurines – what had she been thinking? No wonder he'd buggered off for good. Poor bloke. Maybe she should write and apologise. No. He'd think she was trying to get him back. Would he? Maybe not, if she worded the email carefully enough.

She definitely owed him an apology. He was a sweet man, and she'd been – what? Her usual self. Christ, but she was horrible. No wonder she could never hold onto a boyfriend. Those lads at college, José, Simon... Oh, fuckit. Yes. Write. Now. She booted up the computer and began.

Dear Simon,
No, too formal.
Hi sweetheart!
No.
Wotcha darlin'!
Christ ... How could writing an email be this hard?
Hi.

Okay, that would do. Save as draft. Done. Finish later. Tomorrow. Don't rush this.

She went to bed glad to have made a start on the difficult email, even if it was only one word. Better than nothing.

It was a wild night outside. Rain clattered against her window and the wind thundered along the street, battering the buildings relentlessly. Eventually, in the quiet small hours, the tempest passed and she slept.

Chapter Twenty-four

The next morning she ventured out to inspect the damage caused by the storm. A slithering tile from the previous night lay shattered on the pavement, along with a dead pigeon, reduced to a few damp straggling feathers that nobody would dare touch. The rain might have stopped, but the day was dark and the guttering above creaked and overflowed – she had no idea where all the water was coming from.

She took the tube to Hyde Park and walked along the Serpentine. The sun shot out from between clouds mimicking its midsummer self, teasing forth inquisitive insects. Pigeons huddled in groups on the ground, wary of the plants felled in the night – mostly rose bay willow herb, flattened by the weight of water. Moss under the trees had soaked up the rainfall and turned it into treacherous slime. Victoria tiptoed round it with care. She shivered. Should have worn a warmer coat. London could be deceptive – it generated plenty of its own heat but today, beside the Serpentine, she was cold. Bitterly cold. Lonely too. She hadn't thought about her loneliness for a while. Ought to do something about it. No good having it as a great fat presence next to her that she never dared mention.

She hurried back to the tube station and down the escalators into the warmth below.

'Cynthia!'

'Hey, Vicky – good to see you out and about.'

'Hello Leonardo! Gods, he's so cute.'

In the midst of the blur of commuters surging along the tunnels, Victoria stooped down and kissed the little dog's muzzle. He licked her nose and wagged his tiny tail furiously. The flow of travellers parted around them.

'They'll be jealous,' said Cynthia.

'Jealous?'

'You bet. Half of them will be dying to kneel down and pet a wee doggie, but they won't dare.'

'Heh. I'm sure you're right. He's such a darling. You going anywhere exciting?'

'Just to the park. Our usual walk is too littered with fallen branches this morning. Leonardo insists on running back and forth, so of course his lead gets tangled up horribly. We gave up after ten minutes and decided to set off for the wide open spaces of Hyde Park.'

'Wise choice. It's great there this morning, but bitterly cold.'

'Certainly brought some colour into your cheeks. Seriously, you look much better than you did even a week ago. What's happened?'

'I don't know. Just ... Dunno. Feeling more positive. Bouncing back. Started writing a letter to Simon to apologise.'

'That's good.'

'I hope it is. Hard one to write though. Don't want him to feel obliged to reply or make contact or anything. Though having said that, I'd love to bump into him again one day. Well into the future, hopefully. We could do that whole reminiscing bit of remembering what a cow I was. Oh, how we'd laugh!'

'Vicky!'

'You know what I mean. But yes, I am better. Thank you. And thank you for putting up with my moods for months on end. You've no idea how much I needed your company and support all those weeks in hospital, and afterwards as well. I wasn't taking you for granted, honest. No, that's not true. Of course I was, but I wasn't thinking straight at first. Now that I'm approaching something like normal, I can see how much you were doing for me.'

'That's quite all right, dear. It was a pleasure. Are you going to be coming back to the studio then? Mal's been pining away.'

'Like hell he has. I'm sure I saw him at a distance the other day with his arm round some beautiful creature.'

'Oh. Damn. In that case, my matchmaking plans will come to nothing.'

'Matchmaking? Me and Mal? Oh, Cynthia! There was never any hope of that. He's a pretty boy and very sweet, but that's all.'

'I know. Only teasing.'

'Thank God for that.'

'I'd better go. Look at Leonardo.'

The little dog was straining at the leash, clearly desperate to get to the park and chase pigeons.

'Okay. See you around. 'Bye!'

''Bye!'

Victoria strolled onto the platform for her train which came a few minutes later. She sat down and looked around the carriage.

There was a man, slim and dark, reading a paper. He had hairs on the back of his hands. Victoria's stomach lurched. The man lowered the paper to turn the page. It wasn't John. Victoria felt her colour rise and started murmuring a half-remembered poem under her breath.

'Deep underground, they met on the Bakerloo Line, deep underground, amidst whooshes and rumbling sound, where Waterloo sunset can't shine, but he left on the Northern Line ... deep underground.'

Back in her studio room, Victoria set a new canvas on the easel. Time to consign Simon to paint; the first and last picture. She would take care over this portrait. He didn't deserve to become an oil-slick the way José had. No cadmium yellow. No vermillion. Nothing harsh. Porcelain blue. White. All shades between. Care and precision. A hint of soft green, for kindness.

She primed the canvas with pure white gesso, then stood back, and decided that oddly enough the portrait could well be finished already. She'd leave it for a day or two. No, this was wrong. There had to be more to Simon than a plain white canvas, however carefully painted. He had shape, he had form, he had life. He cared. That must mean some colour, surely? Tricky one. She cleaned the brush and thought hard about it. The painting was in the same state as the email at the moment. "Hi" and gesso. Simon was worth more than that. Maybe if she finished the email it would help her with the painting.

Later. She'd do it later. What now then? Tea? No. She'd had gallons of tea. Didn't need any more. Maybe it was time to wash the kitchen floor. Get rid of the tea stains, the crumbs, the odd scraps of paper, the dried out frozen peas, the sweetcorn, the cobwebs in the corners – Chrissake! How had the kitchen got into such a state?

She found a broom and swept the floor from corner to corner. That made an immediate improvement. Then she mopped it, properly for once: wetted the floor, cleaned it well in its wet state, then went back over it with a squeezed out mop removing every last bit of moisture. Polish? No, that would be overkill.

The tea stains round the bin still showed up slightly. Memo to self: if you drop a teabag, remove the stain straight away. Yes, this was more like it. Organised. House proud.

148

Bored.

What the hell was the point of all this mopping and scrubbing? Who was she trying to impress? Next thing she'd be redecorating the flat and putting up shelves; changing all the lampshades, steam-cleaning the carpets – all to put off writing that pesky email. It wouldn't do. Come on Victoria. Write.

Hi,

Thought it was about time I wrote to say thank you. I've been horribly ungracious, to put it mildly. You were so kind to visit me in hospital, and although I didn't realise it at the time, you were also kind to refuse to bail me out financially. As a result, I've managed to get my act together, and have pretty much paid off my debts. There's certainly no danger of me losing the flat any more. You knew I needed a kick up the backside to do this, so you gave me one, and I'm grateful.

No hard feelings about anything, I hope?

Love,

Victoria xxx

Yes, that would do. She pressed "send" before she could change her mind. Perhaps now she could get on with that painting.

Two hours later she stood back from the canvas and realised she'd painted a pale blue version of Michelangelo's "David". Now there was a surprise. She didn't even particularly like Michelangelo – not at a visceral level, although she couldn't help but acknowledge his astonishing genius as an artist; his passion for physical beauty. He'd have loved Simon as a model. But not as a lover. No. Not even if Simon had been that way inclined. Not to worry. It was a good painting. She'd leave it to dry overnight and continue tomorrow. This one would need a few more sessions to build up the depth she wanted, but at least the outline of her vision was there and she could relax and enjoy the craft of bringing the painting closer to the real Simon.

Chapter Twenty-five

The reply from Simon arrived a week later.

You're welcome. No hard feelings. Simon
.

Victoria stared at the screen. Okay, she hadn't expected a great long letter necessarily, but that was so bloody cold and unemotional. She felt like throwing a tin of scarlet paint at the portrait in the box room. Make him bleed a bit. No, she wouldn't. She was pleased with the finished picture. It wasn't even a portrait of Simon any more; simply a way of sorting out and laying to rest any remaining feelings for him.

Talking of which, she probably ought to visit Tate Modern again. The "crack" had been filled in, apparently. Might be interesting to see if any of it still hung in the air, or if with the loss of its physicality, it was entirely gone. Cynthia had been to see it and had reported back to Victoria that the length and breadth were still very visible as all they'd done was fill it in with some sort of compound. Presumably it would always be there for all to see. Was she ready to look at it? No. Not yet. What if she bumped into John again? No. It wouldn't happen. The coincidence would be too great, but ... no. It would be even more awkward now than the first time.

Victoria spent most of her waking hours determinedly not thinking about John. She refused to compare every man she saw on the street with him. Every portrait might have something about the eyes that was familiar, but that was just coincidence. Every crowd scene included him, but only in a generic way. Travelling on the tube was the worst. She kept "seeing" him in every smartly-dressed middle-aged businessman with dark hairs on the back of his hands.

It didn't help that she'd started writing to Emma again. Despite everything they'd agreed, John had once again become the "name that must not be spoken". They managed to talk about everything else under the sun, but never mentioned that eminent dealer in serpentine furniture, Mr John-bloody-Stephenson.

Emma had a few days holiday owing, and had invited Victoria up for another visit, to stay at the cottage properly this time. She was going to go, of course, but whether they'd manage a long weekend without mentioning the unmentionable was open to question, and if his name did come up, Victoria couldn't exactly say what was on her mind: 'Oh, by the way Emma, I don't half fancy that ex of yours. Now that you've finished with him, could I have a go? And yes, I am conveniently forgetting that he hit you.' Shit. His name had better not come up.

The Friday in late February arrived. Dawn streaked an orange light across the sky, sounding the shepherd's warning and searching with chill beams for a way through the morning gloom. Two starlings shivered in the plane tree outside Victoria's flat. The trains moving in and out of Kings Cross and St Pancras sounded more than usually ghostly – whether due to a trick of the mist, or her own mood, Victoria wasn't sure.

She donned her rucksack, packed this time with art materials, extra jumpers and a couple of changes of underwear, and made her way along York Way to the station. The area was changing. Regents Canal had been smartened up beyond recognition and was now flanked by shiny glass offices. The towpath was entirely free of dog dirt. Very pretty, but soulless. The usual line of limousines queued for the American car wash, emerging spotless a few yards down the road through the next door. The Cross Kings pub still retained something of the authenticity of the old Kings Cross, but everywhere else was becoming unrecognisable. Less sleaze, undoubtedly, but too squeaky clean. Time to move on?

Even Kings Cross station was shrugging off the comfortable mess it used to be and was trying to vie with the sparkling St Pancras next door. The train was already in, so Victoria made her way straight down the platform to carriage F, heaved the rucksack onto the luggage rack and settled into her seat. The last time she'd made this journey had been the ill-fated trip to Alnmouth, via the Durham Botanical Gardens, and the time before had been the day she'd journeyed up to the city to have tea in the bookshop with Emma. On the return journey – oh Gods, yes, it had been that very journey – Simon had spilled his drink in her lap, and then bought her champagne in St Pancras as recompense. In retrospect, that was the best time they'd ever spent together. She'd been totally charmed. He'd been so deliciously apologetic about her jeans. They should have said goodbye after that and never seen each other again. Then they could have lived on the memories, the "what ifs", instead of knowing precisely "what if" and regretting it ever since. Never mind. That was over.

With a lurch, they were off. Victoria looked out of the window as the train slipped along parallel to York Way. She smiled at the life-size automaton that beckoned the limos into the car wash, still just about visible between the buildings, but for how much longer she had no idea. All this redevelopment could mask it any day now. That could be her cue to leave. Yes – when she could no longer see the beckoning hand, that would be it.

The train rumbled through the many tunnels and out into the suburbs. Ally Pally was just visible on the other side through the mist. Victoria remembered waking up on the train, asking Simon where they were, him telling her, and her panicking about the wet patch on her jeans. He'd lent her his paper to cover herself up and save embarrassment. When had that been? Just last summer? Yes, not even nine months ago. Unbelievable. Since then, she'd fallen in and out of love – and now back in again with the wrong man, if she didn't watch her step – and walked under a car with horrible consequences. She stretched her legs out carefully at the thought, relieved that they felt all right, if still a little weird round the knees.

The houses disappeared. She started to doze, and looked out through half-closed eyes as trees loomed out of the mist, twisting at the edge of sanity, trying to pull their roots from the ground as the horizon tipped this way and that. A young sapling, ordered and clean, wouldn't allow the elder to stay in this field of rough grasses. Each felt the rumblings, the snowbound force, the crack as ages-old ice split and sighed far away in the mountains, but neither imagined the force of the flood which would follow the rending of soil, the roiling of waters, the loss of the forest.

The train jolted and Victoria opened her eyes properly. It was just a ploughed field with a few sad looking trees. She enjoyed her imagination, and used it frequently, but sometimes wondered if she should keep a tighter rein on her mind-wanderings. No. Why? Without her imagination, she might as well draw porcelain all her life and have done with it.

Emma was waiting for her at the station.

'Hi, Vic!'

'Emma!'

They ran towards each other – or rather, Emma ran, and Victoria managed a sort of a lope which was all she dared do on her unstable knee – and gave each other a proper hug.

'How was the journey?'

'Fine. Uneventful. Plenty of time for musing.'

'Profitable musing?'

'I don't know. I let my imagination wander. When I do that, ideas sort of stick in my subconscious and turn up at a later date in my paintings, but I never know at the time what will stay and what won't. You look blank.'

'I never did understand your painting processes. Or anyone else's – not really. I'm not the creative type. Love art, of course, and I'm building on all that stuff I did for my degree, but I'll never be an artist. I can draw a little, but that's it.'

'You can draw more than a little.'

'Yeah, maybe.'

She opened the car door.

'Hop in. Weather's looking dodgy. We don't often get snow on the coast, but apparently there's a load of it blowing down from the arctic.'

'Good. I fancy being snowed in. Have you got plenty of firewood?'

'Tons of the stuff. I've been collecting driftwood all through the autumn, half intending to make those sculptures we talked about, but also having at the back of my mind the fact that it will burn beautifully. It's all in the shed, nice and dry.'

'Excellent. So long as you have that, and a pantry full of baked beans, we'll be fine. Plus tea bags of course. You must have inexhaustible stocks of tea bags.'

'No problem. Once I knew you were coming, I got in a good supply. Oh, I hope you don't mind, but John's popping round tonight.'

'What? Emma ...'

'Don't sound so shocked. We're communicating fine now. This whole divorce business has cleared the air. Now that I don't feel officially tied to him, I'm able to cope so much better. He had some stuff of mine that I wanted – mostly art books and so on – and we decided it was easiest if he drove up, especially as he had to come to Newcastle anyway – and dropped them off. I told him you'd be here but he didn't seem to mind.'

'Christ.'

'What's the matter? Is it going to be a problem? I know you don't exactly like him, but you're civilised enough to be polite, aren't you? I'm serious, Vic. If you think it's going to be too difficult, then I'll put him off. He can always drop the books off at the gallery, I suppose, and I could pick them up next week.' She looked miserable at the thought.

'No, no, it's okay. I've been known to swear at him a bit, but I'll bite my tongue. Last time I met him we were quite civilised and talked about art. Those potato prints. Remember them?'

'Oh, yes! Weren't they going to win you the Turner Prize or something?'

'That was the theory. Hasn't happened yet.'

'Maybe you should've used parsnips.'

'Dammit, you're right. Parsnips! Of course! Or carrots. Or a complete medley of vegetables, plus a stock cube, some pearl barley and chopped parsley. Seasoned well. Talking of which, I'm hungry.'

'Don't worry, I've got that larder full of beans.'

'Good.'

They arrived at the cottage to find a message from John on the answer-phone. Something had come up, and he wouldn't be round that evening, but would pop by the following afternoon. Victoria hoped it would snow and stop him coming. She wanted to see him, but not with Emma. Hell, not with Emma, especially an Emma who could not only say the word "John", but seemed to delight in it. She hadn't quite said the word "reconciliation", but it was hanging in the air, without a doubt, and Victoria hated it.

The next morning dawned cold and grey. The sky darkened until it could hold the water back no longer. The air grew very still and then all the rain in the world dropped into Emma's back yard. It eased off at about eleven o'clock, turning to a silvery drizzle that left the roof tiles slick and shiny, reflecting the pale skies. A mist developed – a

154

typical North East haar. It was bitterly cold, but at least the rain had worn itself out for the time being.

'I'm going to have another go at the castle,' said Victoria.

'You're mad – you'll freeze.'

'I know, but I've brought all my stuff, and I need to paint.'

'Stay indoors. Do a still life or something. I've got all that driftwood.'

'No, I *need* to paint. Not to do a picture. There's a difference.'

'Okay. You're feeling driven. That sort of thing?'

'Yes.'

'Still trying to get Simon out of your system?'

'Christ no, he's long gone. I just … need to paint.'

'All right. Do you want to borrow anything? I have some gloves knitted from llamas or something.'

'Probably alpacas.'

'Al whats? Oh yes. Bolivian alpaca. That was it.'

'Or the Lakes.'

'Al Lakers? Nope, that can't be right.'

'There's an alpaca farm near Ullswater.'

'You do know the most random things.'

'One of my few talents. And yes please, I'll borrow the knitted llamas if I may, just for getting down there. Will have to take them off to paint.'

'Okey-doke. Have fun!'

Victoria couldn't wait to get down to the beach. The wind was biting cold, but not so strong that she couldn't wedge the easel so long as she didn't use too large a canvas. It was no good painting a masterpiece only to watch it sail away. Emma hadn't offered to help carry stuff down to the beach, for which Victoria was glad. She needed to be alone. Chatting to Emma about how nice John could be when you weren't married to him was painful.

Once down on the beach, she found a relatively sheltered spot, sunk the legs of the easel into the sand, wedged them with stones, and fixed the canvas. She sat on a rock with her feet on the front legs of the easel, to help keep it steady.

Right. Squeeze out the colours. Make this work before frostbite sets in.

First came vermillion – the colour of anger and loss. Next, lemon yellow for cruelty. She knocked back the wintery sky with ultramarine. Somewhere within the jumble of these colours lay an intimate landscape; somewhere there was a Prussian blue lake, a crack that led deep into a mountain, a place for the haar to escape and evaporate. Each glaze, each scumble, brought her closer to what she desired. The acrylic paint dried virtually instantly in the wind, enabling her to work non-stop for a couple of hours, until the cold became too much.

She stood back and looked at her work. Superficially, the painting showed the castle. In reality, it was the most intensely erotic picture she had yet done, each stroke showing frustrated lust. She knew she was safe: knew Emma would never be able to read the picture. Possibly nobody would. Talk of self-indulgent – but hell, why not? Didn't she deserve to paint like this after the weeks of postcard potboilers? Yes. She did. So there.

She packed up quickly, donned the alpaca gloves, and made her way back to the cottage.

'How did it go?' asked Emma.

'Brrrr.'

'Hehe – told you it was cold. I'll put the kettle on. Let's have a look at the picture. Wow! That's ... I don't know what to say. It's scary. Brilliant, but scary. I'm not sure I could live with it. You don't mind me saying that, do you?'

'No, of course not. It's not an easy picture. You're quite right. It's just something I needed to get out of my system.'

'You know, I wish I could do that. Would have sorted out all those suicidal thoughts I used to have if I could have committed them to canvas like this.'

'You think this picture is suicidal?'

'No, but it's got something of the same power. It frightens me.'

'Oh, sorry about that. I'll put it in my room. Don't want it upsetting you.'

'No, don't. Leave it here. I need to learn to look at things like this. I've spent too much of my life avoiding whatever this is.'

'If you're sure?'

'Yes. C'mon. Let's have something to eat.'

156

Chapter Twenty-six

The dreaded knock at the door came as they were finishing their meal.

'That'll be John,' said Emma, flushing like a teenager.

Victoria didn't say anything. She wiped her mouth slowly as Emma ran to the door. Now then. How to play this. Act natural? What the hell was "natural"? No, try to be normal, whatever that might mean. Pleasant. Ladylike. For Emma's sake.

She heard voices – Emma's bright and cheerful, John's a low rumble. If she'd heard him cry out: 'My darling Emma, how wonderful to see you again!' she'd probably have slit her throat – except that she'd never manage it with the butter knife that was the only implement to hand. She'd have to rummage in her art stuff for a craft knife.

The happy couple came in while she was scanning the room for murderous or suicidal weapons. Emma was positively chirping, like a zebra finch, hopping from branch to branch, sweet and unbearably lovely.

John, on the other hand, looked like John. Dour and unsmiling. He'd been more cheerful when he'd visited Victoria in hospital, despite her swearing at him. Emma couldn't be having the desired effect on him.

'Hello, Victoria. You're looking well.'

'Hi, John. Thanks.'

And that was that. He turned to Emma.

'Here are those books. I think that's it. I don't have anything else of yours.'

'Oh, I bet you can find something if you look hard enough,' said Emma, with a wink.

Victoria cringed. 'I'll clear this stuff away,' she said, hoping to busy herself with the washing up.

'No, don't bother with that now,' said Emma. 'Let's put the kettle on.'

'Not for me,' said John. 'I need to be getting back.'

'No, you can't!'

'Emma, I have work to do.'

He turned, frowning, and spotted Victoria's painting.

'Well, fancy that,' he said.

'Fancy what?'

'I take it you did that, Victoria? Not quite our Emma's style.'

'Yes, it's one of mine. Did it this morning down on the beach.'

'It's quite a contrast to the "David" – or should I say "Simon" – I spotted on your website.'

'How did you know it was Simon?'

'Obvious. Remember, I know him well. And you know him better than I thought you did. I found that interesting. You captured something very subtle with your use of colour. Very subtle indeed.'

'Well, there you go, Vic,' said Emma. 'You should clearly get back together with him. So, John, what about this one Vic painted this morning? What do you make of it? I love to hear you talk about art.'

'That? Clearly supposed to be a self-portrait.'

'It's nothing of the sort!' blurted out Victoria.

'I know,' said John, quietly.

Victoria was aware of Emma's eyes flicking between her and John. Oh God. What was John seeing in the painting? Too much, undoubtedly. And what was Emma thinking? She looked like she might burst into tears any minute. Shit. Do something Victoria.

'I'll just clear these things away.'

This time Emma didn't try to stop her. Victoria made her escape into the kitchenette and turned the hot tap on full, thankful that the plumbing clattered and burbled so that she couldn't hear any further conversation from the other room.

When she went back, John and Emma were talking about the weather. Maybe she'd been imagining things.

'I really do need to be getting back. Looks like it could snow, and I don't want to be stuck out here.'

'Oh, why not. Could be fun,' said Emma.

'No, it wouldn't. Stop this.'

'Stop what?'

'You know.'

Victoria looked around desperately for something to do. This cottage was too damn small. The sooner John left the better. If those frown lines got much deeper he'd never be able to smile again. Why didn't he leave? What was he waiting for? He'd said he had to go, so why was he still here talking with Emma, who was obviously doing nothing for his mood?

'Victoria, would you like a lift to the station?' said John. 'If the weather gets any worse, you could be stranded, and presumably you need to get back to town some time.'

'Thanks for the offer, but I'm sure I'll be all right.'

'No, of course, she doesn't want to go with you!' said Emma. 'Why would she? She's having a lovely holiday. Why would she want to be stuck in a car with you anyway?'

'Emma, please.'

'What, calm down? That's the usual one, isn't it? Don't be hysterical?'

'Fuckfuckfuck,' whispered Victoria under her breath, turning to examine the wallpaper in minute detail.

Emma was unstoppable. 'Don't make a scene? Is that it? Behave yourself in front of Vic? Why? What's Vic to you? Why's she so special? You bastard – you don't bloody change, do you.'

Emma lunged at John while Victoria memorised the precise shade of the wallpaper and started counting the dots that made up the pattern.

John grabbed Emma's wrist.

'Oh no you don't. I won't let you. Not any more.'

He pushed her away firmly. She let out a yelp as her temple hit the side of a bookcase.

That'll make a nice bruise for Emma to show off, thought Victoria. Oh, shit, lost count. Start again. Two, four, six, eight …

'I'll see myself out. 'Bye, Victoria.'

''Bye, John,' she mumbled to the wall.

He exited the room, followed by Emma, screaming at him and most likely hitting him, though Victoria didn't look. She didn't want to see. Christ! What did Emma think she was doing? Arctic weather or not, Victoria needed to get out of the cottage. She turned away from the wretched wallpaper, emptied the paints out of her rucksack, leaving just a sketchbook and a few pencils, donned her jacket and the gloves, and let herself out the back. Once outside the gate, she lurked in the shelter of the yard wall until she saw John's car driving away. The last thing she wanted was to have to talk to him and probably be spotted by Emma. Urrghh! Life. What the fuck was it all about, anyway?

John was an idiot. He shouldn't have come round with those books. What did he think he was doing? He must've known what it would be like.

For the first time in ages, Victoria missed Simon. He would never behave like that. He'd be circumspect. Polite. Wouldn't say anything that would inflame the situation. She remembered the morning after the José debacle, when he'd come round, and despite dying to know why and when and how often she'd slept with him, had made it clear it was none of his business and he wasn't going to ask.

Simon. I wonder …

She took out her mobile. Damn. No signal. Probably for the best. She'd no idea what she'd have said to him. Stupid idea. Leave the poor man alone.

It was a short walk to the dunes. The wind was vicious. Tiny flakes of ice struck her face like needles. She sat down between two of the tallest dunes where the sand was dryish and soft. It was very tempting to curl up and sleep. No, that would only lead to hypothermia and death.

She retrieved the sketchbook and a sharp pencil and divided the page neatly in two. On the left, she drew a portrait of Simon. A clear, sensible, calm portrait. Photorealistic. It was a good likeness. A faint smile on the lips. Very kissable lips. Mmm. Nice.

On the other side, she tried to do the same with John. The deep frown lines were easy, but she couldn't do any more. Couldn't, or wouldn't? Didn't dare? *Come on Victoria. Do this. You need the comparison.* Perhaps she'd already done it in the paintings of "David" and the castle, but the castle portrait was too superficial a rendition of John; too full of her own desires. It showed his anger and unhappiness, true, but the rest had been her, not him. Maybe that's why he'd been so amused by it. He'd known she hadn't discovered the real him. Well, fuck you, Mr John-too-bloody-clever-for-your-own-good-Stephenson. I'm not going to draw your portrait. So there.

She took out a putty rubber and removed all but the two frown lines, which she turned into marram grass on sand dunes, bent almost to breaking point by the freezing wind.

160

When she'd finished, she realised she'd drawn John after all. She put the sketchbook away. Best not to think about it too much. She had to go back and face Emma. Sort her out somehow.

The icy North Sea looked tempting in comparison.

Chapter Twenty-seven

Victoria let herself in by the back door, shut it firmly and took off her jacket. She felt the kettle. It was cold, so Emma couldn't have had a cuppa for a while. Good – she could make the tea, take it in to the living room, have a heart-to-heart, sort everything out. Yeah, right. Oh, come on Victoria. Give it a try. Emma's your friend.

She made two mugs of tea and took them into the living room. Emma lay curled up on the sofa, shivering. Victoria winced when she saw the bruise on her face. Yes, she knew that was from Emma falling against a shelf – Victoria had seen it happen – but that didn't stop her looking like a classic victim of domestic violence, just as she had in Durham. Maybe all those previous bruises had been gained in much the same way? No. There'd been too many of them. Had there? Stop it Victoria. Don't make excuses for John. If he hadn't pushed Emma away, she wouldn't have fallen against the shelf and injured herself in the first place.

'Hi. You all right?'

Emma looked up. 'What do you think?'

'I think you look cold and miserable. Here, have some tea.'

'Thanks.' Emma wrapped her fingers round the mug. 'Where did you disappear off to?'

'The dunes. I thought it best. Do you mind? I felt I was in the way.'

'You weren't, but I understand. You didn't miss much. He left straight after you did. Don't suppose I'll ever see him again.'

'Am I allowed to say "that's probably for the best"?'

'Yeah. Sorry. I know I tend to snap at you when you talk obvious sense. I've made a resolution not to see him any more. I've made lots of resolutions, curled up here slowly freezing to death.'

'Why don't you put some more wood in the stove?'

'Because the wood's out in the shed and it's even colder out there than in here.'

'Not great logic, but I see your point. Tell you what – let's burn the picture.'

'What picture?'

'That garish vile monstrous thing I did of the castle. I've gone right off it.'

162

'Okay, but ... burn a *picture*? Are you sure?'

'You bet. We'll need to slice it up first. You can help.'

Emma took a careful sip of her tea. 'Yes. I'd like that. Good idea. There's a craft knife in that drawer.'

Victoria found the knife and took the canvas over to Emma on the sofa.

'There you are. You go first.'

She handed her the knife.

'You sure about this?'

'Positive.'

Emma put her mug of tea down well out of harm's way and slashed a diagonal from one corner of the painting to the other. Breathing quickly, she handed the knife to Victoria, who stabbed the painting several times. Emma then grabbed a loose edge of canvas and pulled, ripping it away from its frame. Grinning at each other, they proceeded to slash and shred, finally breaking the frame apart. They gathered the pieces together and fed them into the stove. The tongues of flame lapped gently at first, but then took hold and the fire roared.

'That's more like it,' said Emma. She relaxed back onto the sofa and gulped down the rest of her tea. 'I even feel sufficiently energised to be sensible and bring in some wood.'

'Good. Let's do it.'

They took the log basket out to the shed, hurrying across the yard. The promised snow had arrived at last and great white flakes fell mercilessly from the sky.

'You really are the best, nicest person I know,' said Emma, as they piled wood into the basket. 'I hope it snows for months and months now, and you have to stay with me forever.'

'It might well, but I'm going to have to fight my way back down south at some point.'

'Yeah, I know. And I need to get back to Fenham in the next couple of days. As a sensibly salaried person, I do need to turn up for work occasionally, but we can enjoy our snowy idyll for a little longer, can't we?'

'Oh yes, no problem. I need to sort out something in my head. I wonder ... tell you what. Let me show you what I sketched on the dunes. See what you think.'

163

They took the wood back indoors and fed some more into the stove. The cottage warmed up quickly. Victoria retrieved the sketchbook from her rucksack and showed Emma the double page with the portrait on one side, and the marram grass on the other.

'This is Simon, isn't it?'

'Yes. I keep forgetting you've never actually been introduced, even though you must have seen him at Alnwick.'

'We have been introduced. I remember now. John said he was a friend, but didn't seem too keen for me to talk to him. No idea why, except that he is exceptionally good looking, so maybe there was a bit of jealousy. You've made him look kind and gentle. A sweet man.'

'Sounds about right. What do you think of the other picture?'

'That's the marram grass on the dunes, isn't it. Bending over. It looks – I don't know – wistful? Sad? Almost tragic, if it's possible for grass to be tragic. Maybe that's just my mood – or your mood when you drew it.'

'Yes, that'll be it. I wasn't sure. I thought I'd drawn something else, but maybe it was a sort of a self-portrait. My sweet gentle Simon on one side, and me being all tragic and wistful on the other because we're apart.'

'So – are you and Simon going to get back together?'

'Fat chance. He chucked me and made it clear later that he wasn't going to help me in any way. That doesn't exactly bode well, does it?'

'No, but at least he never hated you.'

'Oh, I don't know. He turned into the iceman during that fateful evening in Alnmouth. You don't freeze somebody out if you're still feeling a reasonable amount of affection for them. He despised me by then, and only visited me in hospital later because he's fundamentally such a nice guy.'

'God. We're so bad at all this relationship stuff, aren't we.'

'Hopeless. Cataclysmic.'

'Still, you might as well try with him again. You don't have anything to lose.'

'Self-respect?'

'Overrated. I've lost mine totally, and can't say I miss it. I'm relieved, if anything. I mean, look at me today. Made yet another ridiculous effort to get it together with John, flunked it, made a fool

164

of myself, managed to give myself a black eye into the bargain – all for nothing. Stupid, stupid, stupid. Never again. Never, d'ye hear me?'

'I hear you! Now then – beans, is it?'

'Beans and bangers. And mash.'

'Good. Let comfort food rule. You got any booze? I stopped drinking after Alnwick, but I think it's about time I started again.'

'Good thinking. I've got a cellar – or small cupboard, if you like – with at least two bottles of Vin de Pays d'Oc.'

'Excellent. Corkscrew? I'd hate for you to get my hopes up, only to find we can't open the bottles.'

'We're okay. They're screw tops.'

'Emma, you're perfect. Will you marry me?'

'I'd love to, but I think Simon would be better for you. Let's open those bottles, get plastered, and tell each other ghost stories or something.'

'Hurrah! Haven't done that since I was ten.'

'Me neither. Come on – you're on holiday!'

Victoria woke early the next morning with a throbbing head. She welcomed the hangover as a sign she was getting back to normal. The sobriety of the last few months had been tiresome. She drew back the curtains. More snow had fallen overnight and the sun was rising in a glow of purple, crimson and acid pink. That probably meant more snow later. Damn. Knowing full well she ought to get back to London before she was cut off completely, she snuggled back under the duvet and fell asleep rather than do anything about it.

When she woke up a couple of hours later her headache had nearly gone. She dressed quickly and went into the kitchen, where Emma was standing over the stove stirring a pot of porridge.

'Morning! That looks yummy.'

'Absolutely,' said Emma. 'Porridge: the most effective denial of winter's chill known to mankind.'

There was a kerflump outside the kitchen window as a mini-avalanche slid off the shed roof and landed in the yard.

'Looks like it's melting,' said Emma.

'Good. I don't trust this weather. I really ought to get back to Newcastle this morning for the train. Don't suppose?'

165

'I could give you a lift? Of course. So long as I can move the car. The main roads will be gritted, but we might have to do a bit of shovelling here.'

'No problem. Good for the figure.'

They finished the porridge, left the bowls to soak, and set to work with shovels. Twenty minutes later they'd cleared a wide track to the road, then it was back to the cottage for a cup of tea while Victoria packed her rucksack and Emma sorted out a bag for herself.

'It's a pity we had to cut this so short,' said Emma.

'I agree, but I don't like the look of the sky. It's got that yellowish look now that always presages snow.'

'Yellowish? Yes, see what you mean. Never occurred to me before. This is why you're the artist and I'm not. I never see things like that. John ... used to try to show me, but I never got it. We weren't remotely suited, were we?'

'Nope. Not at all,' said Victoria, cheerfully, confident that Emma wasn't going to get maudlin again.

'Oh well. A couple of years of my life wasted. No great harm done.'

'Not wasted. You've learnt stuff about yourself. You had some good times. Must have done.'

'Yeah, you're right. Not that I can remember any of them. C'mon, let's get this stuff loaded. Snowflake just landed on the back of my neck.'

They put the bags in the boot and set off. The car started straight away, to their relief.

'I've got a lovely chap called Andy who's been looking after it,' said Emma. 'He reckons he can keep it going indefinitely.'

'Everyone needs an Andy.'

'He was something of a find. Cute as anything, too.'

'Really? A cute mechanic?'

'And why not?'

'Why not indeed.'

There was a hairy moment when the car slid over some compacted snow, but once onto the main road, the going was easy enough, and the A1 was completely clear.

166

Conversation during the journey was the most relaxed it had been since university days. They'd set the world to rights the previous evening thanks to the red wine and now were able to talk about anything at all – John, Simon, previous boyfriends, Andy the mechanic, work, art, snow, life – anything.

Newcastle appeared all too quickly.

'We'll have to do this again,' said Emma: 'later in the spring, when the weather's better. You can bring Simon to the cottage for a weekend.'

'You seem very optimistic about me and Simon.'

'Of course. If you want him, you'll get him, no question. You have an unerring ability to get what you want.'

'You reckon? Then why aren't I already a world-famous artist?'

'Give it time. You will be.'

'Thanks, Emma. Maybe you're right.'

'Of course I'm right. I'm always right about everything.'

They both laughed at that, but Emma managed to keep a tight grip on the steering wheel.

'I must concentrate now,' said Emma. The A1 is easy enough, but Newcastle can be a pain. This is our turning. Shout at me if I get into the wrong lane.'

'Okey-doke.'

They arrived at the station ten minutes later, and within half an hour Victoria was on a train heading south. The weather was grim: huge flakes of snow followed by sleet, and then a rattling rain against the window. By Darlington it was snowing again, and Victoria shivered, even though it was perfectly warm in the train. Half an hour further down the line, the weather had settled into a drear grey day of sludge and sleet. It stayed like that all the way to Kings Cross.

Chapter Twenty-eight

As Victoria walked back to her flat she tried to remember this familiar road in its summer guise of heat and humidity with heavy sunbeams filtering through the plane trees. She could remember such weather in theory, but clear recall wasn't possible. The sleet eased off, giving way to a thick fog which turned everything monochrome. It seeped through her jacket and into her pockets, down her boots and round her toes. She stopped on the bridge over the canal and looked into the looming whiteness. For a moment she wanted to turn round and head straight back north to Emma, but she couldn't. She was held here, not through fear of fog or silence or dimming lights, or anything she could recognise. Stepping forward, she breathed the fog into her lungs, held out her fingers and tried to feel the texture of the water vapour. She already loved mist – she knew this – so what was wrong here? She took another deep breath, and couldn't help coughing. Okay, North Sea haar was one thing, but this fog was something else entirely. She shook her head and left the canal, soon arriving at her flat.

The next few days went by in a flurry of uncharacteristically organised activity. She made sure all bills were paid, all outstanding orders for postcards fulfilled – even washed the floor, but this time without going overboard. She did it because it needed doing. There was satisfaction in performing such chores when they had such a marked effect. De-cluttering the studio took a couple of days, but was worth it. She booked an appointment with a hairdresser and did some serious clothes shopping. Nothing flashy, just proper fitting jeans that she would *not* wear for painting, promise, plus a selection of well-fitted tops which gave her what she hoped was an air of understated elegance – or at least stopped her being such a total scruff.

A week later she was ready for her "now or never" moment. She took the bus to St Johns Wood and walked the short distance to Simon's flat in her smart and slightly uncomfortable new shoes. She hadn't phoned in advance. He probably wasn't in. If he was, he'd be polite, maybe offer her a cup of tea, and then send her on her way. Except he wouldn't be in. He'd better not be, because she was likely to throw up with nerves any minute. Chrissake, what was she doing here? He'd chucked her, hadn't he? Twice at least. Emma was wrong. He didn't want her back.

Before she could talk herself out of the expedition, she rang the doorbell, hoping that the small security camera pointing down on her wasn't making her look too ghastly. Moments later, the door buzzed and she pushed it open. This was it. At least he'd let her in. He could have pretended to be out, but he was in, and she wasn't entirely unwelcome. Probably. Maybe.

She went up the stairs and tapped lightly on his door. It opened immediately.

Hi, she said, silently. That was no good. Where the fuck was her voice?

'Victoria. Come in,' said Simon. 'You look lovely.'

'I do? Thank God for that. It's not too over-the-top, is it?'

'You're wearing jeans and a smart coat, not sequins and a feather boa.'

'True.'

'How's the leg?'

'The what? Oh, fine. Much better. Thank you.'

'And to what do I owe this unexpected pleasure?'

Victoria didn't answer. She was looking round the flat, astonished. 'Where have they all gone?' she asked eventually.

'Who?'

'All the figurines. The vases. The ornaments. The pretty stuff.'

'Locked away in cupboards.'

'Why? You love those things. Why hide them away?'

'Because if I have them out, they can get damaged. Visitors come in and they become tense. They barely move. Barely speak. The objects were a barrier to people getting to know me. I think I was using them as protection – or no, camouflage – in an odd sort of way. You made me realise that.'

'I did? Crikey.'

She walked around the room, wondering at its almost virginal appearance. White walls, no pictures, nothing. Just a few pieces of modern furniture.

'Don't you think you've made it a bit – I dunno – soulless?'

'Totally. It needs pictures – there's no question of that. I thought of buying some of yours – anonymously, of course – but I looked at them and ...'

169

'Couldn't stand them?'

'They're too intense. I could live with the little postcards you do, but wasn't sure I wanted twenty near identical views of St Paul's.'

'Don't blame you. I think you're right. My pictures wouldn't work in here, not with all this modern furniture. You need something softer, not my "screamers".'

'That's it exactly. Thank you for not being offended. Would you like a cup of tea?'

'Have you ever known me not want a cup of tea?'

'I'll put the kettle on.'

He went into the kitchen and Victoria thought about his words. No porcelain. That was a revelation. Astonishing. None of her pictures, either. That wasn't surprising, and she appreciated the honest way in which he'd told her they wouldn't work in his life.

She went to join him in the kitchen, being careful not to touch the black granite worktops for fear of leaving greasy fingerprints.

He turned round, looked at her and smiled. 'Would you like to help me pick out some pictures? There's a good selection at a gallery in the high street. Traditional-style stuff, horribly over-priced, but I think they'd be a good foil for the modernist furniture.'

'I'd love to.'

'Good. We'll just have this tea, then go out and see what we can find. This place needs –'

'What – a woman's touch?' She chuckled.

'Not just any woman's.'

'Shit, Simon!'

'Ah, that sounds more like the Victoria I know and love.'

The kettle chose this moment to boil. Victoria silently cursed it. This is where he should have taken her in his arms and kissed her, swearing undying love and begging her forgiveness, not pouring hot water onto tea bags – or more likely, over single estate Darjeeling in a priceless Sèvres teapot.

But no, he was making tea directly in a couple of solid looking mugs. He squidged the tea bags absentmindedly and threw them towards the bin. They went straight in. How did he do that? Just a bloke thing, presumably. He poured in a dash of milk and handed Victoria her mug. Great. No chance of a hug when both were carrying mugs of tea. Never mind. She was optimistic of at least a cursory cuddle before she left.

170

'You're being very nice to me,' she said. 'Why is that?'

'A number of reasons.'

'Such as?'

'Let's sit down.'

'Okay.'

They returned to the living room where Victoria sat down very carefully on the pristine sofa, willing herself not to spill any tea; not the tiniest bit. She managed, thanks in part to the fact that Simon served mugs of tea on saucers.

He didn't sit next to her. Instead, he settled back into an uncomfortable-looking construction of chrome and pale green leather.

'First of all, I regret being so unpleasant when you asked me for help. However well-thought out my reasons may have been, it was still unkind. I think I was right not to lend you money, but I could have helped you sort yourself out. You were in a distressed state, and I should have done something.'

Victoria nodded. 'It's okay. Turned out fine in the end. I got my act together.'

'As I hoped you would, and it may well have been for the best, but I still acted churlishly towards someone who deserved better.'

'Not sure I did.'

'Be honest, Victoria.'

'I am, but if you insist, okay: you were a right bastard and it hurt.'

'That's why I did it, of course. I wanted to hurt you.'

'Christ ...'

'I'm sorry, but at the time I wanted to destroy you. See you suffer. Burn all your paintings.'

'Really? Funny you should say that. Me and Emma chopped up one of my masterpieces and fed it into a wood-burning stove quite recently.'

'You're joking. You? Destroy one of your own works of art?'

'It's like – I take my art very seriously, but I'm not precious about it. That particular painting needed destroying and the act of destruction was cathartic for both of us. We'd just had a slightly torrid time with John and needed to clear the atmosphere. By the way, I think Emma really is over him now. She won't be bothering him any more.'

171

'I'm greatly relieved to hear it. I don't know all the details, of course, as John doesn't confide in anyone, least of all me nowadays, but it's all academic anyhow. He left for New York last week and apparently has no intention of returning for at least six months. He's establishing a foothold in the markets over there and decided being on the spot was the easiest way to do it.'

'Blimey. That's a – I don't know. Bolt from the blue sort of a thing. I never expected him to bugger off. Emma must have hurt him even more than I realised if he felt the need to cross the Atlantic.'

'It won't be all down to Emma. There's his business, after all.'

'Yeah, right. Convenient though, innit? But enough about John. What about you. You said there were reasons. Plural. Okay, you wanted to hurt me, and now you're feeling bad about it. What else?'

This is the point where he should have said, "this"; then risen from the peculiar chair, swept Victoria off the sofa, kissed her passionately, before carrying her into the bedroom. He didn't. He put his cup down, crossed his legs, and sat there looking thoughtful. Great.

'I'll have to think carefully before I answer that. Have you finished your tea? If you have, we'll go and look at some pictures.'

'Give me a moment. You must have an asbestos gullet.'

'Victoria, you're frowning.'

'Of course I'm bloody frowning. I want – oh, I don't know what I want. What do *you* want?'

You, of course. That's the other reason why I'm being so nice to you. He didn't say it, naturally.

'Me? I want to get to the gallery before it closes,' said Simon.

'Chrissake!'

Simon grinned. 'Your language hasn't improved, I see, even if your financial situation has.'

'Well, what the fuck do you expect?' said Victoria, cheerfully. 'Okay. Finished now. Let's go and look at some over-priced prints.'

The gallery proved a delight, and the prices not nearly as exorbitant as expected. They picked out a series of watercolours of Venice and some antiquarian botanical prints before returning to the flat to discuss where to hang them.

'We'll leave it for now,' said Simon eventually. 'I think we know more or less where each is going to go, but it's probably best to sleep on it.'

The word "sleep" hung in the air. Or did it? Certainly did as far as Victoria was concerned, but Simon seemed oblivious. Or was he? Christ, but this was difficult. How did she ever think she could read this man? No wonder everything had gone wrong before. She'd made assumption after assumption, and got the whole bloody lot wrong.

'Can you stay for dinner?'

'Yes. Yes, of course. That would be lovely. You're cooking?'

'No, don't look so concerned. There's a choice of Italian, Greek, Turkish – you name it. We're spoilt for choice round here.'

'Italian will be fine.'

'Good. Pizza it is.'

'Pizza? You're joking.'

'Real pizza. Not some ghastly franchise product with its crust stuffed with cheddar and plastic ham and pineapple dolloped on the top.'

'I like that sort of pizza.'

'Good grief, woman. You don't really, do you?'

'No. Just teasing.'

'Thank heavens. We have an hour or two to kill. Come here.'

He walked over to the bedroom, beckoning her to follow. More discussions about pictures? Or was this where all the porcelain was kept? Victoria braced herself to knock over a stand covered in priceless Sèvres. To her surprise, the bedroom was free of anything that looked as if she could damage it. The only fragile thing in there was Simon, and he seemed a good deal more robust now than the last few times she'd seen him.

'This is the best place to view the garden,' he explained.

Oh, great. Now he expected her to be a horticultural expert; green-fingered but no doubt slightly mad. She could dye her mousey hair orange and tie it in bindweed.

'Okay,' she said: 'it's a garden. A bit dead looking at the moment, but that's hardly surprising given the time of year and the weather. What about it?'

'Looks dead now, true, but it'll come to life in the spring. Already new shoots are growing. Daffodils under the apple trees. It's unstoppable. You know, you can prune things, cut them back – you can hack some plants to bits, but they still come back. If the life force in them is strong enough, they come back.'

She looked at the garden with new interest.

Simon continued: 'Just as you came back.'

This would have been an ideal time for him to throw her onto the bed. He didn't, but at least he took her hand and kissed it. That would have to do for now.

'I could grow to love that garden,' she murmured: 'but I thought you weren't into plants? At Durham, you didn't seem particularly interested.'

'At Durham I was feeling hurt and fed up even before I sprained my ankle. It was much later when I started to replay some of what you'd been trying to say to me that day – things like the grasshopper – that I thought I ought to try and look around at the natural world – see what you were seeing. That was when I remembered I had a garden. Up till then, all that had happened was a succession of anonymous gardeners coming in once a week to keep everything neat and tidy. I let them continue to mow the lawn, but asked them to leave everything else to me. It was a revelation, growing things. Wrong time of year, of course, being early autumn, as nothing much grows then, so it was more a case of watching things decay and moulder away. One of the gardeners, seeing me try to poke my finger into some soil, realised I was a complete ignoramus and suggested I put in some bulbs. They're coming up now. It's unbelievable. I never thought I could do anything like that.'

She squeezed his hand, which still held her own. Okay. Time to make her move.

'Can we go to bed?'

'We *can*, of course, but we won't. Not until we're both sure.'

'Bloody hell, Simon! I *am* sure. Stop dithering, man.'

'To dither hopefully is better than to arrive.'

'You're impossible!'

'So are you. Perhaps we're well-suited after all. Let's go and eat.'

Chapter Twenty-nine

They soon settled into a routine, but this was very different to the last time. Victoria stayed over at Simon's every night, unless he was away on business for some reason. She spent the day working in the tiny studio at her flat, which meant she never had to tidy up, never had to do anything that interfered with her art – just had to make sure she had tea bags in the cupboard and milk in the fridge, and that was it. She became very productive, and the glory of it all was that Simon didn't have to see any of her paintings. They had an unspoken agreement that he would never visit her flat. Her art had been the cause of tension in the past, but now it was a separate part of her life, and nothing to do with him. Daytimes were hers and hers alone. Nighttimes were for them both; for being a couple. It worked. It bloody worked.

She started going to the life drawing sessions again and having regular cups of tea with Cynthia.

'I'm so glad for you, dearie. About time you were settled.'

'Thanks, Cynthia. In some ways it's a compromise, but it works, and that's what matters. I no longer have to try to make Simon into something that he's not.'

'Quite right too. My husband hates dogs, so Leonardo turns into a cat every evening.'

'You what?'

'Only joking.'

'Thing is, if Simon loved my art, he wouldn't be Simon. And Simon is the guy I love.'

'I know. That's plain. You're glowing. Not expecting already are you?'

'Heavens no. I'm not ready for any of that.'

'Okay, but don't leave it too late. If you get settled into a comfortable way of doing things, you'll never be "ready" for anything.'

They carried on sipping tea.

'And Simon – he's happy?' asked Cynthia.

'Deliriously.'

'That's okay then.'

'Yes.'

Cynthia poured another cup.

'How's your art?'

'Great. I'm churning out picture after picture.'

'So you're prolific. That's good. But are the pictures?'

'What, are they good?'

'Yes.'

'I think so.'

'Think so?'

'Cynthia, what are you saying?'

'The old Vicky would "know so", not "think so". She would be passionate about her art. She'd be telling me about the agony it took to produce each painting – each brushstroke.'

'The new Victoria's passion has another outlet, but that doesn't mean the pictures aren't as good as ever. If anything, they're better. Far more technically proficient.'

'I'd like to see them.'

'What, now?'

'Yes. Do you mind?'

'No, not at all, but it's already five, and by the time we get to the flat –'

'You'll have to start preparing yourself for an evening of passion round at Simon's?'

'Something like that. Yes.'

'Another time then.'

'That would be best. We'll arrange something,' said Victoria brightly.

'Of course we will.'

'Cynthia!'

'Well, what do you expect? I've never known you so evasive about your art – and Vicky, I have to say I'm concerned.'

'Isn't it enough that I'm happy?'

'No, it isn't. I thought you were an artist. The real thing.'

'And you have to be miserable to be an artist?'

'To a certain extent, yes.'

'Okay then.' Victoria pulled a long face. 'Miserable enough?'

Cynthia chuckled. 'No! Not nearly enough. You need to look suicidal, not turn up for tea with your hair neatly coiffed. For goodness sake, you've even got nice fingernails. What's all that about then?'

176

'I've been working in pen and ink recently. It doesn't muck up your hands.'

'Right, now we're getting somewhere. The million dollar question is this: are your hands in good nick because you've been working in pen and ink, or are you working in pen and ink to keep your hands in good nick?'

'I don't know. Does it matter?'

'Of course it matters. You were so bloody good. You know you were.'

'Still am.'

'I only have your word for that.'

'You get to see some of the work I do down at the life sessions, don't you?'

'Yes, and I see technical perfection. You're astonishingly good at capturing a photo-realistic likeness these days. It's a useful accomplishment. People always want portraits that even a completely non-artistic person can recognise as being a close physical likeness. But is it art? You might as well buy a camera and have done with it.'

'Ouch.'

'Well, it needed saying. I'm delighted that you're happy with Simon, really I am, but I still can't help missing the old Vicky; the sassy, bad-tempered grouch of a Vicky, whose language used to make poor Mal pass out with shock. He's quite calm these days and has completely got over his lust for you. That's a shame. He lived on that lust for months. It was what made his art so good, though not a patch on yours, of course. Now that it's gone, he's simply a good technician.'

'So what do you want me to do? Chuck Simon and swear at Mal?'

'No, of course not. Oh, we're going round in circles, aren't we? I don't know what the answer is. More tea?'

'That's the answer to most things.'

'But not this, I fear.' Cynthia beckoned to the waitress for the bill. 'No, it's all right, I'll pay for these. You save your pennies.'

'Why? I'm selling pictures, and I don't mean those silly postcard things.'

'So you're up to A5 size now?'

'Yes.'

'That must be very convenient for framing.'

'Yes it is. And what's wrong with that?'

'The old Vicky never designed her artwork around a convenient frame size.'

'You never heard of pragmatism?'

'Of course. The old Vicky –'

'Was never pragmatic? You're right, of course. Dammit, Cynthia. I *have* lost a spark somewhere, haven't I. Where the hell did it go?'

'You see? "Where the hell" – the old Vicky would never have said "Where the hell" – it would have been at least "Where the fuck?"'

'We'd better go. That waitress just gave us a filthy look.'

Cynthia paid the bill while Victoria took Leonardo outside.

'Your cleaned up language is most unnerving,' said Cynthia a few minutes later, taking the little dog's lead from Victoria.

'Simon doesn't like me to swear too much.'

'He's asked you not to?'

'No, not in so many words. I just know he doesn't like it. And we'll have no long drawn out sighs please, Cynthia. I know what you're saying. You think that me settling into domestic bliss has been crap for my art. But you don't know that; you're just making assumptions.'

'Am I? Yes, I suppose I am – but I'm right, dear. I really am right. We're going this way – Leonardo needs a walk.'

'Hyde Park?'

'Yes, thought we'd amble down along the Serpentine.'

'Oh God! I haven't been there in ages. Can I come?'

'Of course. What's the matter? You look upset.'

'It's just the word "Serpentine". It has associations.'

'With snakes?'

'Something like that. Squirmy wriggly things with hidden strength, coiled round trees, stretching up to catch the rooks. Can you hear the rooks?'

'Now *that* was more like the old Vicky. That word – Serpentine – it set you off. I wonder why. And I can see from your look that you're not telling. You want to run off don't you – paint that vision of whatever it was you just saw.'

'Do you mind terribly?'

178

'No, not at all dear. I'll see you next week. Look after yourself.'
'Will do. Thanks, Cynthia. 'Bye!'

Victoria hurried home, dug out an enormous canvas to set on the easel, and started to paint. First of all, a man, standing and gazing out across a broken sea of snow, interrupted by waves of stiff grass which broke against islands of granite, weathered with memories too ancient for words. Ferns – yes, a profusion of ferns: fractals gone mad. Contorted icicles mustered, ready to fall; bedraggled plants shrugged off the weight of the snow in order to peer round bulbous and weathered sandstone shapes.

She put the canvas down, leaned it against the wall and took another, slightly smaller, primed long ago with a swirl of crimson and sap green. She'd paint the turn of the season on this one: a girl dancing in the cold of a pale winter sun amongst stalactites that grew alive like snakes, sending sparks flying this way and that, twisting with the wind. The girl would thread her dreams between charred treetops, delve into woodland and run with shadows through the dark of the forest, beneath firs that would sing her to sleep in a lightless world where the snow couldn't reach … she would wake in the rain, soft, soft rain, to the chatter of finches, a donkey braying, bustling hedgerows and dew drops on cobwebs – would dart out her forked tongue, taste the air, glimpse a dark figure through the trees, know at last the season had turned.

A third canvas. Victoria couldn't stop now. Snow slipped from twigs unaccustomed to its weight. Winter petered out and mist revealed the snow's agonised melting with the promise of a morning when sun-bleached and golden *he* would return; but until then she'd cut the smile from anyone's face who tried to read her paintings.

She stopped, exhausted and shocked by what she had done. It was late. She knew she'd have to call Simon to tell him she'd been caught up in her art and lost track of the time. When she made the call, he sounded sad and very far away, but she promised it wouldn't happen again.

The promise was hollow. The next week it happened again twice, and in the weeks and months that followed, with increasing frequency. She tried to make it up to Simon; tried to be especially affectionate when she was with him. He told her that it didn't matter and that he understood her art was important to her. She didn't believe him for one minute. He'd never understood what art meant to her. There was no way he could.

Chapter Thirty

The new pictures were striking; bold and disturbing and easily good enough for Victoria to find an agent. This made a huge difference to her finances. Yes, the agent took a percentage, and yes, the galleries that exhibited her work swiped a jaw-dropping cut, but at last people were seeing her art properly. Over the next few months, her name appeared with increasing frequency in reviews in the better art journals. A well-known collector bought one of her works, bringing valuable publicity. Within eighteen months she had secured exhibitions in both Amsterdam and New York, as well as in increasingly prestigious galleries at home. Commissions were steady and at last she dared hope she would never have to paint postcard-sized pictures of St Paul's again.

Her day to day life remained outwardly calm and organised, though once in her studio she would work herself into an agonised state as desperation poured onto the canvases – not that Simon knew any of this, as she took care to shield him from the creative process. She still divided her time between her flat and Simon's, but essentially they now lived independent lives and he'd even been to the annual Alnwick dinner without her. She'd quite fancied going, just for "shits and giggles" as her new American friends would say, but the event had clashed with an opening, so that was that.

She rarely attended the life classes any more, due to lack of time, but still occasionally met with Cynthia for a chat or a short stroll through Hyde Park. Leonardo had become grey and arthritic, but still hobbled along, attempting to chase the squirrels, while Victoria poured out her feelings about art to the one person who could offer solace simply by listening and understanding what she was saying.

Emma was easy enough to reach by email or phone, but they didn't communicate regularly. She was now engaged to Andy, the young mechanic who had kept her ancient car running. Her emails were comfortable and jolly: full of plans of how the two of them were going to fix up the cottage when they got married and how many children they would produce. She sounded blissfully happy, and if she mentioned John at all it was only to say: 'Oh my God – how did I stick it out so long? We were so utterly wrong for each other! What rubbish! Andy is *so* much better for me.'

181

So that was that, then. All good.

One morning in late December, Victoria looked out of the bedroom window across Simon's garden and committed to memory the small-scale changes in the familiar view, as she did every day. The seasonal white stuff had departed for the time being, but the wind and rain had howled through the night and she was exhausted through lack of sleep. Simon was still snoring, in a very gentleman-like fashion. Victoria looked over to the bed with its expensive hand-embroidered quilt covering her near-as-dammit perfect boyfriend, and shivered. She crept back into bed and closed her eyes, drifting off to climb a path through twisted oaks, heavy with ice. She sat down exhausted on a step while someone – and she knew damn well who it was, despite never acknowledging the fact – stroked her hair and slipped words between her lips like a kiss. Her current pale existence seeped away as she ran between marble columns, swooping and diving with velvet-winged bats, crying the tears of a salmon on this, the coldest night of the year, when the Thames smelled sweet, and the dome of St Paul's lent closer with whispers and lies …

'Tea?'

'What? Oh, thanks Simon. I must have fallen asleep again. I'm knackered.'

'You work too hard. No reason why you shouldn't ease off a bit.'

'Can't. I'm having too much fun.'

'Fun? Victoria, you have grey circles under your eyes. Every morning.'

'So?'

'So you're overdoing things, and that can't be good for your work. Take a few days off. I don't mean you should go away or anything – just get out. Visit galleries like you used to do. Tell you what; I've got nothing on this morning – why don't we amble along to have a look at the latest peculiarity at Tate Modern? Might be just up your street.'

'Might well be, but I doubt if it would be your sort of thing,' said Victoria.

'That doesn't matter.'

'Yes it does,' she replied in a manner which allowed for no discussion

182

'Okay then,' said Simon. 'How about the Wallace Collection? I haven't been for ages. Used to enjoy the occasional visit.'

'That's a thought. Would you believe I've never been there? Ever?'

'Well, there you go.'

'All right. I suppose I could take one morning off.'

'You certainly should.'

'Yes darling,' she said dutifully.

Simon kissed her cheek. 'I'll get dressed. You take your time drinking that tea. We'll go when you're ready.'

Victoria sipped the tea and glanced over to the window where a pale light peeped through gaps in the ragged clouds, hinting at change. Did she want change? No, everything was perfect, wasn't it? She put the cup of tea down and closed her eyes to think about her latest painting. As usual, she'd done the back view of a man – she never said his name, even in her thoughts – and had shown him walking away from her into loss, past beech trees that dwarfed his physicality, haunted his spirit and hid from all but the artist the faint aroma of leather, of snuggling up to pipe smoke and tweed in an old leather armchair, with the crackle and hiss of echoes – and the pearl necklace she knew so well, the green velvet dress, her elbow cupped in his hand.

The images were clear in her mind but by the time they reached the canvas she hid them so that all that the viewer saw was a mass of abstract brush strokes. She would revel in who and what she'd painted, but nobody else would be allowed to unravel her desires. The most they could hope for would be a feeling of unease; of wariness; of an unexpectedly raised pulse.

Simon had sufficient sensitivity to wince at gallery openings, but he still came occasionally at her request. She liked him to be there to cup her elbow in his hand – not that he ever did, and not that she had ever owned a green velvet dress or worn a pearl necklace. He came through duty and probably love as well, so she welcomed his presence.

Sunlight blazed through a crack in the clouds, blinding her briefly and leaving spots in front of her eyes. She blinked at the wallpaper. Time to get up. The sun backed behind another cloud as she slipped out of bed and padded across the ludicrously soft carpet to the window. Half a dozen pigeons were bathing in a puddle on the patio, enjoying some wing-flapping fun, heedless of all but the moment, lucky things. A couple of dogs barked, each competing with the other, set off no doubt by the beeping of the reversing bin van. Together they produced the usual Wednesday morning cacophony – no good for anyone wanting a lie-in. A blue tit stretched, preened, hopped and flitted away. Side-lit cobwebs trembled in the breeze, but the spider remained hidden. Victoria could have stood there for hours watching the garden, weaving the events into pictures, but no – Simon was taking her out. That hadn't happened in a long while.

Fifteen minutes later she was dressed and ready. Simon insisted she ate a slice of toast and marmalade to keep her blood sugar up, which she thought was a load of old bollocks, and told him so. Eventually he deemed her sufficiently prepared for the treat ahead. They took the tube to Bond Street, walked the short way to Selfridges, and then across Wigmore Street to Manchester Square.

'Beethoven, yes, bloody Beethoven,' said Victoria.

'Beethoven?'

'I was remembering that recital we went to a couple of years ago.' The one where we bumped into your best friend. 'If they're playing Beethoven in the Wallace Collection, I'll scream.'

'You're a Philistine, Victoria, do you know that? And no, they won't be playing Beethoven. All you'll hear is the multiple ticking of antique clocks and perfectly synchronised chimes. They have quite a collection and keep a fair number running, as I recall.'

'That's okay then. Clocks I can cope with. What else do they have?'

'An excellent selection of paintings, some fine porcelain and furniture, and one of the better museum cafés in London.'

'Porcelain? They wouldn't happen to specialise in Sèvres by any chance?'

'They might.'

Simon grinned and Victoria squeezed his hand.

Once inside, they stopped chatting, and started absorbing the *objets d'art*. Soon Victoria's mood changed. She could have looked at the exquisite canvasses by Watteau all day, but unfortunately there were also vast numbers of paintings depicting dead animals and piles of fruit – even one charming family group where the mother was holding a dead hare with glee. The image turned Victoria's stomach.

184

Then there was Franz Hals' smirking Cavalier, a grotesquely overdone landscape by Rubens with badly reflected cows in a river and a rock-solid rainbow overhead, the brief respite of a couple of decent Canalettos, some poor copies of Velasquez, a few okayish Murillos ... and Poussin's tiny *Dance to the Music of Time* which he should have painted ten, twenty times bigger, but at least it was here, and it wasn't a run-of-the-mill painting by Sir Joshua Reynolds, of which there were far too many. Even a finely-rendered Gainsborough left her cold today.

She left the paintings and went to find Simon. He was stood transfixed in front of one of several cabinets of Sèvres porcelain. The brilliant colours of the pieces reflected in his blue eyes and almost made Victoria want to paint him, but as she looked at him standing there, hopelessly in love with what he was seeing, it came to her that she would never paint him again. Instead, she enjoyed the aesthetic qualities of the vision with a feeling of things coming to an inevitable end, though why that should be happening now, today, she didn't know.

She ignored the lure of the paintings around them and stayed still, watching Simon gaze at the pieces of china with their delicate flower designs, his lips parted slightly and his breath coming fast and light. He looked both ecstatic and totally at peace. She'd never been able to make him look like that and there wasn't a chance in hell she'd ever be able to. It was a shame, as he was such a beautiful man – such a perfect human being.

She wandered off and sat down on a badly padded bench; a round thing, with in its centre an ugly porphyry construction of pairs of writhing serpents. It was horrible, but served as a useful reminder of the things that really mattered to her.

Simon caught up a few minutes later.

'Something to eat? Drink?'

'No thanks. I noticed a long and non-moving queue for food. I'm not hungry anyway, not even for a dead hare to suck.'

'Dead hare? Whatever do you mean?'

'Weetabix.'

'Weetabix? I really don't know what you're on about, Victoria. You had your breakfast before we came out.'

'Haven't you noticed? Loads of paintings of dead game by some gadgie called Weetabix or something.'

'Weenix?'

'Might be. I don't know.'

'Victoria, you've gone all grumpy. Whatever's the matter?'

'Sorry. Oh, God, Simon – I'm so sorry!' She felt the tears welling up.

'Good grief. Come on. Let's go and look in the gift shop. You always like gift shops.'

'Yes, and I'm five years old and need humouring.'

He didn't answer.

Once through the shop, they noticed they'd missed the armoury galleries, so wandered along a corridor to view the suits of armour, guns, rows and rows of daggers, knives, swords, more armour, great suits of armour for horses, more knives, more swords. They reminded Victoria of the entrance to Alnwick Castle and she started to cheer up.

'These are beautifully horrid things, aren't they?' she said.

'Not really my cup of tea, darling.'

'I know. I know.' She felt the tears again. 'I'm not really your "cup of tea" either, am I.'

He didn't answer, but took her hand in his and carried on walking slowly. His fingers entwined round hers and he squeezed gently. She responded in kind.

'Oh, Simon. I'm so, so sorry.'

'I know, love.' He kissed the top of her head.

They left the gallery, as close as they'd ever been, now that they'd reached the end. And there, in the middle of Oxford Street, with Christmas shoppers racing by, Simon took Victoria in his arms and hugged her with such affection she thought her heart would break. Except it didn't. She knew it wouldn't.

'I need to get to Tate Modern,' she told him after a while.

'Yes, of course. It's already midday. I ought to get back to work.'

'I'll be round some time to pick up my things. Not sure exactly when.'

'That's fine. Whenever you like. Just let me know.'

'Simon –'

'Yes?'

'Thank you.'

'My pleasure, Victoria. My very great pleasure.'

186

Chapter Thirty-one

Louise Bourgeois' great spider, "Maman", had scuttled away from the front of the Tate Modern a long time ago, but Victoria didn't need her any more. She'd found the confidence to produce the art she needed, though she knew that with each picture she was killing herself, slowly and subtly, and sometime soon she would have to stop the process and find a way of painting without this agonising slow death. Bourgeois had lived to ninety-eight. Not all artists had to die young.

Saying goodbye to Simon had been the start of the recovery process, but she had so very far to go before she was herself again.

She stared up at the towers of the old Bankside Power Station for a few moments longer, wondering why she'd never made the connection with a cathedral before. Ready at last, knowing how to do this task she'd set herself, she drew a deep breath and walked in through the large doors at the end of the turbine hall. A few yards in, she found the remains of Doris Salcerdos' "Shibboleth", the crack that ran through the heart of the building. Yes, it had been filled in. Yes, everything was strong, intact; but the scar was still there, still clearly visible. She wanted to sit down on the floor and stroke it, but didn't quite have the nerve. It would be just her luck if she were kicked out for being a weirdo before she'd found any answers.

John … Yes, she could say his name. She gave herself permission. It had been here. Just this spot. She'd been sitting. No. No, don't sit down Victoria. Don't.

She followed the barely visible crack down through the hall until the halfway point, where she had no option but to raise her eyes. There, at the far end, was the huge dark cube that was Miroslaw Balka's "How it is". The installation was small in comparison to the vastness of the turbine hall, but still filled her with foreboding. Did she really want to do this? Did she dare? She'd heard tales of how some visitors had been traumatised by stepping inside; had felt the echoes of death camps and other agonies. How dare she, a piddling little artist, walk in there and expect her own problems to have anything at all to do with this work of art? How dare she ask for answers?

She looked around. The gallery was quiet this lunchtime. It was now or never. Come on Victoria. You can do this.

She walked to the far end of the turbine hall and surveyed the huge ramp that led up into the abyss, the end of all things – "How it is".

I think you are a coward.

Shut up José.

I think you cannot do this. He is not here. There are no answers.

You don't know that.

I do. You must come back to Spain. I am waiting. The sun is setting. You must come back soon, before it is too late. This darkness is not for you.

No, I need the darkness in order to excise it for good. You are a dream, José. You ceased to exist a long time ago. You know this.

I do not..

You do. You really do. Now go. And don't come back. Ever.

You have said goodbye to Simon?

I have.

And you will say hello to someone who is – how you say – more sexy?

José, for goodness sake. Yes. Much more sexy.

Very well. That is good and I am happy. Adios, my lovely Vicki. Besitos...

And then he was gone. That was a relief. If she'd achieved nothing else on this strange and revelatory day, at least she'd laid one ghost to rest. One amongst dozens, from the looks of things. Staring up into the dark opening, she saw pale ghosts emerge at regular intervals only to turn back into apparently live humans as they approached the bottom of the ramp. She didn't want to walk amongst them and was tempted to creep up the side, holding on to the wall like a non-swimmer working their way round a pool. That was the coward's way. Perhaps she should walk up the centre, hold her head up high, say, "I can do this". No, that was wrong too. She was an artist. She looked at the width of the entrance, and chose a point that instinct told her equated to the golden third. Then she walked steadily up the ramp and entered the darkness.

The black enveloped her, cradled her, held her safe. She could just make out a few other people, but the end of the structure was effectively the void. There was nothing. *Finis rerum.* An end of things.

No, wait a moment. That was wrong. That's not how it was at all. As she walked further inside, she felt her spirits rising. This was good. This was – oh, homely, somehow. How could it be homely? It was hardly womb-like – far too big – yet she felt at her ease, more relaxed than she'd been in ages. She walked on with increased confidence into the structure, and even felt a slight disappointment when she reached the end. It would have been good if this could have gone on and on. She put out a hand to touch, expecting cold metal. Instead she felt velvet. Ah, wonderful! The softness of velvet. She remembered a dress of velvet, a man cupping her elbow in his hand, and she felt such exquisite longing that tears came to her eyes and she knew at last how to heal herself, how to make things right.

Time to head back out. She turned – another revelation. Out of darkness into light – but oh, such light. She remembered how she'd thought the towers of the old power station were like a cathedral. Now she knew she was in a real cathedral, one that spoke to her far more eloquently than the beloved "half church of God, half castle 'gainst the Scot", that clung with such grey necessity to the banks of the River Wear. Durham was but a pale reminder of this, the real thing. Thank you, Miroslaw Balka, and thank you even more, Caspar David Friedrich! *You* would have recognised this. Yes, this was definitely a scene straight out of the German Romantic artist's paintings. Every so often someone would stop on their way out of the structure and be silhouetted against the light, just as Friedrich had painted back views of silhouetted figures against his inspirational landscapes. Just as she'd been doing in her own art for so long.

Okay, done that. Time to move on. Cup of tea? Yes. When transfigured, when enraptured, when overwhelmed, drink tea.

Eyes glistening, she hurried round to the steps and almost ran up to the fourth floor coffee bar, bought a cup of tea and made her way out to the balcony. It was cold and wet but there below was the Thames, and across the river was that other great church, St Paul's Cathedral, which she'd painted so often with contempt, but now looked at with love.

After draining the last dregs of the tea and disposing of the paper cup, she wandered back down through the galleries, coming across another smaller installation by Miroslaw Balka, a warm construct of wood and comfort – and saw it was dedicated to Caspar David Friedrich. Well, there you go. Who'd have thought it? Great minds, and all that.

She returned to the turbine hall, which was now swarming with school parties and tourists. Would the feeling have changed? She walked round and looked into the giant structure to find out. Oh yes. With a vengeance. The quiet had gone and the great cube now thundered with the sound of dozens of school kids running back and forth and squealing. Many wore shoes with lights in their heels that lit up and flickered like fireflies. Tourists ignored the "no phones" sign and lit themselves and their companions with pale luminescence whilst chatting inconsequentially. *It's pitch black and I'm at the end of all things. Would you like me to get some fish for tea? How did Elizabeth get on at the clinic? Don't forget to pick up Malachi from five-a-side.* Camera flashes went off at intervals, adding to the randomness. A gallery attendant grimaced and lit a dim torch which she turned to the ground before going in to sort it all out. Victoria watched her with suppressed giggles. This had become a place of fun, of naughtiness; of pranks and banality.

Simon would have hated it. He wouldn't have understood what she'd felt the first time and he'd be furious at the way thoughtless people were spoiling it for everyone else this time – except that they weren't spoiling it. If José had been here, he'd have come out with some smart aleck comment about it in an attempt to make her feel small and stupid, when actually he knew nothing about any art other than the art of bluffing.

And John? What would John have made of it all? He would have raised one eyebrow in a knowing way, and caught her eye, appearing to know precisely what she was thinking. He must be still in New York, but dear God, he'd better come home soon. She was only dying inside because he was so far away. That much was bloody obvious, though she rarely admitted the fact to herself so directly.

Time to get home and paint. She'd wait for John to call. Of course he'd call. He must. He'd always had an uncanny ability to second-guess her. He'd know how much she needed him; that now was the time.

Back at the flat, the first canvas she created depicted the birth of colour. Rivulets of rose madder poured down the street where a man

190

trod; his footprints creating springs of unadulterated pigment, flowing as greasy oil slicks. She followed, wondering how he sourced such colour from flat grey paving. He knelt down, scooped up the pigment with care, and she knew she need never worry about her paintings again.

In the second painting, she had to flee – a shelter was torn down, she felt exposed to the sky, to anything flying above and even the ants that walked below in ranks across the concrete out to the fields. She could only breathe, could only see through the safety of branches, the filigree patterns of black and white, out of the sight of watchers whose nightly intrusions shrivelled her mind. They couldn't win: she would run across the pasture, over a stile and onto the beach where the shingle was unforgiving but dawn had risen – over there – look at the sky – speckled with dots that grew and swooped like martins.

The phone rang.

There is a point in all potential relationships when you make a decision. Think about this person: pursue the possibilities, even though they may come to naught – or cast them out of your consciousness. Don't allow any fantasy, Victoria. Any. Don't allow yourself to be tempted into dreams. No, really. Don't.

She was on a knife edge. The desire was there, but dear God – the danger of pursuing such a course. Answer the phone or not.

Easy. Answer it.

Christalmighty! That'll teach you to ponder and think great thoughts, you dolt!

The phone stopped ringing before she reached it. When she dialled 1471 to find out who had rung, she got a "caller didn't leave a number" message. Bugger it! Mind, it couldn't have been John. He wouldn't refuse to give a number. Would he? No, be sensible. Chrissake, Victoria, he's in New York, of course he's not going to phone. Pull yourself together.

Or better still, go to bed. It was past midnight. She'd painted herself to a point of exhaustion and parted from her perfect boyfriend for the sake of a nothing; a fleeting piece of imagination; an arrogant man who hit his wife. Ex-wife. Who had been mostly curt and cold when they'd met; who probably hadn't thought of her once since he'd left. Who was now a successful antiques dealer in New York.

Go to bed, Victoria.

Chapter Thirty-two

Two months later he still hadn't called. He wasn't going to call. Victoria threw herself into her art and started producing what her agent called tragic masterpieces, but which Victoria referred to privately as "poor little me" paintings. She worked late into the night and woke before dawn to continue. In many ways she hated living in this state of perpetual exhaustion, but at the same time, she was the happiest she'd ever been. She didn't have John – she didn't have anyone – and she thrived on the loneliness and the freedom to do whatever she liked whenever she liked. This meant painting non-stop, so whether it was really freedom or not was a moot point.

She woke up one morning arguing with herself; trying to ascertain the precise shade of scarlet her desire required. Did she dare risk a splash of cadmium red? Oh please, dare she? She'd been dreaming about John, of course, and the dream had been sufficiently erotic to make her weep with the frustration of waking up. Right. Get painting, Victoria. You know who you want to paint, so paint him. It's the closest you'll get to the real thing. Be honest – might even be better.

She flung the duvet onto the floor and scrabbled around for yesterday's discarded clothes. They smelled clean enough, so she dressed hurriedly, grimaced at herself in the bathroom mirror, and was in the middle of giving her teeth a cursory brush when the doorbell rang. Bugger! The last thing she needed now was interruptions. If this was the bloody Jehovah's Witnesses again, she'd be polite. If it was José, she'd punch him in the jaw, and probably break her hand in the process. It mustn't be Simon – please God, not Simon. She'd sooner it were anyone else.

She opened the door and John walked in – slightly shorter than in her dreams, definitely older, wearing different aftershave, but still undoubtedly John.

'Morning, Victoria. We need to talk. Can you pack an overnight bag?'

'John – you're here.'

'Well spotted.'

'But you're in New York.'

'No, been back for months.'

'Shit. Really? I didn't know. Have you seen Simon?'

'Yes, I saw him as soon as I returned from the States, but he specifically asked me not to make contact with you. We had one of those gentlemanly discussions where he asked me as one of his oldest friends – etcetera, etcetera. I think he was hoping that if you didn't know I was here, he'd be able to hang onto you for a little longer.'

'Oh God ...'

'I obliged, naturally. He was so polite about it all I felt I had little choice. Then I found out the other day by chance that you two weren't together any more. Seems my oldest friend had carefully omitted to tell me the coast was clear. Victoria, don't stand there gawping – pack that bag.'

'Yes, yes, give me a moment.' She hurried off to the bedroom, scrabbled around in her underwear drawer for the most presentable items, grabbed a cleanish T-shirt off the floor, and threw in a toothbrush and comb.

'Done.'

'Good. Bring a warm jacket. Scarf, hat, gloves. That sort of thing. Stout shoes.'

'Do I ever wear anything else?'

'You did at Alnwick.'

'Christ, you noticed what I had on my feet more than two years ago?'

'Yes.'

'Good God.'

She gathered together the necessary clothing, putting on all she could wear and carrying the rest. They went down to John's Mercedes and loaded the bag into the boot.

'So, where are we going? Your secret hideaway in deepest Sussex? That cottage I keep promising myself in Snowdonia?'

'No. We're going up North,' said John, closing the door with a gentle thud.

'Oh, excellent – but not to Bamburgh, I hope.'

'Categorically not.' The engine purred into life. 'I'm not sure I ever want to go there again. You remember – you could hardly forget – my visit to the cottage to deliver those blasted books? Did you ever stop to ask yourself why I didn't post them instead? That would have been much the easiest course of action given the state of play between Emma and myself at that time.'

'I honestly didn't give it much thought, but if I had – I don't know – I'd have assumed they were too valuable to post. Something like that?'

'No, they weren't remotely valuable. I only didn't post them because Emma told me that you were staying with her at the cottage, and I wanted to see you, to find out if what I felt for you was reciprocated in any way.'

'What you felt for me? Oh shit. Really?'

'Yes. You remember that picture you did the previous day on the beach? The vivid, agonised one? The one I teased you was a self-portrait, when I could see straight away it was the way you saw me – no, the way you *wanted* me?'

'Oh God yes. That was the one me and Emma slashed to pieces and fed to her stove shortly after you left.'

'You did that? You pair of scoundrels. I rather liked that picture.'

'It had to go, and it was a very cathartic process, as I recall.'

'And do you remember my comments about what you'd done in the picture? I tried to be as clear as I could, and thought you understood what I was saying.'

'I did. You were being horribly perceptive and got right under my skin.'

'Seems like you saw some of what I wanted to communicate, but not all of it. My declarations of affection do tend to be horribly obtuse, I'm afraid.'

'That was a declaration of affection? Bloody hell.'

'See what I mean? And then when I offered to drive you to the station, you turned me down without a second thought.'

'Did I? Oh. Yes, sorry about that. I was so concerned with Emma's feelings it didn't occur to me to worry about yours.'

'Exactly. You weren't remotely interested.'

'No, I didn't *show* interest. Different thing entirely.'

'Not from my point of view, so I ran off to the States feeling sorry for myself.'

'That's an awfully long way to run just because someone refuses your offer of a lift.'

'I know. I'm like that, I'm afraid,' said John. 'A tendency towards dramatic gestures and wallowing in misery.'

194

He put his foot on the pedal and the car shot onto the motorway, smoothly overtaking everyone else.

'Aha. So *you* are the suicidal king. Not José at all.'

'The "suicidal king"? Who or what might that be?'

'It's a picture I drew ages ago – student days – it reminded me of an ex-boyfriend of mine, but it's far more like you. I reckon I've been drawing and painting you for ever – must have started long before I met you.'

'That's a clever trick.'

'Isn't it just. And now my portraits of you are exhibited all over the world.'

'I know. I went into a gallery in New York and didn't know where to look. It's a strange feeling to walk into an exhibition when every single picture is a portrait of you, but nobody else in the world – other than the artist – realises it. That's when I knew I had to come back. If you were painting me so obsessively, you must either hate me with a vengeance or be – I don't know. "In love" sounds too mild.'

'Know what you mean. I don't do mild. Neither do you. That was part of the problem Emma had. She couldn't do the swinging from chandeliers thing.'

'The *what*?'

'Those were her words.'

'She was right. Clever little Emma. You know, I'm still fond of her despite everything – not that I'd ever tell her. Not now.'

'Christ, no! She's got her mechanic and half a dozen kids on the way. Last thing she needs is you turning up and giving her another black eye.'

'I never gave her a black eye – not directly – and anyway, I've got you now. I don't need her.'

'You take a lot for granted, don't you?'

'Yes.'

They drove on in silence for a while.

'Look at that sign,' said Victoria. '"Hatfield and the North." Forget Shakespeare – *that* is the most poetic line in the English language.'

'Couldn't agree more.'

'So where precisely *are* we going?'

'Alnmouth.'

'You're joking.'

'No, not at all,' said John. 'It's time to lay some ghosts.'

'You sound like me. I did exactly the same thing a few months back. Went to Tate Modern and saw the crack – what's left of it, that is. Then I went into "How it is".'

John nodded. 'Thought you might. I went there too, but presumably not on the same day, or we might have bumped into each other. Literally.'

'What did you think of it?'

'I found it a curiously optimistic piece. It gave me hope, though I'm not exactly sure why. Walking into a pitch black shipping container is not the obvious course to take when seeking the light.'

'I felt much the same. But – Alnmouth?'

'I've been back a couple of times since you were there. Chatted to Simon at one of those blasted dinners up at Alnwick Castle. We both skirted round the issue. There we were, surrounded by all those weapons of war, each dying to grab a sword and eviscerate the other, but having to engage in small talk instead.'

'I wish I'd known.'

'Best you didn't.'

'But I've been all alone.'

'Quite right too. It's enabled you to produce your best artwork yet. Staggering pieces compared to your earlier stuff.'

'So you're saying I need to be miserable to produce great art? That's a load of old bollocks.'

'Possibly.'

She looked across to him to see if he was smiling. He wasn't.

'Victoria, you do realise that I'm a difficult person – nearly as bad as you? I think between us we'll be able to conjure up enough stress and misery to keep your artwork on track, just so long as we don't kill each other in the process.'

'Good. That's all right then. How long is it going to take us to get there? To Alnmouth, I mean, not into the promised perpetual state of misery.'

'About five hours in this car, now that the A1's been upgraded.'

Five hours in a sleek black Mercedes sitting next to John, with him in complete control. Victoria decided to savour every moment. God knows she'd waited long enough.

196

They arrived at Alnmouth late in the afternoon. A few other cars had struggled through the rain to park on the front by the golf links.

John switched the engine off. They sat without speaking for several minutes, looking out across the grey North Sea.

'This is where I come in my darkest moments,' he said, eventually.

'This isn't a dark moment, is it?'

'No, but I used to come here when I didn't know what to do about Emma; when my life was collapsing and she seemed further away than ever from the lovely girl I thought I'd married. I'd stand here in the wind and freeze – trying to numb myself, I suppose, but I didn't have the strength to withstand the buffeting of the wind. I failed every time, then went home to Emma, and ...'

'And the buffeting continued?'

'Something like that. I'm a fighter. I have to fight back, even though everyone – except Emma, presumably – will tell you I'm not a violent man.'

'No, you're wrong about Emma. She told me ages back that you weren't violent. I couldn't understand what the hell she meant, not when –'

'When her face was bruised and you knew I'd hit her?'

'Yes.'

'I've never come closer to slitting my wrists. It happened on more than one occasion – you need to know that.'

'I do know.'

'She told you?'

'She told me pretty much everything.'

'Hellfire.'

'Hey – it's okay. I think.'

'It will be, I promise. Come on. Let's walk.'

They retrieved their jackets from the boot, donned scarves and hats and set off along the side of the estuary.

'Before I met Emma, I honestly didn't know I had such behaviour in me, but with her, everything changed. I couldn't bear it when the beautiful girl I thought I could mould into a perfect wife turned into a cloud of misery draped over my shoulders. I had to survive, but at the risk of losing everything. And I did lose everything: Emma, my self-respect – everything. Drowned and gone forever, just like that village.'

'What village?'

'There.' He pointed up the estuary. 'The land was swept away, isolating Alnmouth when the river changed course one night. There were probably only a few cottages lost, but there was life here, under this dead water, these waves. Once. I'm not even sure how long ago.'

'It's a thought isn't it. People going about their lives like fish.' Victoria made a fish face and blew imaginary bubbles.

'Not like fish!'

Victoria giggled. 'I know.'

'That's the huge difference between you and Emma.'

'What, I take the piss? She took you too seriously?'

'Yes, that's it precisely. You laugh at me. Swear at me. You're completely dismissive at times. You puncture my pomposity, and God knows it needs puncturing. Emma never had the nerve.'

'That's because she was afraid of you – or if not afraid, at least in awe, right from the start.'

'Am I such a scary man?'

'No, but you frightened Emma long before you did anything to justify that fear, first with your erudition and your assumption of superiority and then with your expectations of what she should be. She knew she'd never achieve the saintly state of perfect mate to Mr John-aren't-I-so-erudite-and-cultured-Stephenson. Hadn't a hope.'

John frowned.

'That's one of the reasons she goaded you,' said Victoria.

'"Goaded" me?'

'Yes, that was the word she used.'

'She knew what she was doing?'

'And how. She needed to justify the fear; turn you into a wife-beater and herself into an innocent victim.'

'Dear God. She pretty much succeeded. Far too successful for her own good. My poor little Emma.'

'Poor little Emma, my arse. Calculating, clever little Emma. Manipulative, scheming little Emma. Fully aware of what she was doing, justifying it to herself because ... I don't know. That's a toughie. She loved the idea of you, but the actuality was too strong for her to take, so she turned the tables and pretty much turned you into the victim. She's my best friend, but she's also a right bloody cow at times.'

'Victoria, you do me good.'

A gull flew overhead. On the shore, a sand martin bobbed back and forth looking for food. The water lapped gently and the ghosts slept peacefully under green stones. The rain-clouds parted and a little weak sunlight broke through.

Victoria looked up at the profile of this man, this almost stranger who she had been painting for so long. Needing for so long.

'Remember "Shibboleth"?' she said. 'You have wounds. They fester. They never heal.'

'You understand that? Really understand?'

'Yes.'

He took hold of her hand and held it tight.

Victoria leaned her head on his shoulder and looked up. 'It's clouding over. I thought we might get a bit more sun, but it doesn't look like it's going to happen. Astonishing how quickly the weather can turn here. Do you want to go?'

'No, I want to stay here a little longer. There is beauty in mist.'

'You don't mind the lack of sun?'

'I don't think either of us is exactly a "sunshine" person.'

'We thrive on doom and gloom?'

'Victoria, I've seen your pictures. Remember?'

'Yes.'

She put her arms round him and hugged him tightly while the wind swept round as if to bind them together. His kiss, when it came, was sudden and vivid, and completely different from her slow and languorous dreams; far more dangerous, far more intimate. She knew at once that she needed more; needed to find out if her idea of this man was going to be different in other ways too. The direct approach had rarely worked well with Simon, but she had a feeling it wouldn't be a problem with John.

'Bed?' she said.

'Who needs a bed? We have a deserted beach, plus the golf links.'

'You've got to be joking! It's freezing!'

'Where's your sense of adventure, woman?'

'You're laughing at me.'

'Indeed I am. Come on. We'll be able to get a room in one of the hotels here, I have no doubt.'

'Good. I'm hungry.'

'As am I.'

He kissed her again with a swiftness and intensity that made her want to use the golf links after all, to save time.

Chapter Thirty-three

'Sorry about the state of these things,' said Victoria, as she stripped off her tatty and mismatched underwear and threw it into a corner of the bedroom.

'It's what's inside that interests me,' said John.

'Good.' She was pleased to see that he was equally untidy with the way he flung his clothes about, and clearly in a hurry.

Their lovemaking was intense and explosive. He had a penchant for pinning her to the bed and rendering her helpless, which suited her mood briefly, but then she turned the tables and attempted to do the same to him, causing much hilarity. Gods, but this was fun! Why had sex never been fun before? Perfunctory with José, sweet and loving with Simon, but never sheer blinding fun like this. It was exhausting too, and after they'd finished, she felt like crying, she was so drained. She snuggled up to John and he pulled the covers over her. She was asleep in minutes.

She woke up about an hour later.

'About time,' said John. 'Now for some lazy loving.'

'Lazy loving?'

'Slow and ... like this ... and this ...'

'Mmm ...'

This was not swinging from chandeliers so much as swimming through syrup – sensuous and ultimately overwhelming. The thought passed through her mind that she was going to be a physical wreck tomorrow. Did she care? Did she hell. And yes, she'd be bruised, but they'd be the right sort of bruises, and they wouldn't show, so that was all right. Or was it? Yes, of course it was. Shut up Victoria. Enjoy the moment.

And then it was over and they were in the shower, kissing between sneezes and splutters, dropping the soap and collecting more bumps and bruises, but somehow getting clean enough to go down to the bar without telltale odours letting everyone know what they'd doing for the last couple of hours.

They settled down in the corner with a couple of large gins. John leaned back and shut his eyes and Victoria took the opportunity to study his face in detail. The frown lines were less obvious than usual; the whole face as contented as she'd ever seen it. This was right.

This was how it should be. This was … how she'd never painted him. She'd never given him any sort of a post-coital glow. That would be the next picture, definitely. He was going to look different in her artwork from now on. Much more alive. No more back views, staring moodily into the distance. Now she would allow him to turn round. She poured the tonic into her glass, and took a long drink, feeling the delicious frisson of ice and heat as it slipped down her throat. Simon had never approved of her drinking. John wouldn't mind, she was sure. She gulped some more down. Mmm, that was good. Very good.

John took hold of her hand and brushed it against his lips.

'Can we go upstairs again? Now?' she said, downing the rest of her drink in one go. 'Please?'

'You're drunk. Not very, but –'

'Does it matter?'

'No, not at all.' He finished his own drink, then led her by the hand straight back to their room. This time he was more experimental and took his time coaxing her to do things she didn't know "nice" people did at all, but she was game, and after all, when had anyone ever accused her of being "nice"? At one point she got an attack of hiccups, which he found highly amusing.

'I've never had that effect on anyone before,' he whispered into her ear, before doing something that shocked her hiccups into submission.

Afterwards, she looked at the state of the bed. 'Blimey. We'll have to pay for that, won't we?'

'No problem. They're used to me here. They know I tip well.'

Victoria was starting to feel out of her depth. What was she getting into? Emma's chandelier swinging comment was making more and more sense. She'd known sex with John would be more adventurous than anything she'd known before, but – oh, fuck it. But nothing. This is what she'd been gagging for ever since that first visit to Tate Modern, wasn't it? Of course it was. She was just drunk. What did they call it – "tired and emotional"? Yes. That was it. More like bloody knackered.

'I'm ravenous,' said John. 'Fancy something to eat?'

'Food?'

'Yes. As in the sort of stuff they serve in restaurants. Or would you sooner go for a walk first?'

'Walk?'

'Yes, as in one foot in front of the other. Victoria! Pull yourself together, woman.'

'I'd better get dressed.'

'It would be advisable, yes.' He leaned over and kissed her lightly on the lips. 'You all right? I wasn't too – I don't know –'

'I'm fine. Just not used to exerting so much energy. I need to paint. No, eat, I mean. I need to eat.'

'You need both, I suspect, but I doubt if you thought to pack any painting materials. Don't look so crestfallen, my love. I'll take you back home tomorrow and you can paint huge erotic canvases to your heart's content.'

Victoria had little idea of what she ate that night. She felt sick from too much gin and frightened by the thought of making love to John again. This was the man who had hit Emma, more than once. What was she doing with him? She pushed the food about on her plate. Perhaps she should make her excuses and leave. What, and walk down the estuary into the mist? Shit, Victoria – what's the matter with you? Don't go down that road. Just don't. This is what you wanted, isn't it?

John grabbed her hand and held it firmly.

'Victoria, what's the matter?'

'Nerves.'

'Okay, fair enough. We'll finish up here and then go and get some air.'

He spoke quietly and kindly. She'd never thought of John as "kind" before. It was a revelation of sorts. A quiet, gentle one – exactly what she needed.

'Do you want coffee?' he said.

'No, let's not bother.'

Five minutes later, suitably clad once more in hats and coats, they were walking along the side of the estuary, hand in hand. The horizon darkened as they watched, and the terns came down in a cloud and settled onto a sand spit. Victoria stooped down and picked up a handful of shells and clutched them tightly. Their sharp edges would stop her from drifting; keep her focused. She needed to know this man better: needed to talk to him about anything and everything, to find the real John and exorcise the figment of her imagination she'd been painting for so long. But how? They had by-passed pretty much all of the "getting to know you" small talk and she didn't know how to backtrack; how to initiate it. She saw a boulder, half-submerged, its rounded form reminding her obliquely of apricots. When had her flat last smelled of apricots?

'Do you like plums?' she said. 'Apricots? That sort of thing?'

'What a strange question. Yes, I like all those fruits; I like them when they're slightly overripe and their skin bruises easily; I like their sweetness, their succulence.'

He kissed the top of her head.

'And the marram? The grass? Do you like that?'

'Yes; the way the wind whips it in the twilight, sinking to grey, to an otherworldliness.'

'Gorse?'

'The surprising yellow? The – how would you put it – the prickly certitude?'

Victoria laughed. 'Yes, that sounds about right.'

'Any more random questions? I can tell you about my first day at school; my odd experience at age five when seeing a porcupine at the zoo; my childhood collection of matchboxes; the time I nearly drowned – literally; the day I saw my first piece of serpentine furniture and knew, just *knew*, that my matchbox collecting days were over. And the day I first saw you and wondered at my wife's taste in friends – wondered what this scruffy girl with the mousey hair was doing at my otherwise smart wedding. You were rude to me even back then, you know. You took one look and scowled, as if to say, "Emma, what the fuck? Who is this guy?"'

'Bloody hell. Didn't know I was so obvious. Sorry!'

'You're forgiven. Your reaction was prescient in many ways, as I later came to realise.'

'Look, there's *Marean.*'

'Who? Ah yes, I see.'

'Have you ever sailed?'

'Not properly. I tried to crew for a friend of mine once at university and ended up with a bump like a conker on my forehead and blisters on my hands that took weeks to heal – quite apart from the near drowning. Not really my thing. But I remember him telling me about the draw of the sea. He would wax lyrical going on about – oh, I don't know, I don't know the terminology, but his enthusiasm drew me into his world for a while and I didn't want to leave.'

They walked on in silence for a while. Victoria half-closed her eyes, checking the way the sky could be painted and how the sea turned and strained to be free of the moon's gravitational pull.

They reached the yacht and Victoria ran her hands along its cracked paintwork.

'She's almost derelict, isn't she. Poor old thing. Looks exhausted.'

'No, I don't think so. Wouldn't take much make her float again. A little care,

some patching up, a shove, and she'd sail again.'

'You reckon?'

'Oh yes.'

Victoria fingered the shells in her pocket, feeling the fine sand which slipped into the seam of her jacket, becoming part of its substance; an indelible memory of this moment.

Yes, it was going to be all right. She didn't have to worry, didn't have to be afraid.

John put his arms round her and held her for a very long time. She snuggled into his coat, smelling a mixture of tweed and brine and a hint of after-shave; homely and comforting. After a while, the wind got up. Victoria shivered. John stroked her cheek.

'Let's get back and get you warmed up. Come on.'

Back at the hotel they went straight up to their room, kissed and cuddled and snuggled into bed. John fell asleep quickly, but Victoria stayed awake, watching him in the quiet blue light that filtered through the curtains.

205

Chapter Thirty-four

They drove back the following day, stopping off in Durham to overlay any awkward old memories with new ones. The cathedral's towers were dressed in white rags as usual – protection for the workers on the scaffolding, or else a bridal garb to welcome the spring. Victoria liked the idea of the latter.

'The circus is coming,' she said, as they entered the building. 'Can you feel it? Winding round columns, down aisles, across transepts, up spirals, into every stone, every joint, every flaw. Come, flights of jesters; colour my mind with bog myrtle, ashes and heather. Acrobats, claw your way through the zigzags, the herringbones – tumble to other dimensions, for today is midsummer and misrule is the only rule.'

'Quite right too,' said John: 'very lyrical. But it's only February, and you're barking, you know that? Did you ever think of becoming a poet?'

'I already am. In paint.'

'True enough.'

'Oh look. What a miserable little man.'

Victoria pointed to a priest who'd entered through a side door from the cloister.

'I've a feeling he looks exactly as I used to do,' said John.

'What, black-hearted and heavy with bile?'

'Something like that.'

'Maybe, but that's as far as it goes. You create light out of darkness, which is what he should be doing, given his calling, but look at his expression – he's doing the precise opposite. Can you see that path etched out behind him like the slime from a vitriolic slug? I know he's wearing a dog collar, but it might as well be a hangman's noose.'

'I like the vitriolic slug idea. You should use that.'

'I will.'

They watched the priest creep round the stony corners and out into the middle of the nave, tapping his teeth with a biro as he went.

'I don't like him,' said Victoria. 'He looks like he wants to desecrate the place. He's spreading wrongness around him. Shouldn't be allowed. Not in here.'

The priest waved his arms about in slow motion, as if rehearsing some arcane ritual in semaphore. A couple of old ladies stopped and watched him, peering myopically at his tai chi style movements.

Victoria committed the scene to memory; imagined the ladies as spinster sisters – she would call them the Misses Frobisher – safe and protected from the priest by layers of powdery-pink foundation and lipstick that ran down the cracks of their soft mouths.

'Have you ever noticed that window?' said John, breaking through her train of thought.

Victoria looked where he pointed. The stained glass depicted a scene of St Cuthbert preaching in a northern village. 'No, not really. What about it?'

'I've always loved the way the congregation are wearing the traditional Pennine farmer's garb – you know, generous flowing robes in royal blue and crimson.'

'Oh, classic! You're right. That's absolutely hilarious.'

'Yes, but it's beautiful in its way. The background reminds me of upper Teesdale. Cow Green reservoir,' said John. 'That's another place we should definitely visit some time. You have no idea how depressed I've been up there in the past.'

'Sounds like a plan,' said Victoria, giggling. She squeezed his arm before running a finger along the slanting carved stonework, as she'd done so many times before in her student days.

'I want to see the trilobites,' she said. 'Come on. They're up here.'

He offered her a rare smile and she felt her face flush with desire for him.

They walked hand in hand to the pulpit, where they stopped to examine its columns of Frosterley marble teeming with long-dead sea creatures, condemned to a stony immortality

A birdlike chattering alerted Victoria to a large group of choristers who had appeared in the nave. Victoria caught an unexpected look of terror on the priest's face. The boys formed a huddle in blue and quietened down to listen to instructions from their teacher. Bright-eyed tourists watched and waited, presumably hoping for music but no – it seemed the boys weren't choristers after all, just a school party, clutching clipboards rather than psalters.

By the time John and Victoria reached the transept, the boys had gone, but then, as if time were repeating itself, an identical group started bearing down on them.

'I don't fancy being trampled,' said Victoria.

'Me neither,' said John, pulling her into a side chapel.

Victoria slipped her other hand into John's and ran her thumb over the short black hairs on the back of his hand that had caused her many a frisson of desire in the past. His finger stroked her palm, her wrist, her pulse. She looked up – there was a high place; a corridor in the tower. No one would see them up there, but everyone would hear them. She stifled a laugh, imagined a "Yes! Yes! Yes!" ringing out during evensong. Nothing wrong with a bit of rapture, especially in a church, she reckoned, knowing John would agree.

'Look up there,' she said.

John followed her pointing finger. 'Ah, yes. Very good. Just room for my arm round your shoulder, and your leg round my waist, don't you think?

'Definitely.'

He leaned over and kissed the top of her head. 'Later,' he promised. 'Though maybe not here.'

'You don't want to get arrested?'

'No, it would be most inconvenient.'

Another group of faux choristers had entered the cathedral. They sat in the pews halfway down the nave and stared at the priest, who made a hurried sign of the cross. He clearly couldn't cope with wave upon wave of blue children and looked as if he were drowning in revulsion.

'Look at the Misses Frobisher,' said Victoria.

'The who?'

'Those two old ladies. They've been moving around in a single unit kind of a way. Probably once conjoined twins.'

John spluttered. 'Victoria! For goodness sake!'

'No, really. I bet in their youth they once went on a trip to Barcelona; passed the window of *Louis Vuitton,* and ever since that time, whenever they're in holy places, they stand together in prayerful silence, remembering the incident with their matching pink frocks, their lumpy calves and brogues.'

'How revolting. These Miss Frobishers; do they have individual names?'

208

'Of course. Lettuce and Violet. Lettuce is telling Violet that their roots need some attention. Look! Violet's nodding. She agrees. Do you suppose they'll consult the priest on the matter?'

'I hope so. Anything to frighten him off.'

'You don't like him, do you?'

'No. As I said, he's like me before I found you. Far too familiar.'

A beam of light streamed through a high lancet window. The children in the nave stood up as one, and swarmed forward.

'The tide of blue goblins cannot be stopped,' said Victoria. 'Wait till they reach the Miss Frobishers. This could be fun. The ladies will scream, forced apart, trampled by orcs, hacked to pieces by dwarvish axes. They will exude a faint smell of lilies, of death and funerals, but no lingering incense, which is a shame, as that alone might have saved them.'

'You seriously need to get back to your studio, don't you,' said John.

'You bet. Shall we go? No, wait. The botanicals.'

'The who?'

'Botanical gardens. That's where me and Simon first went seriously wrong – or rather, I did. He just twisted his ankle, poor lamb. I'd like to go there again to see it with you; to make some new memories. Is that okay?'

'Absolutely. I'm in no rush.'

The gardens were angular today; the bamboo erect and insistent, the steel sculpted insects imbued with preternatural strength and industrial vigour. Victoria tried to remember the heat and stillness in the blazing sunshine when she'd been here with Simon – quite different to the chilly stiff breeze that had accompanied her and John everywhere over the last couple of days.

'Why is it always stormy round you?' she said.

'It isn't. I think you're causing it.'

'Sounds reasonable. Come on. I want to show you something.'

She raced ahead and stopped by a blue conifer. Peering between its branches, she found a tiny black bug.

'There,' she said, as he caught up. 'What do you think?'

He peered into the branches to see what she was seeing.

'I think you're testing me.'

'Of course. And you've just passed. Thank you, thank you, thank you!'

'For what?'

'For being interested. For looking where I look. For trying to work out what I'm thinking. For knowing me, even though you hardly know me.'

'That's easy. I've been going round galleries and looking at your art for long enough. Buying a few pieces too – and not just those delightful potato prints. Some of your more recent horrendously over-priced pieces as well.'

'They're worth every penny.'

'No they're not. They're not bad, and I bought them because you painted them, but you can do much better, you know. Will have to if you're going to get anywhere.'

'You what? How do you mean, "much better"? What's wrong with them?'

'They're half-hearted. Childish. You need to grow up and mature as an artist. You will, of course. I think possibly you need to travel; have your eyes opened to what's going on elsewhere. You're desperately parochial you know, my dear.'

'Christ! You bastard!'

'I told you I wasn't very nice. I am, however, scrupulously honest. Did Simon ever advise you about your art? Or did he simply say, "That's nice dear," and let you get on with it, making mistakes, churning out average paintings, but never anything truly great?'

'Simon's into Sèvres porcelain. Of course he wouldn't advise me on my art.'

'So just because someone likes Mozart, they're not allowed to have an opinion on Wagner? Just because they read Milton, they can't also read Sylvia Plath?'

'I hate you.'

'Of course you do. Come on. Let's get back. It's a long drive to London.'

'And I hate Durham Botanical Gardens. Why do I always have to be so bloody miserable here?'

'You're not miserable, you're just sulking.'

'Fuck off.'

And with that, she pulled her hand away and marched off up the bank, willing herself to cry – tears were always useful in such

210

situations. They wouldn't come. There was an absolute and adamant refusal for any genuine unhappiness to be displayed by her traitorous eyes. She slowed down. John was right, of course. Her paintings were still naïve. That would change with time and encouragement. She turned round and looked at him. He was smiling.

'I knew you wouldn't be upset,' he said.

'Shut up, you bastard.'

'That's more like it. Now let's talk seriously about what we can do about your art.'

Much of the drive back to London passed in discussion of the direction Victoria could take her career with John's help. She liked the idea of this partnership. There was already a solidity in her relationship with John that she'd hadn't come close to achieving with Simon. He was taking her for granted, of course. Her acquiescence in his plans matched his assumption of her acquiescence in bed. She wasn't sure whether to be contented or seriously pissed off, but decided contented would make for a very much more pleasurable existence, at least for the time being.

He dropped her off at her flat, saying he had to sort out some things at the office, and then needed to pop over to Amsterdam, but would see her again next week. Next week?

'What do you mean, next week?'

'Today's Wednesday. I'll see you after the weekend. Monday afternoon. I'm busy until then, and I'm sure you are too. Bye-bye for now. Be good.'

'Good? What the fuck?'

'And be angry. Go and paint that anger.'

'You controlling bastard.'

'That's the idea. Until Monday.'

And with that, he let himself out of the flat and disappeared. Victoria had picked up a small porcelain figurine and was about to hurl it after him when she stopped, gasping. The figurine – it was one she'd bought months ago with her increased earnings, intending it as a gift for Simon – a little token of affection. Oh God – it was so brittle, so perfect.

The tears started to flow now, helplessly and horribly. Simon! Chrissake – what have I done?

She put the figurine down with care and walked slowly into the bedroom, undressed, and looked at her naked body in the mirror. She looked battered and bruised, much as Emma had done. What sort of a monster was this John?

José? Advice please? Help me?

No answer. Damn. Cup of tea? No. Not this time. Bath? Yes. Hot and soothing. Bubbles. Lots of bubbles. Yes, that's what she needed. Bubbles.

Chapter Thirty-five

The next day Victoria took out her sketch pad and pencil and drew frantically, almost with her eyes closed. She made lightning sketches of Marean, Durham Cathedral, John, the sea, the wind, John, waves of marram grass, John. He looked kind and loving and infinitely desirable in the pictures. Then she drew Simon. He looked perfect, but he didn't look like Simon. He'd become a stranger, and she could no longer capture his likeness.

She rang Cynthia.

'Can we meet? Usual café?'

'Of course we can. What's up?'

'I'm ... urrghh ... errm ...'

'Oh. Like that. Okay. Eleven o'clock suit you?'

'Fine. Thanks. See ya.'

She put the phone down and wondered what she was going to say.

In the event, it was easy. She told Cynthia that she loved John and needed him as she'd never needed anyone before; but that she could foresee things being very difficult because he could be both infuriating and hurtful in equal measure and was far too forthright for comfort. He brought out the worst in her: illogicality, bad temper and hysterics. Cynthia's response was to look delighted and say: 'Oh good – I'm so relieved. You have no idea.'

That was encouraging if unexpected.

'Remember how worried I was when you were so content with Simon?' said Cynthia.

'Yes, of course, and in many ways you were right, but at the same time –'

'Oh lordy!'

'What?'

Victoria turned round to see what Cynthia was looking at.

'Shit. Buggery hell.'

Simon had walked into the coffee shop with an elfin sprite. The woman was gorgeous. Unspeakably beautiful. They made the most ridiculously perfect couple she'd ever seen.

Victoria tried to remember if she'd brushed her hair this morning. She was pretty sure she'd cleaned her teeth, but didn't think she'd done much else. She looked down at her jeans. They were grimy and smudged. Her top was splattered with tea stains. Her clothes weren't as bad as they might have been, but they made her look rough, scruffy and uncaring. She ran her fingers through her hair and they got stuck. There was an enormous tangle on the back of her head, where it usually formed. Bloody typical.

'Cynthia, I look a mess, don't I.'

'Yes, but not to worry. He hasn't seen you. Oh. Spoke too soon. They're coming over. Smile nicely.'

'Victoria!' Simon looked pleasantly surprised and completely charming.

'Simon. Lovely to see you.'

Victoria kissed him decorously on the cheek. It seemed to be expected.

'This is Melissa. Darling, I'd like you to meet Victoria and Cynthia. They're artists.'

The elf-maiden came forward for the obligatory air kiss. Then she smiled, showing perfect teeth, which Victoria had a sudden urge to knock out – but as she smiled she dimpled and turned into a human being rather than an enviable accessory. The look Simon gave her was one of pure adoration. Victoria wondered if vomiting all over the chintzy tablecloth would be allowable at this point, but decided against it.

'May we?' said Simon.

May you what? Tell me how dowdy and awful I look next to your perfect new girlfriend? Tell me that I could have had you but I totally blew it? Oh, may you join us, you mean. Yes, why not. Go ahead. Complete my humiliation.

Simon and the delightful Melissa pulled up chairs. The waitress came straight over to take their order. She never came straight over for Victoria. Bar staff, yes. Waitresses? Never.

Victoria tried not to stare, but Melissa was absurdly beautiful. There were cake knives on the table. Not especially sharp, but it shouldn't take much to sever the carotid artery, not if the victim were taken by surprise. Blood would gush out, spurting all over the place. Victoria's top and jeans were mucky anyway. Wouldn't make much difference.

They all drank tea and chatted politely. Cynthia was on fine form and filled any gaps in the conversation with ease. Melissa turned out

214

to be charming. Of course she was charming. Of course Simon was happy. Of course they'd both have to be killed, very nastily, then melted down and ground into pigment for a series of art installations called "Death in Sèvres", or something stupid like that. Of course, of course, of course.

Then, thankfully, it was all over. Mr and Mrs McPerfect left the café unscathed. Cynthia started giggling.

'Vicky, how you managed to get through that, I shall never know. Your face was a picture. Talk of conflicting emotions!'

'Shut up, Cynthia,' said Victoria affectionately. 'I would now like to slit my wrists. No, I want to drown myself in the Serpentine. That'll do. Far more appropriate. Or get swallowed by a giant python. Strangled by a boa constrictor.'

'She's nice, isn't she.'

'Of course she's bloody nice. She's Simon's girlfriend. How could she not be nice. Fuck's sake, even I was occasionally nice when I was with him. Thank God I've got John now. I'd go mad with Simon. I *did* go mad with Simon. Is it Monday yet?'

'No, why?'

'I'm seeing John on Monday. I think I'll get very drunk tonight. I want to sleep away the time until he returns.'

'I recognise that quote – something about mandragora root, isn't it?'

'Yeah, that's the one. Cleopatra needing her Antony. Shakespeare knew stuff, didn't he.'

'He did indeed, but you don't need alcohol, you need something much stronger. If I were you, I'd go home and paint. Remember how I once asked you which was more important to you, Simon or your art?'

'Yes. And I answered "my art", of course, but I didn't feel disloyal to Simon for saying so, because they were two completely different things.'

'Right. And I said they shouldn't be. So. Same question. Which is more important to you: John or your art?'

'They can't be separated.'

'Exactly.'

'Thank you, Cynthia.'

'You're welcome. Now run along home and paint.'

About the Author

Catherine Edmunds was born in Kent, England, and educated at Dartington College of Arts and Goldsmith's College, London. After a successful career as a professional musician, she reinvented herself as a portrait artist, illustrator and writer. She still teaches music, but also works professionally as an illustrator and author with more than 350 poems and short stories in print.

Catherine has provided cover art for a wide range of publications. Her illustrations – featuring exploding dogs, quills inserted into veins, and rotting toads – can be see in *The A-Z of Punisment and Torture* (BeWrite Books), *Anomalous Appetites* (Editor John Irvine) and the ebook version of her solo poetry collection, *wormwood, earth and honey* (Circaidy Gregory Press), as well as several Earlyworks Press anthologies.

Her magical realism novel, *Small Poisons* (Circaidy Gregory Press) was published in 2009 and is available as both paperback and ebook. Catherine has frequently been placed in writing competitions, including two short-listings for the 2010 Bridport Prize. Reviews, competition successes and full listings of published work may be found on Catherine's website at

www.freewebs.com/catherineedmunds/

By the same author …

Small Poisons
a novel by

Catherine Edmunds

A contemporary novel for Midsummer Night's Dreamers

With charm, wit and magical style
Catherine Edmunds conjures a
fairy tale for grown ups, in a place
where dreams and stark reality
meet.

- Neil Marr, BeWrite Books

'Small Poisons' by Catherine Edmunds
ebook ISBN 978-1-906451-41-7
paperback ISBN 978-1-906451-16-5
Paperback £7.99+P&P from www.circaidygregory.co.uk

wormwood, earth and honey
selected poems by Cathy Edmunds

Accessible but never trivial; warm, earthy, intelligent and – just
when you begin to snuggle into the intimacy of it – spiked with fire
and venom.

What's it like? Asked for a blurb, Cathy wrote....

> teasel scratches, bramble catches
> deep inside my den of mischief
> mud pies splatter, cracked plates clatter
> if you dare to enter here
>
> insects bite you, ferrets fight you
> creepers catch you, magpies snatch you
> hidden dangers trap all strangers
> don't you try it; don't you dare
>
> I will chuckle, smirk and giggle
> deep inside my den of mischief
> faith is forfeit, friendship fickle
> if you dare to enter here.

Paperback ISBN 978-1-906451-04-2 UK Price £6.50 New, illustrated ebook edition
ISBN 978-1-906451-27-1